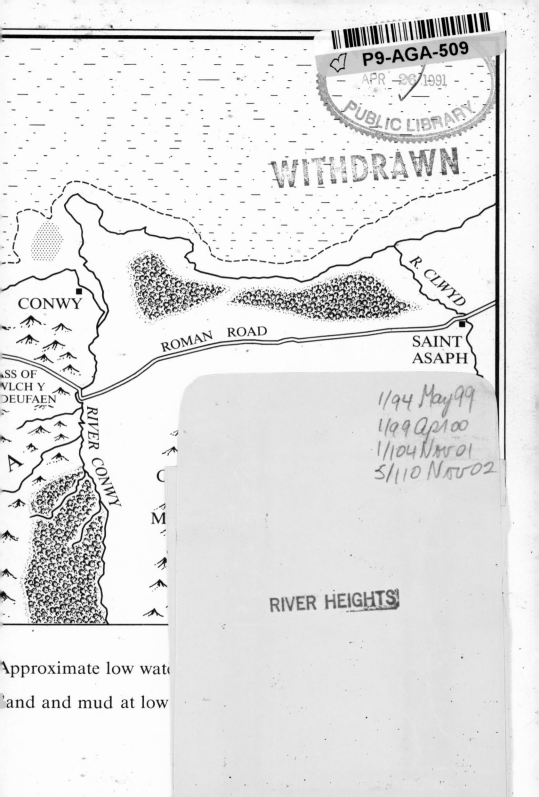

CONWY

R. CLWYD

ROMAN ROAD

SAINT
ASAPH

SS OF
VLCH Y
DEUFAEN

RIVER CONWY

A

1/94 May 99
1/99 Ap 100
1/104 Nov 01
5/110 Nov 02

Approximate low wate

and and mud at low

The
Summer
of the Danes

The Summer of the Danes

The Eighteenth Chronicle
of Brother Cadfael

Ellis Peters

Brother
CADFAEL

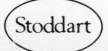

Stoddart

First published in 1991 by
Stoddart Publishing Co. Limited
34 Lesmill Road
Toronto, Canada
M3B 2T6

Published in Great Britain by
Headline Book Publishing PLC
Headline House
79 Great Titchfield Street
London W1P 7FN
England

10 9 8 7 6 5 4 3 2 1

Canadian Cataloguing in Publication Data

Peters, Ellis, 1913–
The summer of the Danes

ISBN 0-7737-2482-6

I. Title.

PR6031.A49S85 1991   823'.912   C91-093443-6

Printed and bound in Great Britain by
Richard Clay Ltd, Bungay, Suffolk

The
Summer
of the Danes

Chapter One

Chapter One

HE EXTRAORDINARY events of that summer of 1144 may properly be said to have begun the previous year, in a tangle of threads both ecclesiastical and secular, a net in which any number of diverse people became enmeshed, clerics, from the archbishop down to Bishop Roger de Clinton's lowliest deacon, and the laity from the princes of North Wales down to the humblest cottager in the trefs of Arfon. And among the commonalty thus entrammelled, more to the point, an elderly Benedictine monk of the Abbey of Saint Peter and Saint Paul, at Shrewsbury.

Brother Cadfael had approached that April in a mood of slightly restless hopefulness, as was usual with him when the birds were nesting, and the meadow flowers just beginning to thrust their buds up through the new grass, and the sun to rise a little higher in the sky every noon. True, there were troubles in the world, as there always had been. The vexed affairs of England, torn in two by two cousins contending for the throne, had still no visible hope of a solution. King Stephen still held his own in the south and most of the east; the Empress Maud, thanks to her loyal half-brother, Robert of Gloucester, was securely established in the southwest and

1

maintained her own court unmolested in Devizes. But for some months now there had been very little fighting between them, whether from exhaustion or policy, and a strange calm had settled over the country, almost peace. In the Fens the raging outlaw Geoffrey de Mandeville, every man's enemy, was still at liberty, but a liberty constricted by the king's new encircling fortresses, and increasingly vulnerable. All in all, there was room for some cautious optimism, and the very freshness and lustre of the Spring forbade despondency, even had despondency been among Cadfael's propensities.

So he came to chapter, on this particular day at the end of April, in the most serene and acquiescent of spirits, full of mild good intentions towards all men, and content that things should continue as bland and uneventful through the summer and into the autumn. He certainly had no premonition of any immediate change in this idyllic condition, much less of the agency by which it was to come.

As though compelled, half fearfully and half gratefully, to the same precarious but welcome quietude, the business at chapter that day was modest and aroused no dispute, there was no one in default, not even a small sin among the novices for Brother Jerome to deplore, and the schoolboys, intoxicated with the Spring and the sunshine, seemed to be behaving like the angels they certainly were not. Even the chapter of the Rule, read in the flat, deprecating tones of Brother Francis, was the 34th, gently explaining that the doctrine of equal shares for all could not always be maintained, since the needs of one might exceed the needs of another, and he who received more accordingly must not preen himself on being supplied beyond his brothers, and he that received less but enough must not grudge the extra bestowed on his brothers. And above all, no grumbling, no envy. Everything was placid,

2

conciliatory, moderate. Perhaps, even, a shade on the dull side?

It is a blessed thing, on the whole, to live in slightly dull times, especially after disorder, siege and bitter contention. But there was still a morsel somewhere in Cadfael that itched if the hush continued too long. A little excitement, after all, need not be mischief, and does sound a pleasant counterpoint to the constant order, however much that may be loved and however faithfully served.

They were at the end of routine business, and Cadfael's attention had wandered away from the details of the cellarer's accounts, since he himself had no function as an obedientiary, and was content to leave such matters to those who had. Abbot Radulfus was about to close the chapter, with a sweeping glance around him to make sure that no one else was brooding over some demur or reservation, when the lay porter who served at the gatehouse during service or chapter put his head in at the door, in a manner which suggested he had been waiting for this very moment, just out of sight.

'Father Abbot, there is a guest here from Lichfield. Bishop de Clinton has sent him on an errand into Wales, and he asks lodging here for a night or two.'

Anyone of less importance, thought Cadfael, and he would have let it wait until we all emerged, but if the bishop is involved it may well be serious business, and require official consideration before we disperse. He had good memories of Roger de Clinton, a man of decision and solid good sense, with an eye for the genuine and the bogus in other men, and a short way with problems of doctrine. By the spark in the abbot's eye, though his face remained impassive, Radulfus also recalled the bishop's last visit with appreciation.

'The bishop's envoy is very welcome,' he said, 'and may

3

lodge here for as long as he wishes. Has he some immediate request of us, before I close this chapter?'

'Father, he would like to make his reverence to you at once, and let you know what his errand is. At your will whether it should be here or in private.'

'Let him come in,' said Radulfus.

The porter vanished, and the small, discreet buzz of curiosity and speculation that went round the chapterhouse like a ripple on a pond ebbed into anticipatory silence as the bishop's envoy came in and stood among them.

A little man, of slender bones and lean but wiry flesh, diminutive as a sixteen-year-old boy, and looking very much like one, until discerning attention discovered the quality and maturity of the oval, beardless face. A Benedictine like these his brothers, tonsured and habited, he stood erect in the dignity of his office and the humility and simplicity of his nature, as fragile as a child and as durable as a tree. His straw-coloured ring of cropped hair had an unruly spikiness, recalling the child. His grey eyes, formidably direct and clear, confirmed the man.

A small miracle! Cadfael found himself suddenly presented with a gift he had often longed for in the past few years, by its very suddenness and improbability surely miraculous. Roger de Clinton had chosen as his accredited envoy into Wales not some portly canon of imposing presence, from the inner hierarchy of his extensive see, but the youngest and humblest deacon in his household, Brother Mark, sometime of Shrewsbury abbey, and assistant for two fondly remembered years among the herbs and medicines of Cadfael's workshop.

Brother Mark made a deep reverence to the abbot, dipping his ebullient tonsure with a solemnity which still retained, until he lifted those clear eyes again, the slight echo and charm of absurdity which had always clung about the mute waif Cadfael first recalled. When he stood erect he was again the ambassador; he would always be both man and child from this time forth, until the day when he became priest, which was his passionate desire. And that could not be for some years yet, he was not old enough to be accepted.

'My lord,' he said, 'I am sent by my bishop on an errand of goodwill into Wales. He prays you receive and house me for a night or two among you.'

'My son,' said the abbot, smiling, 'you need here no credentials but your presence. Did you think we could have forgotten you so soon? You have here as many friends as there are brothers, and in only two days you will find it hard to satisfy them all. And as for your errand, or your lord's errand, we will do all we can to forward it. Do you wish to speak of it? Here, or in private?'

Brother Mark's solemn face melted into a delighted smile at being not only remembered, but remembered with obvious pleasure. 'It is no long story, Father,' he said, 'and I may well declare it here, though later I would entreat your advice and counsel, for such an embassage is new to me, and there is no one could better aid me to perform it faithfully than you. You know that last year the Church chose to restore the bishopric of Saint Asaph, at Llanelwy.'

Radulfus agreed, with an inclination of his head. The fourth Welsh diocese had been in abeyance for some seventy years, very few now living could remember when there had been a bishop on the throne of Saint Kentigern. The location of the see, with a foot either side the border, and all the power of Gwynedd to westward, had always made it difficult to maintain. The cathedral stood on land held by the earl of Chester, but all the Clwyd valley above it was in Owain

Gwynedd's territory. Exactly why Archbishop Theobald had resolved on reviving the diocese at this time was not quite clear to anyone, perhaps not even the archbishop. Mixed motives of Church politics and secular manoeuvring apparently required a firmly English hold on this borderland, for the appointed man was a Norman. There was not much tenderness towards Welsh sensitivities in such a preferment, Cadfael reflected ruefully.

'And after his consecration last year by Archbishop Theobald, at Lambeth, Bishop Gilbert is finally installed in his see, and the archbishop wishes him to receive assurance he has the support of our own bishop, since the pastoral duties in those parts formerly rested in the diocese of Lichfield. I am the bearer of letters and gifts to Llanelwy on my lord's behalf.'

That made sense, if the whole intent of the Church was to gain a firm foothold well into Welsh land, and demonstrate that it would be preserved and defended. A marvel, Cadfael considered, that any bishop had ever contrived to manage so huge a see as the original bishopric of Mercia, successively shifting its base from Lichfield to Chester, back again to Lichfield, and now to Coventry, in the effort to remain in touch with as diverse a flock as ever shepherd tended. And Roger de Clinton might not be sorry to be quit of those border parishes, whether or not he approved the strategy which deprived him of them.

'The errand that brings you back to us, even for a few days, is dearly welcome,' said Radulfus. 'If my time and experience can be of any avail to you, they are yours, though I think you are equipped to acquit yourself well without any help from me or any man.'

'It is a weighty honour to be so trusted,' said Mark very gravely.

6

'If the bishop has no doubts,' said Radulfus, 'neither need you. I take him for a man who can judge very well where to place his trust. If you have ridden from Lichfield you must be in need of some rest and refreshment, for it's plain you set out early. Is your mount being cared for?'

'Yes, Father.' The old address came back naturally.

'Then come with me to my lodging, and take some ease, and use my time as you may wish. What wisdom I have is at your disposal.' He was already acutely aware, as Cadfael was, that this apparently simple mission to the newly made and alien bishop at Saint Asaph covered a multitude of other calculated risks and questionable issues, and might well send this wise innocent feeling his way foot by foot through a quagmire, with quaking turf on every hand. All the more impressive, then, that Roger de Clinton had placed his faith in the youngest and least of his attendant clerics.

'This chapter is concluded,' said the abbot, and led the way out. As he passed the visitor by, Brother Mark's grey eyes, at liberty at last to sweep the assembly for other old friends, met Cadfael's eyes, and returned his smile, before the young man turned and followed his superior. Let Radulfus have him for a while, savour him, get all his news from him, and all the details that might complicate his coming journey, give him the benefit of long experience and unfailing commonsense. Later on, when that was done, Mark would find his own way back to the herb garden.

'The bishop has been very good to me,' said Mark, shaking off firmly the idea of any special preference being shown him in his selection for this mission, 'but so he is to all those close about him. There's more to this than favour to me. Now that he's set up Bishop Gilbert in Saint Asaph, the archbishop knows very well how shaky his position must be, and wants to make sure his throne is secured by every support possible. It was his wish – indeed his command – that our bishop should pay the new man this complimentary visit, seeing it's from his diocese most of Gilbert's new see has been lopped. Let the world see what harmony there is among bishops – even bishops who have had a third of their territory whipped from under their feet. Whatever Bishop Roger may be thinking of the wisdom of planting a Norman, with not a word of Welsh, in a see nine-tenths Welsh, he could hardly refuse the archbishop. But it was left to him how he carried out the order. I think he chose me because he does not wish to make too lavish and flattering a show. His letter is formal and beautifully executed, his gift is more than suitable. But I – I am a judicious half-measure!'

They were gathered in conference in one of the carrels of the north walk, where the Spring sunshine still reached slanting fingers of pale gold even in late afternoon, an hour or so before Vespers. Hugh Beringar had ridden down from his house in the town as soon as word of Brother Mark's arrival had reached him, not because the sheriff had any official business in this clerical embassage, but for the pleasure of seeing again a young man he held in affectionate remembrance, and to whom, in this present instance, he might be able to give some help and advice. Hugh's relations with North Wales were good. He had a friendly agreement with Owain Gwynedd, since neither of them trusted their mutual neighbour the earl of Chester, and they could accept each other's word without question. With Madog ap Meredith of Powis the sheriff had a more precarious relationship. The Shropshire border was constantly alert against sporadic and almost playful raids from beyond the dyke, though at this

8

present time all was comparatively quiet. What the conditions of travel were likely to be on this ride to Saint Asaph, Hugh was the most likely man to know.

'I think you are too modest,' he said seriously. 'I fancy the bishop knows you well enough by now, if he's had you constantly about him, to have a very good opinion of your wit, and trusts you to step gently where a weightier ambassador might talk too much and listen too little. Cadfael here will tell you more than I can about Welsh feeling in Church matters, but I know where politics enter into it. You can be sure that Owain Gwynedd has a sharp eye on the doings of Archbishop Theobald in his domain, and Owain is always to be reckoned with. And only four years ago there was a new bishop consecrated in his own home diocese of Bangor, which is totally Welsh. There at least they did sanction a Welshman, one who at first refused to swear fealty to King Stephen or acknowledge the dominance of Canterbury. Meurig was no hero, and did finally give way and do both, and it cost him Owain's countenance and favour at the time. There was strong resistance to allowing him to take his seat. But they've come to terms and made up their differences since then, which means they'll certainly work together to keep Gwynedd from being wholly subservient to Theobald's influence. To consecrate a Norman now to Saint Asaph is a challenge to princes as well as prelates, and whoever undertakes a diplomatic mission there will have to keep a sharp eye on both.'

'And Owain at least,' Cadfael added shrewdly, 'will be keeping a sharp eye on what his people are feeling, and an ear open to what they are saying. It behoves Gilbert to do the same. Gwynedd has no mind to give way to Canterbury, they have saints and customs and rites of their own.'

'I have heard,' said Mark, 'that formerly, a long time ago,

9

St David's was the metropolitan see of Wales, with its own archbishop not subject to Canterbury. There are some Welsh churchmen now who want that rule restored.'

Cadfael shook his head rather dubiously at that. 'Better not to look too closely into the past, we're hearing more of that claim the more the writ of Canterbury is urged on us. But certainly Owain will be casting his shadow over his new bishop, by way of a reminder he's in alien territory, and had better mind his manners. I hope he may be a wise man, and go gently with his flock.'

'Our bishop is very much in agreement with you,' said Mark, 'and I'm well briefed. I did not tell the whole of my errand in chapter, though I have told it to Father Abbot since. I have yet another letter and gift to deliver. I am to go on to Bangor – oh, no, this is certainly not at Archbishop Theobald's orders! – and pay the same courtesy to Bishop Meurig as to Bishop Gilbert. If Theobald holds that bishops should stand together, then Roger de Clinton's text is that the principle applies to Norman and Welsh alike. And we propose to treat them alike.'

The 'we', as applying to Mark in common with his illustrious superior, sounded an echoing chord in Cadfael's ears. He recalled just as innocent a presumption of partnership some years back, when this boy had been gradually emerging from his well-founded wariness of all men into warmth and affection, and this impulsive loyalty to those he admired and served. His 'we', then, had signified himself and Cadfael, as if they were two venturers keeping each the other's back against the world.

'More and more,' said Hugh appreciatively, 'I warm to this bishop of ours. But he's sending you even on this longer journey alone?'

'Not quite alone.' Brother Mark's thin, bright face flashed for an instant into a slightly mischievous smile, as though he had still some mysterious surprise up his sleeve. 'But *he* would not hesitate to ride across Wales alone, and neither would I. He takes it for granted the Church and the cloth will be respected. But of course I shall be glad of any advice you can give me about the best way. You know far better than I or my bishop what conditions hold good in Wales. I thought to go directly by Oswestry and Chirk. What do you think?'

'Things are quiet enough up there,' Hugh agreed. 'In any event, Madog, whatever else he may be, is a pious soul where churchmen are concerned, however he may treat the English laity. And for the moment he has all the lesser lads of Powys Fadog on a tight rein. Yes, you'll be safe enough that way, and it's your quickest way, though you'll find some rough upland riding between Dee and Clwyd.'

By the brightness and speculation of Mark's grey eyes he was looking forward to his adventure. It is a great thing to be trusted with an important errand when you are the latest and least of your lord's servants, and for all his awareness that his humble status was meant to temper the compliment, he was also aware how much depended on the address with which he discharged his task. He was meant not to flatter, not to exalt, but nevertheless to present in his person the real and formidable solidarity of bishop with bishop.

'Are there things I should know,' he asked, 'about affairs in Gwynedd? The politics of the Church must reckon with the politics of state, and I am ignorant about things Welsh. I need to know on what subjects to keep my mouth shut, and when to speak, and what it would be wise to say. All the more as I am to go on to Bangor. What if the court should be there? I

11

may have to account for myself to Owain's officers. Even to Owain himself!'

'True enough,' said Hugh, 'for he usually contrives to know of every stranger who enters his territory. You'll find him approachable enough if you do encounter him. For that matter, you may give him my greetings and compliments. And Cadfael has met him, twice at least. A large man, every way! Just say no word of brothers! It may still be a sore point with him.'

'Brothers have been the ruin of Welsh princedoms through all ages,' Cadfael observed ruefully. 'Welsh princes should have only one son apiece. The father builds up a sound principality and a strong rule, and after his death his three or four or five sons, in and out of wedlock, all demand by right equal shares, and the law says they should have them. Then one picks off another, to enlarge his portion, and it would take more than law to stop the killing. I wonder, sometimes, what will happen when Owain's gone. He has sons already, and time enough before him to get more. Are they, I wonder, going to undo everything he's done?'

'Please God,' said Hugh fervently, 'Owain's going may not be for thirty years or more. He's barely past forty. I can deal with Owain, he keeps his word and he keeps his balance. If Cadwaladr had been the elder and got the dominance we should have had border war along this frontier year in, year out.'

'This Cadwaladr is the brother it's best not to mention?' Mark asked. 'What has he done that makes him anathema?'

'A number of things over the years. Owain must love him, or he would have let someone rid him of the pest long ago. But this time, murder. Some months ago, in the autumn of last year, a party of his closest men ambushed the prince of

Deheubarth and killed him. God knows for what mad reason! The young fellow was in close alliance with him, and betrothed to Owain's daughter, there was no manner of sense in such an act. And for all Cadwaladr did not appear himself in the deed, Owain for one was in no doubt it was done on his orders. None of them would have dared, not of their own doing.'

Cadfael recalled the shock of the murder, and the swift and thorough retribution. Owain Gwynedd in outraged justice had sent his son Hywel to drive Cadwaladr bodily out of every furlong of land he held in Ceredigion, and burn his castle of Llanbadarn, and the young man, barely past twenty, had accomplished his task with relish and efficiency. Doubtless Cadwaladr had friends and adherents who would give him at least the shelter of a roof, but he remained landless and outcast. Cadfael could not but wonder, not only where the offender was lurking now, but whether he might not end, like Geoffrey of Mandeville in the Fens, gathering the scum of North Wales about him, criminals, malcontents, natural outlaws, and preying on all law-abiding people.

'What became of this Cadwaladr?' asked Mark with understandable curiosity.

'Dispossession. Owain drove him out of every piece of land he had to his name. Not a toehold left to him in Wales.'

'But he's still at large, somewhere,' Cadfael observed, with some concern, 'and by no means the man to take his penalty tamely. There could be mischief yet to pay. I see you're bound into a perilous labyrinth. I think you should not be going alone.'

Hugh was studying Mark's face, outwardly impassive, but with a secretive sparkle of fun in the eyes that watched Cadfael so assiduously. 'As I recall,' said Hugh mildly, 'he said: "Not quite alone!" '

'So he did!' Cadfael stared into the young face that confronted him so solemnly, but for that betraying gleam in the eyes. 'What is it, boy, that you have not told us? Out with it! Who goes with you?'

'But I did tell you,' said Mark, 'that I am going on to Bangor. Bishop Gilbert is Norman, and speaks both French and English, but Bishop Meurig is Welsh, and he and many of his people speak no English, and my Latin would serve me only among the clerics. So I am allowed an interpreter. Bishop Roger has no competent Welsh speaker close to him or in his confidence. I offered a name, one he had not forgotten.' The sparkle had grown into a radiance that lit his face, and reflected not only light but enlightenment back into Cadfael's dazzled eyes. 'I have been keeping the best till last,' said Mark, glowing. 'I got leave to win my man, if Abbot Radulfus would sanction his absence. I have as good as promised him the loan will be for only ten days or so at the most. So how can I possibly miscarry,' asked Mark reasonably, 'if you are coming with me?'

It was a matter of principle, or perhaps of honour, with Brother Cadfael, when a door opened before him suddenly and unexpectedly, to accept the offer and walk through it. He did so with even more alacrity if the door opened on a prospect of Wales; it might even be said that he broke into a trot, in case the door slammed again on that enchanting view. Not merely a brief sally over the border into Powis, this time, but several days of riding, in the very fellowship he would have chosen, right across the coastal regions of Gwynedd, from Saint Asaph to Carnarvon, past Aber of the princes, under the tremendous shoulders of Moel Wnion. Time to talk over every day of the time they had been apart, time to reach the companionable silences when all that needed to be said was said. And all this the gift of Brother Mark. Wonderful what riches a man can bestow who by choice and vocation possesses nothing! The world is full of small, beneficent miracles.

'Son,' said Cadfael heartily, 'for such refreshment I'll be your groom along the way, as well as your interpreter. There's no way you or any man could have given me more pleasure. And did Radulfus really say I'm free to go?'

'He did,' Mark assured him, 'and the choice of a horse from the stables is yours. And you have today and tomorrow to make your preparations with Edmund and Winfrid for the days you're absent, and to keep the hours of the Office so strictly that even your errant soul shall go protected to Bangor and back.'

'I am wholly virtuous and regenerate,' said Cadfael with immense content. 'Has not heaven just shown it by letting me loose into Wales? Do you think I am going to risk disapprobation now?'

Since at least the first part of Mark's mission was meant to be public and demonstrative, there was no reason why every soul in the enclave should not take an avid interest in it, and there was no lack of gratuitous advice available from all sides as to how it could best be performed, especially from old Brother Dafydd in the infirmary, who had not seen his native cantref of Duffryn Clwyd for forty years, but was still convinced he knew it like the palm of his ancient hand. His pleasure in the revival of the diocese was somewhat soured by the appoint-ment of a Norman, but the mild excitement had given him a new interest in life, and he reverted happily to his own lan-guage, and was voluble in counsel when Cadfael visited him. Abbot Radulfus, by contrast, contributed nothing but his blessing. The mission belonged to Mark, and must be left scrupulously in his hands. Prior Robert forebore from comment, though his silence bore a certain overtone of disapproval. An envoy of his dignity and presence would have been more appropriate in the courts of bishops.

Brother Cadfael reviewed his medical supplies, committed his garden confidently to Brother Winfrid, and paid a precautionary visit to Saint Giles to ensure that the hospital cupboards were properly provided, and Brother Oswin in serene command of his flock, before he repaired to the stables to indulge in the pleasure of selecting his mount for the journey. It was there that Hugh found him early in the afternoon, contemplating with pleasure an elegant light roan with a cream-coloured mane, that leaned complacently to his caressing hand.

'Too tall for you,' said Hugh over his shoulder. 'You'd need a lift into the saddle, and Mark could never hoist you.'

'I am not yet grown so heavy nor so shrunken with age that I cannot scramble on to a horse,' said Cadfael with dignity. 'What brings you here again and looking for me?'

'Why, a good notion Aline had, when I told her what you and Mark are up to. May is on the doorstep already, and in a week or two at the most I should be packing her and Giles off to Maesbury for the summer. He has the run of the manor there, and it's better for him out of the town.' It was his usual custom to leave his family there until after the wool clip had been taken and the fields gleaned, while he divided his time between home and the business of the shire. Cadfael was familiar with the routine. 'She says, why should we not hasten the move by a week, and ride with you tomorrow, to set you on your way as far as Oswestry? The rest of the household can follow later, and we could have one day, at least, of your

16

company, and you could bide the night over with us at Maesbury if you choose. What do you say?'

Cadfael said yes, very heartily, and so, when it was put to him, did Mark, though he declined, with regret, the offer of a night's lodging. He was bent on reaching Llanelwy in two days, and arriving at a civilised time, at the latest by mid-afternoon, to allow time for the niceties of hospitality before the evening meal, so he preferred to go beyond Oswestry and well into Wales before halting for the night, to leave an easy stage for the second day. If they could reach the valley of the Dee, they could find lodging with one of the churches there, and cross the river in the early morning.

So it seemed that everything was already accounted for, and there remained nothing to be done but go reverently to Vespers and Compline, and commit this enterprise like all others to the will of God, but perhaps also with a gentle reminder to Saint Winifred that they were bound into her country, and if she felt inclined to let her delicate hand cover them along the way, the gesture would be very much appreciated.

The morning of departure found a little cavalcade of six horses and a pack-pony winding its way over the westward bridge and out of the town, on the road to Oswestry. There was Hugh, on his favourite self-willed grey, with his son on his saddle-bow, Aline, unruffled by the haste of her preparations for leaving town, on her white jennet, her maid and friend Constance pillion behind a groom, a second groom following with the pack-pony on a leading rein, and the two pilgrims to Saint Asaph merrily escorted by this family party. It was the last of April, a morning all green and silver. Cadfael and Mark had left before Prime, to join Hugh and his party in the town. A shower, so fine as to be almost imperceptible in the air, had followed them over the bridge, where the Severn ran full but peaceful, and before they had assembled in Hugh's courtyard the sun had come out fully, sparkling on the leaves and grasses. The river was gilded in every ripple with capricious, scintillating light. A good day to be setting out, and no great matter why or where.

The sun was high, and the pearly mist of morning all dissolved when they crossed the river at Montford. The road was good, some stretches of it with wide grass verges where the going was comfortable and fast, and Giles demanded an occasional canter. He was much too proud to share a mount with anyone but his father. Once established at Maesbury the little pack-pony, sedate and goodhumoured, would become his riding pony for the summer, and the groom who led it his discreet guardian on his forays, for like most children who have never seen cause to be afraid, he was fearless on horseback – Aline said foolhardy, but hesitated to issue warnings, perhaps for fear of shaking his confidence, or perhaps out of the certainty that they would not be heeded.

They halted at noon under the hill at Ness, where there was a tenant of Hugh's installed, to rest the horses and take refreshment. Before mid-afternoon they reached Felton, and there Aline and the escort turned aside to take the nearest way home, but Hugh elected to ride on with his friends to the outskirts of Oswestry. Giles was transferred, protesting but obedient, to his mother's arms.

'Go safely, and return safely!' said Aline, her primrose head pale and bright as the child's, the gloss of Spring on her face and the burnish of sunlight in her smile. And she signed a little cross on the air between them before she wheeled her jennet into the lefthand track.

Delivered of the baggage and the womenfolk, they rode on

at a brisker pace the few miles to Whittington, where they halted under the walls of the small timber keep. Oswestry itself lay to their left, on Hugh's route homeward. Mark and Cadfael must go on northward still, but here they were on the very borderland, country which had been alternately Welsh and English for centuries before ever the Normans came, where the names of hamlets and of men were more likely to be Welsh than English. Hugh lived between the two great dykes the princes of Mercia had constructed long ago, to mark where their holding and writ began, so that no force should easily encroach, and no man who crossed from one side to the other should be in any doubt under which law he stood. The lower barrier lay just to the east of the manor, much battered and levelled now; the greater one had been raised to the west, when Mercian power had been able to thrust further into Wales.

'Here I must leave you,' said Hugh, looking back along the way they had come, and westward towards the town and the castle. 'A pity! I could gladly have ridden as far as Saint Asaph with you in such weather, but the king's officers had best stay out of Church business and avoid the crossfire. I should be loth to tread on Owain's toes.'

'You have brought us as far as Bishop Gilbert's writ, at any rate,' said Brother Mark, smiling. 'Both this church and yours of Saint Oswald are now in the see of Saint Asaph. Did you realise that? Lichfield has lost a great swathe of parishes here in the northwest. I think it must be Canterbury policy to spread the diocese both sides the border, so that the line between Welsh and English can count for nothing.'

'Owain will have something to say to that, too.' Hugh saluted them with a raised hand, and began to wheel his horse towards the road home. 'Go with God, and a good journey!

19

We'll look to see you again in ten days or so.' And he was some yards distant when he looked back over his shoulder and called after them: 'Keep him out of mischief! If you can!' But there was no indication to which of them the plea was addressed, or to which of them the misgiving applied. They could share it between them.

Chapter Two

'I AM TOO OLD,' Brother Cadfael observed complacently, 'to embark on such adventures as this.'

'I notice,' said Mark, eyeing him sidelong, 'you say nothing of the kind until we're well clear of Shrewsbury, and there's no one to take you at your word, poor aged soul, and bid you stay at home.'

'What a fool I should have been!' Cadfael willingly agreed.

'Whenever you begin pleading your age, I know what I have to deal with. A horse full of oats, just let out of his stall, and with the bit between his teeth. We have to do with bishops and canons,' said Mark severely, 'and they can be trouble enough. Pray to be spared any worse encounters.' But he did not sound too convinced. The ride had brought colour to his thin, pale face and a sparkle to his eyes. Mark had been raised with farm horses, slaving for the uncle who grudged him house-room and food, and he still rode farm fashion, inelegant but durable, now that the bishop's stable had provided him a fine tall gelding in place of a plodding farm drudge. The beast was nutbrown, with a lustrous copper sheen to his coat, and buoyantly lively under such a light weight.

21

They had halted at the crest of the ridge overlooking the lush green valley of the Dee. The sun was westering, and had mellowed from the noon gold into a softer amber light, gleaming down the stream, where the coils of the river alternately glimmered and vanished among its fringes of woodland. Still an upland river here, dancing over a rocky bed and conjuring rainbows out of its sunlit spray. Somewhere down there they would find a night's lodging.

They set off companionably side by side, down the grassy track wide enough for two. 'For all that,' said Cadfael, 'I never expected, at my age, to be recruited into such an expedition as this. I owe you more than you know. Shrewsbury is home, and I would not leave it for any place on earth, beyond a visit, but every now and then my feet itch. It's a fine thing to be heading home, but it's a fine thing also to be setting out from home, with both the going and the return to look forward to. Well for me that Theobald took thought to recruit allies for his new bishop. And what is it Roger de Clinton's sending him, apart from his ceremonial letter?' He had not had time to feel curiosity on that score until now. Mark's saddle-roll was too modest to contain anything of bulk.

'A pectoral cross, blessed at the shrine of Saint Chad. One of the canons made it, he's a good silversmith.'

'And the same to Meurig at Bangor, with his brotherly prayers and compliments?'

'No, Meurig gets a breviary, a very handsome one. Our best illuminator had as good as finished it when the archbishop issued his orders, so he added a special leaf for a picture of Saint Deiniol, Meurig's founder and patron. I would rather have the book,' said Mark, winding his way down a steep woodland ride and out into the declining sun towards the valley. 'But the cross is meant as the more formal tribute.

22

After all, we had our orders. But it shows, do you not think, that Theobald knows that he's given Gilbert a very awkward place to fill?'

'I should not relish being in his shoes,' Cadfael admitted. 'But who knows, he may delight in the struggle. There are those who thrive on contention. If he meddles too much with Welsh custom he'll get more than enough of that.'

They emerged into the green, undulating meadows and bushy coverts along the riverside, the Dee beside them reflecting back orange gleams from the west. Beyond the water a great grassy hill soared, crowned with the man-made contours of earthworks raised ages ago, and under the narrow wooden bridge the Dee dashed and danced over a stony bed. Here at the church of Saint Collen they asked and found a lodging for the night with the parish priest.

On the following day they crossed the river, and climbed over the treeless uplands from the valley of the Dee to the valley of the Clwyd, and there followed the stream at ease the length of a bright morning and into an afternoon of soft showers and wilful gleams of sun. Through Ruthin, under the outcrop of red sandstone crowned with its squat timber fortress, and into the vale proper, broad, beautiful, and the fresh green of young foliage everywhere. Before the sun had stooped towards setting they came down into the narrowing tongue of land between the Clwyd and the Elwy, before the two rivers met above Rhuddlan, to move on together into tidal water. And there between lay the town of Llanelwy and cathedral of Saint Asaph, comfortably nestled in a green, sheltered valley.

Hardly a town at all, it was so small and compact. The low wooden houses clustered close, the single track led into the heart of them, and disclosed the unmistakable long roof and

23

timber bell-turret of the cathedral at the centre of the village. Modest though it was, it was the largest building to be seen, and the only one walled in stone. A range of other low roofs crowded the precinct, and on most of them some hasty repairs had been done, and on others men were still busily working, for though the church had been in use, the diocese had been dormant for seventy years, and if there were still canons attached to this centre their numbers must have dwindled and their houses fallen into disrepair long ago. It had been founded, many centuries past, by Saint Kentigern, on the monastic principle of the old Celtic clas, a college of canons under a priest-abbot, and with one other priest or more among the members. The Normans despised the clas, and were busy disposing all things religious in Wales to be subject to the Roman rite of Canterbury. Uphill work, but the Normans were persistent people.

But what was astonishing about this remote and rural community was that it seemed to be over-populated to a startling degree. As soon as they approached the precinct they found themselves surrounded by a bustle and purpose that belonged to a prince's llys rather than a church enclave. Besides the busy carpenters and builders there were men and women scurrying about with pitchers of water, armfuls of bedding, folded hangings, trays of new-baked bread and baskets of food, and one strapping lad hefting a side of pork on his shoulders.

'This is more than a bishop's household,' said Cadfael, staring at all the activity. 'They are feeding an army! Has Gilbert declared war on the valley of Clwyd?'

'I think,' said Mark, gazing beyond the whirlpool of busy people to the gently rising hillside above, 'they are entertaining more important guests than us.'

Cadfael followed where Mark was staring, and saw in the shadow of the hills points of colour patterning a high green level above the little town. Bright pavilions and fluttering pennants spread across the green, not the rough and ready tents of a military encampment, but the furnishings of a princely household.

'Not an army,' said Cadfael, 'but a court. We've strayed into lofty company. Had we not better go quickly and find out if two more are welcome? For there may be business afoot that concerns more than staunch brotherhood among bishops. Though if the prince's officers are keeping close at Gilbert's elbow, a reminder from Canterbury may not come amiss. However cool the compliment!'

They moved forward into the precinct and looked about them. The bishop's palace was a new timber building, hall and chambers, and a number of new small dwellings on either side. It was the better part of a year since Gilbert had been consecrated at Lambeth, and clearly there had been hasty preparations to restore some semblance of a cathedral enclave in order to receive him decently. Cadfael and Mark were dismounting in the court when a young man threaded a brisk way to them through the bustle, and beckoned a groom after him to take their horses.

'Brothers, may I be of service?'

He was young, surely not more than twenty, and certainly not one of Gilbert's ecclesiastics, rather something of a courtier in his dress, and wore gemstones about a fine, sturdy throat. He moved and spoke with an easy confidence and grace, bright of countenance and fair in colouring, his hair a light, reddish brown. A tall fellow, with something about him that seemed to Cadfael elusively familiar, though he had certainly never seen him before. He had addressed them first in

Welsh, but changed easily to English after studying Mark from head to foot in one brilliant glance.

'Men of your habit are always welcome. Have you ridden far?'

'From Lichfield,' said Mark, 'with a brotherly letter and gift for Bishop Gilbert from my bishop of Coventry and Lichfield.'

'He will be heartily glad,' said the young man, with surprising candour, 'for he may be feeling the need of reinforcements.' His flashing grin was mischievous but amiable. 'Here, let me get someone to bring your saddle-rolls after us, and I'll bring you where you can rest and take refreshment. It will be a while yet to supper.'

A gesture from him brought servants running to unstrap the pack-rolls and follow hard on the visitors' heels as the young man led them across the court to one of the new cells built out from the hall.

'I am without rights to command here, being a guest myself, but they have got used to me.' It was said with an assured and slightly amused confidence, as if he knew good reason why the bishop's circle should accommodate him, and was forbearing enough not to presume upon it too far. 'Will this suffice?'

The lodging was small but adequate, furnished with beds, bench and table, and full of the scent of seasoned wood freshly tooled. New brychans were piled on the beds, and the smell of good wool mingled with the newness of timber.

'I'll send someone with water,' said their guide, 'and find one of the canons. His lordship has been selecting where he can, but his demands come high. He's having trouble in filling up his chapter. Be at home here, Brothers, and someone will come to you.'

And he was gone, with his blithe long strides and springing tread, and they were left to settle and stretch at ease after their day in the saddle.

'Water?' said Mark, pondering this first and apparently essential courtesy. 'Is that by way of taking salt, here in Wales?'

'No, lad. A people that goes mostly afoot knows the value of feet and the dust and aches of travel. They bring water for us to bathe our feet. It is a graceful way of asking: Are you meaning to bide overnight? If we refuse it, we intend only a brief visit in courtesy. If we accept it, we are guests of the house from that moment.'

'And that young lord? For he's too fine for a servant, and certainly no cleric. A guest, he said. What sort of an assembly have we blundered into, Cadfael?'

They had left the door wide for the pleasure of the evening light and the animation to be viewed about the court. A girl came threading her way through the purposeful traffic with a long, striding grace in her step, bearing before her a pitcher in a bowl. The water-carrier was tall and vigorous. A braid of glassy blue-black hair thick as her wrist hung over her shoulder, and stray curls blew about her temples in the faint breeze. A pleasure to behold, Cadfael thought, watching her approach. She made them a deep reverence as she entered, and kept her eyes dutifully lowered as she served them, pouring water for them, unlatching their sandals with her own long, shapely hands, no servant but a decorous hostess, so surely in a position of dominance here that she could stoop to serve without at any point abasing herself. The touch of her hands on Mark's lean ankles and delicate, almost girlish feet brought a fiery blush rising from his throat to his brow, and then, as if she had felt it scorch her forehead, she did look up.

27

It was the most revealing of glances, though it lasted only a moment. As soon as she raised her eyes, a face hitherto impassive and austere was illuminated with a quicksilver sequence of expressions that came and passed in a flash. She took in Mark in one sweep of her lashes, and his discomfort amused her, and for an instant she considered letting him see her laughter, which would have discomforted him further; but then she relented, indulging an impulse of sympathy for his youth and apparent fragile innocence, and restored the gravity of her oval countenance.

Her eyes were so dark a purple as to appear black in shadow. She could not be more than eighteen years of age. Perhaps less, for her height and her bearing gave her a woman's confidence. She had brought linen towels over her shoulder, and would have made a deliberate and perhaps mildly teasing grace of drying Mark's feet with her own hands, but he would not let her. The authority that belonged not in his own small person but in the gravity of his office reached out to take her firmly by the hand and raise her from her knees. She rose obediently, only a momentary flash of her dark eyes compromising her solemnity. Young clerics, Cadfael thought, perceiving that he himself was in no danger, might have trouble with this one. For that matter, so might elderly clerics, if in a slightly different way.

'No,' said Mark firmly. 'It is not fitting. Our part in the world is to serve, not to be served. And from all we have seen, outside there, you have more than enough guests on your hands, more demanding than we would wish to be.'

At that she suddenly laughed outright, and clearly not at him, but at whatever thoughts his words had sparked in her mind. Until then she had spoken no word but her murmured greeting on the threshold. Now she broke into bubbling speech in Welsh, in a lilting voice that made dancing poetry of language.

'More than enough for his lordship Bishop Gilbert, and more than he bargained for! Is it true what Hywel said, that you are sent with compliments and gifts from the English bishops? Then you will be the most welcome pair of visitors here in Llanelwy tonight. Our new bishop feels himself in need of all the encouragement he can get. A reminder he has an archbishop behind him will come in very kindly, seeing he's beset with princes every other way. He'll make the most of you. You'll surely find yourselves at the high table in hall tonight.'

'Princes!' Cadfael echoed. 'And Hywel? Was that Hywel who spoke with us when we rode in? Hywel ab Owain?'

'Did you not recognise him?' she said, astonished.

'Child, I never saw him before. But his reputation we do know.' So this was the young fellow who had been sent by his father to waft an army across the Aeron and drive Cadwaladr headlong out of North Ceredigion with his castle of Llanbadarn in flames behind him, and had made a most brisk and workmanlike job of it, without, apparently, losing his composure or ruffling his curls. And he looking barely old enough to bear arms at all!

'I thought there was something about him I should know! Owain I have met, we had dealings three years back, over an exchange of prisoners. So he's sent his son to report on how Bishop Gilbert is setting about his pastoral duties, has he?' Cadfael wondered. Trusted in both secular and clerical matters, it seemed, and probably equally thorough in both.

'Better than that,' said the girl, laughing. 'He's come himself! Did you not see his tents up there in the meadows? For these few days Llanelwy is Owain's llys, and the court of

29

Gwynedd, no less. It's an honour Bishop Gilbert could have done without. Not that the prince makes any move to curb or intimidate him, bar his simply being there, for ever in the corner of the bishop's eye, and 'ware of everything he does or says. The prince of courtesy and consideration! He expects the bishop to house only himself and his son, and provides for the rest himself. But tonight they all sup in hall. You will see, you came very opportunely.'

She had been gathering up the towels over her arm as she talked, and keeping a sharp eye now and then on the comings and goings in the courtyard. Following such a glance, Cadfael observed a big man in a black cassock sailing impressively across the grass towards their lodging.

'I'll bring you food and mead,' said the girl, returning abruptly to the practical; and she picked up bowl and pitcher, and was out at the door before the tall cleric could reach it. Cadfael saw them meet and pass, with a word from the man, and a mute inclination of the head from the girl. It seemed to him that there was a curious tension between them, constrained on the man's part, coldly dutiful on the girl's. His approach had hastened her departure, yet the way he had spoken to her as they met, and in particular the way he halted yet again before reaching the lodging, and turned to look after her, suggested that he was in awe of her rather than the other way round, and she had some grievance she was unwilling to give up. She had not raised her eyes to look at him, nor broken the vehement rhythm of her gait. He came on more slowly, perhaps to reassemble his dignity before entering to the strangers.

'Goodday, Brothers, and welcome!' he said from the threshold. 'I trust my daughter has looked after your comfort well?'

That established at once the relationship between them. It was stated with considered clarity as if some implied issue was likely to come up for consideration, and it was as well it should be properly understood. Which might well be the case, seeing this man was undoubtedly tonsured, in authority here, and a priest. That, too, he chose to state plainly: 'My name is Meirion, I have served this church for many years. Under the new dispensation I am a canon of the chapter. If there is anything wanting, anything we can provide you, during your stay, you have only to speak, I will see it remedied.'

He spoke in formal English, a little hesitantly, for he was obviously Welsh. A burly, muscular man, and handsome in his own black fashion, with sharply cut features and a very erect presence, the ring of his cropped hair barely salted with grey. The girl had her colouring from him, and her dark, brilliant eyes, but in her eyes the spark was of gaiety, even mischief, and in his it gave an impression of faint uneasiness behind the commanding brow. A proud, ambitious man not quite certain of himself and his powers. And perhaps in a delicate situation now that he had become one of the canons attendant on a Norman bishop? It was a possibility. If there was an acknowledged daughter to be accounted for, there must also be a wife. Canterbury would hardly be pleased. They assured him that the lodging provided them was in every way satisfactory, even lavish by monastic principles, and Mark willingly brought out from his saddle-roll Bishop Roger's sealed letter, beautifully inscribed and superscribed, and the little carved wood casket which held the silver cross. Canon Meirion drew pleased breath, for the Lichfield silversmith was a skilled artist, and the work was beautiful.

'He will be pleased and glad, of that you may be sure. I need not conceal from you, as men of the Church, that his lordship's situation here is far from easy, and any gesture of support is a help to him. If you will let me suggest it, it would be well if you make your appearance in form, when all are assembled at table, and there deliver your errand publicly. I will bring you into the hall as your herald, and have places left for you at the bishop's table.' He was quite blunt about it, the utmost advantage must be made of this ceremonious reminder not simply from Lichfield, but from Theobald and Canterbury, that the Roman rite had been accepted and a Norman prelate installed in Saint Asaph. The prince had brought up his own power and chivalry on one side, Canon Meirion meant to deploy Brother Mark, inadequate symbol though he might appear, upon the other.

'And, Brother, although there is no need for translation for the bishop's benefit, it would be good if you would repeat in Welsh what Deacon Mark may say in hall. The prince knows some English, but few of his chiefs understand it.' And it was Canon Meirion's determined intent that they should all, to the last man of the guard, be well aware of what passed. 'I will tell the bishop beforehand of your coming, but say no word as yet to any other.'

'Hywel ab Owain already knows,' said Cadfael.

'And doubtless will have told his father. But the spectacle will not suffer any diminution by that. Indeed, it's a happy chance that you came on this of all days, for tomorrow the royal party is leaving to return to Aber.'

'In that case,' said Mark, choosing to be open with a host who was certainly being open with them, 'we can ride on among his company, for I am the bearer of a letter also to Bishop Meurig of Bangor.'

The canon received this with a short pause for reflection, and then nodded approvingly. He was, after all, a Welshman himself, even if he was doing his able best to hold on to favour with a Norman superior. 'Good! Your bishop is wise. It puts us on a like footing, and will please the prince. As it chances, my daughter Heledd and I will also be of the party. She is to be betrothed to a gentleman in the prince's service, who holds land in Anglesey, and he will come to meet us at Bangor. We shall be companions along the way.'

'Our pleasure to ride in company,' said Mark.

'I'll come for you as soon as they take their places at table,' the canon promised, well content, and left them to an hour of rest. Not until he was gone did the girl come back, bearing a dish of honey cakes and a jar of mead. She served them in silence, but made no move to go. After a moment of sullen thought she asked abruptly: 'What did he tell you?'

'That he and his daughter are bound for Bangor tomorrow, as we two are. It seems,' said Cadfael equably, and watching her unrevealing face, 'that we shall have a prince's escort as far as Aber.'

'So he does still own he is my father,' she said with a curling lip.

'He does, and why should he not profess it proudly? If you look in your mirror,' said Cadfael candidly, 'you will see very good reason why he should boast of it.' That coaxed a reluctant smile out of her. He pursued the small success: 'What is it between you two? Is it some threat from the new bishop? If he's bent on ridding himself of all the married priests in his diocese he has an uphill row to hoe. And your father seems to me an able man, one a new incumbent can ill afford to lose.'

'So he is,' she agreed, warming, 'and the bishop wants to keep him. His case would have been much worse, but my mother was in her last illness when Bishop Gilbert arrived, and it seemed she could not last long, so they waited! Can you conceive of it? Waiting for a wife to die, so that he need not part with her husband, who was useful to him! And die she did, last Christmas, and ever since then I have kept his house, cooked and cleaned for him, and thought we could go on so. But no, I am a reminder of a marriage the bishop says was unlawful and sacrilegious. In his eyes I never should have been born! Even if my father remains celibate the rest of his life, *I* am still here, to call to mind what he wants forgotten. Yes, *he*, not only the bishop! I stand in the way of his advancement.'

'Surely,' said Mark, shocked, 'you do him injustice. I am certain he feels a father's affection for you, as I do believe you feel a daughter's for him.'

'It never was tested before,' she said simply. 'No one grudged us a proper love. Oh, he wishes me no ill, neither does the bishop. But very heartily they both wish that I may go somewhere else to thrive, so far away I shall trouble them no more.'

'So that is why they've planned to match you with a man of Anglesey. As far away,' said Cadfael ruefully, 'as a man could get and still be in North Wales. Yes, that would certainly settle the bishop's mind. But what of yours? Do you know the man they intend for you?'

'No, that was the prince's doing, and he meant it kindly, and indeed I take it kindly. No, the bishop wanted to send me away to a convent in England, and make a nun of me. Owain Gwynedd said that would be a wicked waste unless it was my wish, and asked me there in front of everyone in the hall if I had any mind to it, and very loudly and clearly I said no. So he proposed this match for me. His man is looking for a wife, and they tell me he's a fine fellow, not so young but barely past thirty, which is not so old, and good to look at, and well regarded. Better at least,' she said without great enthusiasm, 'than being shut up behind a grid in an English nunnery.'

'So it is,' agreed Cadfael heartily, 'unless your own heart drives you there, and I doubt that will ever happen to you. Better, too, surely, than living on here and being made to feel an outcast and a burden. You are not wholly set against marriage?'

'No!' she said vehemently.

'And you know of nothing against this man the prince has in mind?'

'Only that I have not chosen him,' she said, and set her red lips in a stubborn line.

'When you see him you may approve him. It would not be the first time,' said Cadfael sagely, 'that an intelligent matchmaker got the balance right.'

'Well or ill,' she said, rising with a sigh, 'I have no choice but to go. My father goes with me to see that I behave, and Canon Morgant, who is as rigid as the bishop himself, goes with us to see that we both behave. Any further scandal now, and goodbye to any advancement under Gilbert. I could destroy him if I so wished,' she said, dwelling vengefully on something she knew could never be a possibility, for all her anger and disdain. And from the evening light in the doorway she looked back to add: 'I can well live without him. Soon or late, I should have gone to a husband. But do you know what most galls me? That he should give me up so lightly, and be so thankful to get rid of me.'

Canon Meirion came for them as he had promised, just as the bustle in the courtyard was settling into competent quietness, building work abandoned for the day, all the domestic preparations for the evening's feast completed, the small army of servitors mustered into their places, and the household, from princes to grooms, assembled in hall. The light was still bright, but softening into the gilded silence before the sinking of the sun.

Dressed for ceremony, the canon was brushed and immaculate but plain, maintaining the austerity of his office, perhaps, all the more meticulously to smooth away from memory all the years when he had been married to a wife. Time had been, once, long ago in the age of the saints, when celibacy had been demanded of all Celtic priests, just as insistently as it was being demanded now by Bishop Gilbert, by reason of the simple fact that the entire structure of the Celtic Church was built on the monastic ideal, and anything less was a departure from precedent and a decline in sanctity. But long since even the memory of that time had grown faint to vanishing, and there would be just as indignant a reaction to the reimposition of that ideal as there must once have been to its gradual abandonment. For centuries now priests had lived as decent married men and raised families like their parishioners. Even in England, in the more remote country places, there were plenty of humble married priests, and certainly no one thought the worse of them. In Wales it was not unknown for son to follow sire in the cure of a parish, and worse, for the sons of bishops to take it for granted they should succeed their mitred fathers, as though the supreme offices of the Church had been turned into heritable fiefs. Now here came this alien bishop, imposed from without, to denounce all such practices as abominable sin, and clear his diocese of all but the celibate clergy.

And this able and impressive man who came to summon them to the support of his master had no intention of suffering diminution simply because, though he had buried his wife just in time, the survival of a daughter continued to accuse him. Nothing against the girl, and he would see her provided for, but somewhere else, out of sight and mind.

To do him justice, he made no bones about going straight for what he wanted, what would work to his most advantage. He meant to exploit his two visiting monastics and their mission to his bishop's pleasure and satisfaction.

'They are just seated. There will be silence until princes and bishop are settled. I have seen to it there is a clear space below the high table, where you will be seen and heard by all.'

Do him justice, too, he was no way disappointed or disparaging in contemplating Brother Mark's smallness of stature and plain Benedictine habit, or the simplicity of his bearing; indeed he looked him over with a nod of satisfied approval, pleased with a plainness that would nevertheless carry its own distinction.

Mark took the illuminated scroll of Roger de Clinton's letter and the little carved casket that contained the cross in his hands, and they followed their guide across the courtyard to the door of the bishop's hall. Within, the air was full of the rich scent of seasoned timber and the resiny smoke of torches, and the subdued murmur of voices among the lower tables fell silent as the three of them entered, Canon Meirion leading. Behind the high table at the far end of the hall an array of faces, bright in the torchlight, fixed attentively upon the small procession advancing into the cleared space below the dais. The bishop in the midst, merely a featureless presence at this distance, princes on either side of him, the rest clerics and Welsh noblemen of Owain's court disposed alternately, and all eyes upon Brother Mark's small, erect figure, solitary in the open space, for Canon Meirion had stepped aside to give him the floor alone, and Cadfael had remained some paces behind him.

'My lord bishop, here is Deacon Mark, of the household of the bishop of Lichfield and Coventry, asking audience.'

'The messenger of my colleague of Lichfield is very welcome,' said the formal voice from the high table.

Mark made his brief address in a clear voice, his eyes fixed on the long, narrow countenance that confronted him. Straight, wiry steel-grey hair about a domed tonsure, a long, thin blade of a nose flaring into wide nostrils, and a proud, tight-lipped mouth that wore its formal smile somewhat unnervingly for lack of practice.

'My lord, Bishop Roger de Clinton bids me greet you reverently in his name, as his brother in Christ and his neighbour in the service of the Church, and wishes you long and fruitful endeavour in the diocese of Saint Asaph. And by my hand he sends you in all brotherly love this letter, and this casket, and begs you accept them in kindness.'

All of which Cadfael took up, after the briefest of pauses for effect, and turned into ringing Welsh that brought an approving stir and murmur from his fellow-countrymen among the assembly.

The bishop had risen from his seat, and made his way round the high table to approach the edge of the dais. Mark went to meet him, and bent his knee to present letter and casket into the large, muscular hands that reached down to receive them.

'We accept our brother's kindness with joy,' said Bishop Gilbert with considered and gratified grace, for the secular power of Gwynedd was there within earshot, and missing nothing that passed. 'And we welcome his messengers no less gladly. Rise, Brother, and make one more honoured guest at our table. And your comrade also. It was considerate indeed of Bishop de Clinton to send a Welsh speaker with you into a Welsh community.'

Cadfael stood well back, and followed only at a distance on to the dais. Let Mark have all the notice and the attention, and be led to a place of honour next to Hywel ab Owain, who sat at the bishop's left. Was that Canon Meirion's doing, the bishop's own decision to make the most of the visit, or had Hywel had a hand in it? He might well be interested in learning more about what other cathedral chapters thought of the resurrection of Saint Kentigern's throne, and its bestowal on an alien prelate. And probing from him might be expected to find a more guileless response than if it came from his formidable father, and produce a more innocent and lavish crop. A first occasion, it might be, for Mark to say little and listen much.

Cadfael's own allotted place was much further from the princely centre, near the end of the table, but it gave him an excellent view of all the faces ranged along the seats of honour. On the bishop's right sat Owain Gwynedd, a big man every way, in body, in breadth of mind, in ability, very tall, exceeding by a head the average of his own people, and flaxen-fair by contrast with their darkness, for his grandmother had been a princess of the Danish kingdom of Dublin, more Norse than Irish, Ragnhild, a granddaughter of King Sitric Silk-Beard, and his mother Angharad had been noted for her golden hair among the dark women of Deheubarth. On the bishop's left Hywel ab Owain sat at ease, his face turned towards Brother Mark in amiable welcome. The likeness was clear to be seen, though the son was of a darker colouring, and had not the height of the sire. It struck Cadfael as ironic that one so plainly signed with his father's image should be regarded by the cleric who sat beside him as illegitimate, for he had been born before Owain's marriage, and his mother, too, was an Irishwoman. To the Welsh a son acknowledged was as much a son as those born in marriage, and Hywel on reaching manhood had been set up honourably in South Ceredigion, and now, after his uncle's fall, possessed the whole of it. And very well capable, by his showing so far, of holding on to his own. There were three or four more Welshmen of Owain's party, all arranged turn for turn with Gilbert's canons and chaplains, secular and clerical perforce rubbing shoulders and exchanging possibly wary conversation, though now they had the open casket and its filigree silver cross as a safe topic, for Gilbert had opened it and set it on the board before him to be admired, and laid de Clinton's scroll beside it, doubtless to await a ceremonial reading aloud when the meal was drawing to its close.

Meantime, mead and wine were oiling the wheels of diplomacy, and by the rising babel of voices successfully. And Cadfael had better turn his attention to his own part in this social gathering, and begin to do his duty by his neighbours.

On his right hand he had a middle-aged cleric, surely a canon of the cathedral, well-fleshed and portly, but with a countenance of such uncompromising rectitude that Cadfael judged he might well be that Morgant whose future errand it was to see that both father and daughter conducted themselves unexceptionably on the journey to dispose of Heledd to a husband. Just such a thin, fastidious nose seemed suitable to the task, and just such chill, sharp eyes. But his voice when he spoke, and his manner to the guest, were gracious enough. In every situation he would be equal to events, and strike the becoming note, but he did not look as if he would be easy on shortcomings in others.

On Cadfael's left sat a young man of the prince's party, of the true Welsh build, sturdy and compact, very trim in his dress, and dark of hair and eye. A very black, intense eye, that focussed on distance, and looked through what lay before his gaze, men and objects alike, rather than at them. Only when he looked along the high table, to where Owain and Hywel sat, did the range of his vision shorten, fix and grow warm in recognition and acknowledgement, and the set of his long lips soften almost into smiling. One devoted follower at least the princes of Gwynedd possessed. Cadfael observed the young man sidewise, with discretion, for he was worth study, very comely in his black and brooding fashion, and tended to a contained and private silence. When he did speak, in courtesy to the new guest, his voice was quiet but resonant, and moved in cadences that seemed to Cadfael to belong elsewhere than in Gwynedd. But the most significant thing about his person did not reveal itself for some time, since he ate and drank little, and used only the right hand that lay easy on the board under Cadfael's eyes. Only when he turned directly towards his neighbour, and rested his left elbow on the edge of the table, did it appear that the left forearm terminated only a few inches below the joint, and a fine linen cloth was drawn over the stump like a glove, and secured by a thin silver bracelet.

It was impossible not to stare, the revelation came so unexpectedly; but Cadfael withdrew his gaze at once, and forbore from any comment, though he could not resist studying the mutilation covertly when he thought himself unobserved. But his neighbour had lived with his loss long enough to accustom himself to its effect on others.

'You may ask, Brother,' he said, with a wry smile. 'I am not ashamed to own where I left it. It was my better hand once, though I could use both, and can still make shift with the one I have left.'

Since curiosity was understood and expected of him, Cadfael made no secret of it, though he was already hazarding a guess at the possible answers. For this young man was almost certainly from South Wales, far from his customary kin here in Gwynedd.

'I am in no doubt,' he said cautiously, 'that wherever you may have left it, the occasion did you nothing but honour. But if you are minded to tell me, you should know that I have carried arms in my time, and given and taken injury in the field. Where you admit me, I can follow you, and not as a stranger.'

'I thought,' said the young man, turning black, brilliant eyes on him appraisingly, 'you had not altogether the monastic look about you. Follow, then, and welcome. I left my arm lying over my lord's body, the sword still in my hand.'

'Last year,' said Cadfael slowly, pursuing his own prophetic imaginings, 'in Deheubarth.'

'As you have said.'

'Anarawd?'

'My prince and my foster-brother,' said the maimed man. 'The stroke, the final stroke, that took his life from him took my arm from me.'

Chapter Three

'HOW MANY,' asked Cadfael carefully, after a moment of silence, 'were with him then?'

'Three of us. On a simple journey and a short, thinking no evil. There were eight of them. I am the only one left who rode with Anarawd that day.' His voice was low and even. He had forgotten nothing and forgiven nothing, but he was in complete command of voice and face.

'I marvel,' said Cadfael, 'that you lived to tell the story. It would not take long to bleed to death from such a wound.'

'And even less time to strike again and finish the work,' the young man agreed with a twisted smile. 'And so they would have done if some others of our people had not heard the affray and come in haste. Me they left lying when they rode away. I was taken up and tended after his murderers had run. And when Hywel came with his army to avenge the slaying, he brought me back here with him, and Owain has taken me into his own service. A one-armed man is still good for something. And he can still hate.'

'You were close to your prince?'

'I grew up with him. I loved him.' His black eyes rested steadily upon the lively profile of Hywel ab Owain, who

43

surely had taken Anarawd's place in his loyalty, in so far as one man can ever replace another.

'May I know your name?' asked Cadfael. 'And mine is, or in the world it was, Cadfael ap Meilyr ap Dafydd, a man of Gwynedd myself, born at Trefriw. And Benedictine though I may be, I have not forgotten my ancestry.'

'Nor should you, in the world or out of it. And my name is Cuhelyn ab Einion, a younger son of my father, and a man of my prince's guard. In the old days,' he said, darkling, 'it was disgrace for a man of the guard to return alive from the field on which his lord was slain. But I had and have good reason for living. Those of the murderers whom I knew I have named to Hywel, and they have paid. But some I did not know. I keep the faces in mind, for the day when I see them again and hear the names that go with the faces.'

'There is also one other, the chief, who has paid only a blood-price in lands,' said Cadfael. 'What of him? Is it certain he gave the orders for this ambush?'

'Certain! They would never have dared, otherwise. And Owain Gwynedd has no doubts.'

'And where, do you suppose, is this Cadwaladr now? And has he resigned himself to the loss of everything he possessed?'

The young man shook his head. 'Where he is no one seems to know. Nor what mischief he has next in mind. But resigned to his loss? That I doubt! Hywel took hostages from among the lesser chiefs who served under Cadwaladr, and brought them north to ensure there should be no further resistance in Ceredigion. Most of them have been released now, having sworn not to bear arms against Hywel's rule or offer service again to Cadwaladr, unless at some time to come he should pledge reparation and be restored. There's one still left

44

captive in Aber, Gwion. He's given his parole not to attempt escape, but he refuses to forswear his allegiance to Cadwaladr or promise peace to Hywel. A decent enough fellow,' said Cuhelyn tolerantly, 'but still devoted to his lord. Can I hold that against a man? But such a lord! He deserves better for his worship.'

'You bear no hatred against him?'

'None, there is no reason. He had no part in the ambush, he is too young and too clean to be taken into such a villainy. After a fashion, I like him as he likes me. We are two of a kind. Could I blame him for holding fast to his allegiance as I hold fast to mine? If he would kill for Cadwaladr's sake, so would I have done, so I did, for Anarawd. But not by stealth, in double force against light-armed men expecting no danger. Honestly, in open field, that's another matter.'

The long meal was almost at its end, only the wine and mead still circling, and the hum of voices had mellowed into a low, contented buzzing like a hive of bees drunken and happy among summer meadows. In the centre of the high table Bishop Gilbert had taken up the fine scroll of his letter and broken the seal, and was on his feet with the vellum leaf unrolled in his hands. Roger de Clinton's salutation was meant to be declaimed in public for its full effect, and had been carefully worded to impress the laity no less than the Celtic clergy, who might be most in need of a cautionary word. Gilbert's sonorous voice made the most of it. Cadfael, listening, thought that Archbishop Theobald would be highly content with the result of his embassage.

'And now, my lord Owain,' Gilbert pursued, seizing the mellowed moment for which he must have been waiting throughout the feast, 'I ask your leave to introduce a petitioner, who comes asking your indulgence for a plea on behalf of another. My appointment here gives me some right, by virtue of my office, to speak for peace, between individual men as between peoples. It is not good that there should be anger between brothers. Just cause there may have been at the outset, but there should be a term to every outlawry, every quarrel. I ask an audience for an ambassador who speaks on behalf of your brother Cadwaladr, that you may be reconciled with him as is fitting, and restore him to his lost place in your favour. May I admit Bledri ap Rhys?'

There was a brief, sharp silence, in which every eye turned upon the prince's face. Cadfael felt the young man beside him stiffen and quiver in bitter resentment of such a breach of hospitality, for clearly this had been planned deliberately without a word of warning to the prince, without any prior consultation, taking an unfair advantage of the courtesy such a man would undoubtedly show towards the host at whose table he was seated. Even had this audience been sought in private, Cuhelyn would have found it deeply offensive. To precipitate it thus publicly, in hall before the entire household, was a breach of courtesy only possible to an insensitive Norman set up in authority among a people of whom he had no understanding. But if the liberty was as displeasing to Owain as it was to Cuhelyn, he did not allow it to appear. He let the silence lie just long enough to leave the issue in doubt, and perhaps shake Gilbert's valiant self-assurance, and then he said clearly:

'At your wish, my lord bishop, I will certainly hear Bledri ap Rhys. Every man has the right to ask and to be heard. Without prejudice to the outcome!'

It was plain, as soon as the bishop's steward brought the petitioner into the hall, that he had not come straight from travel to ask for this audience. Somewhere about the bishop's enclave he had been waiting at ease for his entry here, and had prepared himself carefully, very fine and impressive in his dress and in his person, every grain of dust from the roads polished away. A tall, broad-shouldered, powerful man, black-haired and black-moustached, with an arrogant beak of a nose, and a bearing truculent rather than conciliatory. He swept with long strides into the centre of the open space fronting the dais, and made an elaborate obeisance in the general direction of prince and bishop. The gesture seemed to Cadfael to tend rather to the performer's own aggrandisement than to any particular reverence for those saluted. He had everyone's attention, and meant to retain it.

'My lord prince – my lord bishop, your devout servant! I come as a petitioner here before you.' He did not look the part, nor was his full, confident voice expressive of any such role.

'So I have heard,' said Owain. 'You have something to ask of us. Ask it freely.'

'My lord, I was and am in fealty to your brother Cadwaladr, and I dare venture to speak for his right, in that he goes deprived of his lands, and made a stranger and disinherited in his own country. Whatever you may hold him guilty of, I dare to plead that such a penalty is more than he has deserved, and such as brother should not visit upon brother. And I ask of you that measure of generosity and forgiveness that should restore him his own again. He has endured this despoiling a year already, let that be enough, and set him up again in his lands of Ceredigion. The lord bishop will add his voice to mine for reconciliation.'

'The lord bishop has been before you,' said Owain drily, 'and equally eloquent. I am not, and never have been, adamant against my brother, whatever follies he has committed, but murder is worse than folly, and requires a measure of penitence before forgiveness is due. The two, separated, are of no value, and where the one is not, I will not waste the other. Did Cadwaladr send you on this errand?'

'No, my lord, and knows nothing of my coming. It is he who suffers deprivation, and I who appeal for his right to be restored. If he has done ill in the past, is that good reason for shutting him out from the possibility of doing well in the future? And what has been done to him is extreme, for he has been made an exile in his own country, without a toehold on his own soil. Is that fair dealing?'

'It is less extreme,' said Owain coldly, 'than what was done to Anarawd. Lands can be restored, if restoration is deserved. Life once lost is past restoration.'

'True, my lord, but even homicide may be compounded for a blood-price. To be stripped of all, and for life, is another kind of death.'

'We are not concerned with mere homicide, but with murder,' said Owain, 'as well you know.'

At Cadfael's left hand Cuhelyn sat stiff and motionless in his place, his eyes fixed upon Bledri, their glance lengthened to pierce through him and beyond. His face was white, and his single hand clenched tightly upon the edge of the board, the knuckles sharp and pale as ice. He said no word and made no sound, but his bleak stare never wavered.

'Too harsh a name,' said Bledri fiercely, 'for a deed done in heat. Nor did your lordship wait to hear my prince's side of the quarrel.'

'For a deed done in heat,' said Owain with immovable composure, 'this was well planned. Eight men do not lie in wait in cover for four travellers unsuspecting and unarmed, in hot blood. You do your lord's cause no favour by defending

48

his crime. You said you came to plead. My mind is not closed against reconciliation, civilly sought. It is proof against threats.'

'Yet, Owain,' cried Bledri, flaring like a resinous torch, 'it behoves even you to weigh what consequences may follow if you are obdurate. A wise man would know when to unbend, before his own brand burns back into his face.'

Cuhelyn started out of his stillness, quivering, and was half rising to his feet when he regained control, and sank back in his place, again mute and motionless. Hywel had not moved, nor had his face changed. He had his father's formidable composure. And Owain's unshaken and unshakable calm subdued in a moment the uneasy stir and murmur that had passed round the high table and started louder echoes down in the floor of the hall.

'Am I to take that as threat, or promise, or a forecast of a doom from heaven?' asked Owain, in the most amiable of voices, but none the less with a razor edge to the tone that gave it piercing sweetness, and caused Bledri to draw back his head a little as if from a possible blow, and for a moment veil the smouldering fire of his black eyes, and abate the savage tightness of his lips. Somewhat more cautiously he responded at last:

'I meant only that enmity and hatred between brothers is unseemly among men, and cannot but be displeasing to God. It cannot bear any but disastrous fruit. I beg you, restore your brother his rights.'

'That,' said Owain thoughtfully, and eyeing the petitioner with a stare that measured and probed beyond the words offered, 'I am not yet ready to concede. But perhaps we should consider of this matter at more leisure. Tomorrow morning I and my people set out for Aber and Bangor, together with some of the lord bishop's household and these visitors from Lichfield. It is in my mind, Bledri ap Rhys, that you should ride with us and be our guest at Aber, and on the way, and there at home in my llys, you may better develop your argument, and I better consider on those consequences of which you make mention. I should not like,' said Owain in tones of honey, 'to invite disaster for want of forethought. Say yes to my hospitality, and sit down with us at our host's table.'

It was entirely plain to Cadfael, as to many another within the hall, that by this time Bledri had small choice in the matter. Owain's men of the guard had fully understood the nature of the invitation. By his tight smile, so had Bledri, though he accepted it with every evidence of pleasure and satisfaction. No doubt it suited him to continue in the prince's company, whether as guest or prisoner, and to keep his eyes and ears open on the ride to Aber. All the more if his hint of dire consequences meant more than the foreshadowing of divine disapproval of enmity between brothers. He had said a little too much to be taken at his face value. And as a guest, free or under guard, his own safety was assured. He took the place that was cleared for him at the bishop's table, and drank to the prince with a discreet countenance and easy smile.

The bishop visibly drew deep breath, relieved that his well-meaning effort at peace-making had at least survived the first skirmish. Whether he had understood the vibrating undertones of what had passed was doubtful. The subtleties of the Welsh were probably wasted on a forthright and devout Norman, Cadfael reflected. The better for him, he could speed his departing guests, thus augmented by one, and console himself that he had done all a man could do to bring about reconciliation. What followed, whatever it might be, was no responsibility of his.

50

The mead went round amicably, and the prince's harper sang the greatness and virtues of Owain's line and the beauty of Gwynedd. And after him, to Cadfael's respectful surprise, Hywel ab Owain rose and took the harp, and improvised mellifluously on the women of the north. Poet and bard as well as warrior, this was undoubtedly an admirable shoot from that admirable stem. He knew what he was doing with his music. All the tensions of the evening dissolved into amity and song. Or if they survived, at least the bishop, comforted and relaxed, lost all awareness of them.

In the privacy of their own lodging, with the night still drowsily astir outside the half-open door, Brother Mark sat mute and thoughtful on the edge of his bed for some moments, pondering all that had passed, until at last he said, with the conviction of one who has reviewed all circumstances and come to a firm conclusion: 'He meant nothing but good. He is a good man.'

'But not a wise one,' said Cadfael from the doorway. The night without was dark, without a moon, but the stars filled it with a distant, blue glimmer that showed where occasional shadows crossed from building to building, making for their rest. The babel of the day was now an almost-silence, now and then quivering to the murmur of low voices tranquilly exchanging goodnights. Rather a tremor on the air than an audible sound. There was no wind. Even the softest of movements vibrated along the cords of the senses, making silence eloquent.

'He trusts too easily,' Mark agreed with a sigh. 'Integrity expects integrity.'

'And you find it missing in Bledri ap Rhys?' Cadfael asked respectfully. Brother Mark could still surprise him now and then.

51

'I doubt him. He comes too brazenly, knowing once received he is safe from any harm or affront. And he feels secure enough in Welsh hospitality to threaten.'

'So he did,' said Cadfael thoughtfully. 'And passed it off as a reminder of heaven's displeasure. And what did you make of that?'

'He drew in his horns,' said Mark positively, 'knowing he had gone a step too far. But there was more in that than a pastoral warning. And truly I wonder where this Cadwaladr is now, and what he is up to. For I think that was a plain threat of trouble here and now if Owain refused his brother's demands. Something is in the planning, and this Bledri knows of it.'

'I fancy,' said Cadfael placidly, 'that the prince is of your opinion also, or at least has the possibility well in mind. You heard him. He has given due notice to all his men that Bledri ap Rhys is to remain in the royal retinue here, in Aber, and on the road between. If there's mischief planned, Bledri, if he can't be made to betray it, can be prevented from playing any part in it, or letting his master know the prince has taken the warning, and is on his guard. Now I wonder did Bledri read as much into it, and whether he'll go to the trouble to put it to the test?'

'He did not seem to me to be put out of his stride,' said Mark doubtfully. 'If he did understand it so, it did not disquiet him. Can he have provoked it purposely?'

'Who knows? It may suit him to go along with us to Aber, and keep his eyes and ears open along the way and within the llys, if he's spying out the prince's dispositions for his master. Or for himself!' Cadfael conceded thoughtfully, 'Though what's the advantage to him, unless it's to put him safely out of the struggle, I confess I don't see.' For a prisoner who

52

enjoys officially the status of a guest can come to no harm, whatever the issue. If his own lord wins, he is delivered without reproach, and if his captor is the victor he is immune just as surely, safe from injury in the battle or reprisals after it. 'But he did not strike me as a cautious man,' Cadfael owned, rejecting the option, though with some lingering reluctance.

A few threads of shadow still crossed the gathering darkness of the precinct, ripples on a nocturnal lake. The open door of the bishop's great hall made a rectangle of faint light, most of the torches within already quenched, the fire turfed down but still glowing, distant murmurs of movement and voices a slight quiver on the silence, as the servants cleared away the remnants of the feast and the tables that had borne it.

A tall, dark figure, wide-shouldered and erect against the pale light, appeared in the doorway of the hall, paused for a long moment as though breathing in the cool of the night, and then moved leisurely down the steps, and began to pace the beaten earth of the court, slowly and sinuously, like a man flexing his muscles after being seated a while too long. Cadfael opened the door a little wider, to have the shadowy movements in view.

'Where are you going?' asked Mark at his back, anticipating with alert intelligence.

'Not far,' said Cadfael. 'Just far enough to see what rises to our friend Bledri's bait. And how he takes it!'

He stood motionless outside the door for a long moment, drawing the door to behind him, to accustom his eyes to the night, as doubtless Bledri ap Rhys was also doing as he trailed his coat to and fro, nearer and nearer to the open gate of the precinct. The earth was firm enough to make his crisp, deliberate steps audible, as plainly he meant them to be. But nothing stirred and no one took note of him, not even the few servants drifting away to their beds, until he turned deliberately and walked straight towards the open gate. Cadfael had advanced at leisure along the line of modest canonical houses and guest lodgings, to keep the event in view.

With admirable aplomb two brisk figures heaved up into the gateway from the fields without, amiably wreathed together, collided with Bledri in mid-passage, and untwined themselves to embrace him between them.

'What, my lord Bledri!' boomed one blithe Welsh voice. 'Is it you? Taking a breath of air before sleeping? And a fine night for it!'

'We'll bear you company, willingly,' the second voice offered heartily. 'It's early to go to bed yet. And we'll see you safe to your own brychan, if you lose your way in the dark.'

'I'm none so drunk as to go astray,' Bledri acknowledged without surprise or concern. 'And for all the good company there is to be had in Saint Asaph tonight, I think I'll get to my bed. You gentlemen will be needing your sleep, too, if we're off with the morn tomorrow.' The smile in his voice was clear to be sensed. He had the answer he had looked for, and it caused him no dismay, rather a measure of amusement, perhaps even satisfaction. 'Goodnight to you!' he said, and turned to saunter back towards the hall door, still dimly lighted from within.

Silence hung outside the precinct wall, though the nearest tents of Owain's camp were not far away. The wall was not so high that it could not be climbed, though wherever a man mounted, there would be someone waiting below on the other side. But in any case Bledri ap Rhys had no intention of removing himself, he had merely been confirming his expectation that any attempt to do so would very simply and neatly be frustrated. Owain's orders were readily understood even when obliquely stated, and would be efficiently carried out. If Bledri had been in any doubt of that, he knew better now. And as for the two convivial guards, they withdrew again into the night with an absence of pretence which was almost insulting.

And that, on the face of it, was the end of the incident. Yet Cadfael continued immobile and detachedly interested, invisible against the dark bulk of the timber buildings, as if he expected some kind of epilogue to round off the night's entertainment.

Into the oblong of dim light at the head of the steps came the girl Heledd, unmistakable even in silhouette by the impetuous grace of her carriage and her tall slenderness. Even at the end of an evening of serving the bishop's guests and the retainers of his household she moved like a fawn. And if Cadfael observed her appearance with impersonal pleasure, so did Bledri ap Rhys, from where he stood just aside from the foot of the steps, with a startled appreciation somewhat less impersonal, having no monastic restraints to hold it in check. He had just confirmed that he was now, willing or otherwise, a member of the prince's retinue at least as far as Aber, and in all probability he already knew, since he was lodged in the bishop's own house, that this promising girl was the one who would be riding with the party at dawn. The prospect offered a hope of mild pleasure along the way, to pass the time agreeably. At the very least, here was this moment, to round off an eventful and enjoyable evening. She was descending, with one of the embroidered drapings of the high table rolled up in her arms, on her way to the canonical dwellings across the precinct. Perhaps wine had been spilled on the cloth, or some of the gilt threads been snagged by a belt buckle or the rough setting of a dagger hilt or a bracelet, and she was charged with its repair. He had been about to ascend, but waited aside instead, for the pleasure of watching her at ever closer view as she came down, eyes lowered to be sure of stepping securely. He was so still and she so preoccupied that she had not observed him. And when she had reached the third step from the ground he suddenly reached out and took her by the waist between his hands, very neatly, and swung her round in a half-circle, and so held her suspended, face to face with him and close, for a long moment before he set her quite gently on her feet. He did not, however, relinquish his hold of her.

It was done quite lightly and playfully, and for all Cadfael could see, which was merely a shadow play, Heledd received it without much trace of displeasure, and certainly none of alarm, once the surprise was past. She had uttered one small, startled gasp as he plucked her aloft, but that was all, and once set down she stood looking up at him eye to eye, and made no move to break away. It is not unpleasant to any woman to be admired by a handsome man. She said something to him, the words indistinguishable but the tone light and tolerant to Cadfael's ear, if not downright encouraging. And something he said in return to her, at the very least with no sign of discouragement. No doubt Bledri ap Rhys had a very good opinion of himself and his attractions, but it was in Cadfael's mind that Heledd, for all she might enjoy his attentions, was also quite capable of keeping them within decorous bounds. Doubtful if she was considering letting him get very far. But from this pleasurable brush with him she could extricate herself whenever she chose. They were neither of them taking it seriously.

In the event she was not to be given the opportunity to conclude it in her own fashion. For the light from the open doorway above was suddenly darkened by the bulk of a big man's body, and the abrupt eclipse cast the linked pair below into relative obscurity. Canon Meirion paused for a moment to adjust his vision to the night, and began to descend the steps with his usual selfconscious dignity. With the dwindling of his massive shadow renewed light fell upon Heledd's glossy hair and the pale oval of her face, and the broad shoulders and arrogant head of Bledri ap Rhys, the pair of them closely linked in what fell little short of an embrace.

It seemed to Brother Cadfael, watching with unashamed interest from his dark corner, that both of them were very well aware of the stormcloud bearing down on them, and neither was disposed to do anything to evade or placate it. Indeed, he perceived that Heledd softened by a hair the stiffness of her stance, and allowed her head to tilt towards the descending light and glitter into a bright and brittle smile, meant rather for her father's discomfort than for Bledri's gratification. Let him sweat for his place and his desired advancement! She had said that she could destroy him if she so willed. it was something she would never do, but if he was so crass, and knew so little of her, as to believe her capable of bringing about his ruin, he deserved to pay for his stupidity.

The instant of intense stillness exploded into a flurry of movement, as Canon Meirion recovered his breath and came seething down the steps in a turmoil of clerical black, like a sudden thundercloud, took his daughter by the arm, and wrenched her firmly away from Bledri's grasp. As firmly and competently she withdrew herself from this new compulsion, and brushed the very touch of his hand from her sleeve. The dagger glances that must have strained through the dimness between sire and daughter were blunted by the night. And

Bledri suffered his deprivation gracefully, without stirring a step, and very softly laughed.

'Oh, pardon if I have trespassed on your rights of warren,' he said, deliberately obtuse. 'I had not reckoned with a rival of your cloth. Not here in Bishop Gilbert's household. I see I have undervalued his breadth of mind.'

He was being provocative deliberately, of course. Even if he had had no notion that this indignant elder was the girl's father, he certainly knew that this intervention could hardly bear the interpretation he was placing upon it. But had not the impulse of mischief originated rather with Heledd? It did not please her that the canon should have so little confidence in her judgement as to suppose she would need help in dealing with a passing piece of impudence from this questionably welcome visitor. And Bledri was quite sufficiently accomplished in the study of women to catch the drift of her mild malice, and play the accomplice, for her gratification as readily as for his own amusement.

'Sir,' said Meirion with weighty and forbidding dignity, curbing his rage, 'my daughter is affianced, and shortly to be married. Here in his lordship's court you will treat her and all other women with respect.' And to Heledd he said brusquely, and with a sharp gesture of his hand towards their lodging under the far wall of the enclave: 'Go in, girl! The hour is late already, you should be withindoors.'

Heledd, without haste or discomposure, gave them a slight, curt inclination of her head to share between them, and turned and walked away. The rear view of her as she went was expressive, and disdainful of men in general.

'And a very fine girl, too,' said Bledri approvingly, watching her departure. 'You may be proud of your getting, Father. I hope you are marrying her to a man who'll appreciate beauty. The small courtesy of hefting the lass down the steps to level ground can hardly have blemished his bargain.' His clear, incisive voice had dwelt fondly on the word 'Father', well aware of the dual sting. 'Well, what the eye has not seen, the heart need not grieve, and I hear the bridegroom is well away in Anglesey. And no doubt you can keep a still tongue where this match is concerned.' The plain implication was there, very sweetly insinuated. No, Canon Meirion was exceedingly unlikely to make any move that could jeopardise his cleansed and celibate and promising future. Bledri ap Rhys was very quick on the uptake, and well informed about the bishop's clerical reforms. He had even sensed Heledd's resentment at being so ruthlessly disposed of, and her impulse to take her revenge before departing.

'Sir, you are a guest of prince and bishop, and as such are expected to observe the standards due to their hospitality.' Meirion was stiff as a lance, and his voice thinned and steely as a sword-blade. Within his well-schooled person there was a ferocious Welsh temper under arduous control. 'If you do not, you will rue it. Whatever my own situation, I will see to that. Do not approach my daughter, or attempt to have any further ado with her. Your courtesies are unwelcome.'

'Not, I think, to the lady,' said Bledri, with the most complacent of smiles implicit in the very tone of his voice. 'She has a tongue, and a palm, and I fancy would have been ready enough to use both if I had caused her any displeasure. I like a lass of spirit. If she grants me occasion, I shall tell her so. Why should she not enjoy the admiration she is entitled to, these few hours on the road to her marriage?'

The brief silence fell like a stone between them; Cadfael felt the air quiver with the tension of their stillness. Then Canon

Meirion said, through gritted teeth and from a throat constricted with the effort to contain his rage: 'My lord, do not think this cloth I wear will prove any protection to you if you affront my honour, or my daughter's good name. Be warned, and keep away from her, or you shall have excellent cause to regret it. Though perhaps,' he ended, even lower and more malevolently, 'too brief time!'

'Time enough,' said Bledri, not noticeably disturbed by the palpable threat, 'for all the regretting I'm likely to do. It's something I've had small practice in. Goodnight to your reverence!' And he passed by Meirion so close their sleeves brushed, perhaps intentionally, and began to climb the steps to the hall door. And the canon, wrenching himself out of his paralysis of rage with an effort, composed his dignity about him as best he could, and stalked away towards his own door.

Cadfael returned to his own quarters very thoughtfully, and recounted the whole of this small incident to Brother Mark, who was lying wakeful and wide-eyed after his prayers, by some private and peculiar sensitivity of his own already aware of turbulent cross-currents trembling on the night air. He listened, unsurprised.

'How much, would you say, Cadfael, is his concern only for his own advancement, how much truly for his daughter? For he does feel guilt towards her. Guilt that he resents her as a burden to his prospects, guilt at loving her less than she loves him. A guilt that makes him all the more anxious to put her out of sight, far away, another man's charge.'

'Who can decypher any man's motives?' said Cadfael resignedly. 'Much less a woman's. But I tell you this, she would do well not to drive him too far. The man has a core of

60

violence in him. I would not like to see it let loose. It could be a killing force.'

'And against which of them,' wondered Mark, staring into the dark of the roof above him, 'would the lightning be launched, if ever the storm broke?'

Chapter Four

HE PRINCE'S cortège mustered in the dawn, in a morning hesitant between sullenness and smiles. There was the moisture of a brief shower on the grasses as Cadfael and Mark crossed to the church for prayer before saddling up, but the sun was shimmering on the fine drops, and the sky above was the palest and clearest of blues, but for a few wisps of cloud to eastward, embracing the rising orb of light with stroking fingers. When they emerged again into the courtyard it was already full of bustle and sound, the baggage horses being loaded, the brave city of tents along the hillside above folded and on the move, and even the frail feathers of cloud dissolved into moist and scintillating radiance.

Mark stood gazing before him with pleasure at the preparations for departure, his face flushed and bright, a child embarking on an adventure. Until this moment, Cadfael thought, he had not fully realised the possibilities, the fascinations, even the perils of the journey he had undertaken. To ride with princes was no more than half the tale, somewhere there was a lurking threat, a hostile brother, a prelate bent on reforming a way of life which in the minds of its population needed no reform. And who could guess what might happen between here and Bangor, between bishop and bishop, the stranger and the native?

'I spoke a word in the ear of Saint Winifred,' said Mark, flushing almost guiltily, as though he had appropriated a patroness who by rights belonged to Cadfael. 'I thought we must be very close to her here, it seemed only gracious to let her know of our presence and our hopes, and ask her blessing.'

'If we deserve!' said Cadfael, though he had small doubt that so gentle and sensible a saint must look indulgently upon this wise innocent.

'Indeed! How far is it, Cadfael, from here to her holy well?'

'A matter of fourteen miles or so, due east of us.'

'Is it true it never freezes? However hard the winter?'

'It is true. No one has ever known it stilled, it bubbles always in the centre.'

'And Gwytherin, where you took her from the grave?'

'That lies as far south and west of us,' said Cadfael, and refrained from mentioning that he had also restored her to her grave in that same place. 'Never try to limit her,' he advised cautiously. 'She will be wherever you may call upon her, and present and listening as soon as you cry out your need.'

'That I never doubted,' said Mark simply, and went with a springy and hopeful step to put together his small belongings and saddle his glossy nutbrown gelding. Cadfael lingered a few moments to enjoy the bright bustle before him, and then followed more sedately to the stables. Outside the walls of the enclave Owain's guards and noblemen were already marshalling, their encampment vanished from the greensward, leaving behind only the paler, flattened patches which would soon spring back into lively green, and erase even the memory of their visitation. Within the wall grooms whistled and called, hooves stamped lively, muffled rhythms in the hard-packed earth, harness jingled, maidservants shrilled to one another above the general babel of male voices, and the faint dust of all this vigorous movement rose into the sunlight and shimmered in gilded mist overhead.

The company gathered as blithely as if they were going maying, and certainly so bright a morning invited to so pleasant a pastime. But there were certain graver reminders to be remarked as they mounted. Heledd made her appearance cloaked and ready, serene and demure of countenance, but with Canon Meirion keeping close on one side of her, with tight lips and downdrawn brows, and Canon Morgant on the other, equally tightlipped but with brows arched into uncompromising severity, and sharp eyes dwelling alternately on father and daughter, and with no very assured approval of either. And for all their precautions, at the last moment Bledri ap Rhys stepped between them and lifted the girl into the saddle with his own large and potentially predatory hands, with a courtesy so elaborate that it glittered into insolence: and, worse, Heledd accepted the service with as gracious an inclination of her head, and a cool, reserved smile, ambiguous between chaste reproof and discreet mischief. To take exception to the behaviour of either party would have been folly, so well had both preserved the appearance of propriety, but both canons perceptibly beheld the incident with raised hackles and darkening frowns if they kept their mouths shut.

Nor was that the only sudden cloud in this clear sky, for Cuhelyn, appearing already mounted in the gateway, too late to have observed any present cause for offence, sat his horse with drawn brows, while his intent eyes ranged the entire company within until he found Bledri, and there settled and brooded, a long-memoried man of intense passions, measuring an enemy. It seemed to Cadfael, surveying the scene with a thoughtful eye, that there would be a considerable weight of illwill and not a few grudges among the rich baggage of this princely party.

The bishop came down into the courtyard to take leave of his royal guests. This first encounter had passed off successfully enough, considering the strain he had put upon it by inviting Cadwaladr's envoy into conference. He was not so insensitive that he had not felt the momentary tension and displeasure, and no doubt he was drawing relieved breath now at having survived the danger. Whether he had the humility to realise that he owed it to the prince's forbearance was another matter, Cadfael reflected. And here came Owain side by side with his host, and Hywel at his back. At his coming the whole bright cortège quivered into expectant life, and as he reached for bridle and stirrup, so did they all. Too tall for me, eh, Hugh? Cadfael thought, swinging aloft into the roan's high saddle, with a buoyancy that set him up in a very gratifying conceit of himself. I'll show you whether I have lost my appetite for travel and forgotten everything I learned in the east before ever you were born.

And they were away, out of the wide-open gate and heading westward after the prince's lofty fair head, uncovered to the morning sun. The bishop's household stood to watch them depart, warily content with one diplomatic encounter successfully accomplished. Such threats as lingered uneasily from last night's exchanges cast their shadows on these departing guests. Bishop Gilbert, if he had believed in them at all, could let them withdraw unchallenged, for they were no threat to him.

As those within the enclave emerged into the green track

without, Owain's officers from the encampment fell into neat
order about them, lining either flank, and Cadfael observed
with interest but without surprise that there were archers
among them, and two keeping their station a few yards behind
Bledri ap Rhys's left shoulder. Given this particular guest's
undoubted quickness of perception, he was equally aware of
them, and just as clearly he had no objection to their presence,
for in the first mile he did not let it inhibit him from changing
his position two or three times to speak a civil word in Canon
Morgant's ear, or exchange courtesies with Hywel ab Owain,
riding close at his father's back. But he did not make any
move to edge his way through the attendant file of guards. If
they were keeping him in mind of his virtual captivity, so was
he bent on assuring them that he was perfectly content, and
had no intention of attempting to remove himself. Indeed,
once or twice he looked to left and right to take the measure of
the prince's unobtrusive efficiency, and seemed not unfavour-
ably impressed by what he saw.

All of which was of considerable interest to an inquisitive
man, even if at this stage it remained undecypherable. Put it
away at the back of the mind, along with everything else of
oddity value in this expedition, and the time would come
when its meaning would be revealed. Meantime, here was
Mark, silent and happy at his elbow, the road westward
before him, and the sun bright on Owain's pennant of bright
hair at the head of the column. What more could any man ask
on a fine May morning?

They did not, as Mark had expected, bear somewhat north-
wards towards the sea, but made due west, over softly rolling
hills and through well-treed valleys, by green trails sometimes
clearly marked, sometimes less defined, but markedly

keeping a direct line uphill and down alike, here where the lie of the land was open and the gradients gentle enough for pleasant riding.

'An old, old road,' said Cadfael. 'It starts from Chester, and makes straight for the head of Conwy's tidal water, where once, they say, there was a fort the like of Chester. At low tide, if you know the sands, you can ford the river there, but with the tide boats can ply some way beyond.'

'And after the river crossing?' asked Mark, attentive and glowing.

'Then we climb. To look westward from there, you'd think no track could possibly pass, but pass it does, up and over the mountains, and down at last to the sea. Have you ever seen the sea?'

'No. How could I? Until I joined the bishop's household I had never been out of the shire, not even ten miles from where I was born.' He was straining his eyes ahead as he rode now, with longing and delight, thirsty for all that he had never seen. 'The sea must be a great wonder,' he said on a hushed breath.

'A good friend and a bad enemy,' said Cadfael, beckoned back into old memories. 'Respect it, and it will do well by you, but never take liberties.'

The prince had set a steady, easy pace that could be maintained mile by mile in this undulating countryside, green and lush, patterned with hamlets in the valleys, cottages and church snugly huddled together, the fringe of cultivable fields a woven tapestry round them, and here and there solitary, scattered throughout the tref, the households of the free landowners, and no less solitary, somewhere among them, their parish church.

'These men live lonely,' said Mark, taking in the distinction with some wonder.

'These are the freeborn men of the tribe. They own their land, but not to do as they please with it, it descends by strict law of inheritance within the family. The villein villages till the soil among them, and pay their communal dues together, though every man has his dwelling and his cattle and his fair share of the land. We make sure of that by overseeing the distribution every so often. As soon as sons grow to be men they have their portion at the next accounting.'

'So no one there can inherit,' Mark deduced reasonably.

'None but the youngest son, the last to grow into a portion of his own. He inherits his father's portion and dwelling. His elder brothers by then will have taken wives and built houses of their own.' It seemed to Cadfael, and apparently to Mark also, a fair, if rough and ready, means of assuring every man a living and a place in which to live, a fair share of the work and a fair share of the profit of the land.

'And you?' asked Mark. 'Was this where you belonged?'

'Belonged and could not belong,' Cadfael acknowledged, looking back with some surprise at his own origins. 'Yes, I was born in just such a villein tref, and coming up to my fourteenth birthday and a slip of land of my own. And would you believe it now? – I did not want it! Good Welsh earth, and I felt nothing for it. When the wool merchant from Shrewsbury took a liking to me, and offered me work that would give me licence to see at least a few more miles of the world, I jumped at that open door as I've jumped at most others that ever came my way. I had a younger brother, better content to sit on one strip of earth lifelong. I was for off, as far as the road would take me, and it took me half across the world before I understood. Life goes not in a straight line, lad, but in a circle. The first half we spend venturing as far as the world's end from home and kin and stillness, and the latter half brings us back by roundabout ways but surely, to that state from which we set out. So I end bound by vow to one narrow place, but for the rare chance of going forth on the business of my house, and labouring at a small patch of earth, and in the company of my closest kin. And content,' said Cadfael, drawing satisfied breath.

They came over the crest of a high ridge before noon, and there below them the valley of the Conwy opened, and beyond, the ground rose at first gently and suavely, but above these green levels there towered in the distance the enormous bastions of Eryri, soaring to polished steel peaks against the pale blue of the sky. The river was a winding silver thread, twining a tortuous course through and over shoals of tidal mud and sand on its way northward to the sea, its waters at this hour so spread and diminished that it could be forded without difficulty. And after the crossing, as Cadfael had warned, they climbed.

The first few green and sunny miles gave way to a rising track that kept company with a little tributary river, mounting steeply until the trees fell behind, and they emerged gradually into a lofty world of moorland, furze and heather, open and naked as the sky. No plough had ever broken the soil here, there was no visible movement but the ruffling of the sudden wind among the gorse and low bushes, no inhabitants but the birds that shot up from before the foremost riders, and the hawks that hung almost motionless, high in air. And yet across this desolate but beautiful wilderness marched a perceptible causeway laid with stones and cushioned with rough grass, raised clear of the occasional marshy places, straddling the shallow pools of peat-brown water, making straight for the lofty wall of honed rock that seemed to Brother Mark utterly impenetrable. In places where the firm rock broke

through the soil and gave solid footing, the raised sarn
remained visible as a trodden pathway needing no ramp of
stones, but always maintained its undeviating line ahead.

'Giants made this,' said Brother Mark in awe.

'Men made it,' said Cadfael. It was wide where it was
clearly to be seen, wide enough for a column of men marching
six abreast, though horsemen had to ride no more than three
in line, and Owain's archers, who knew this territory well,
drew off on either flank and left the paved way to the company they guarded. A road, Cadfael thought, made not for
pleasure, not for hawking or hunting, but as a means of moving a great number of men from one stronghold to another as
quickly as possible. It took small count of gradients, but set its
sights straight ahead, deviating only where that headlong line
was rankly impossible to maintain, and then only until the
obstacle was passed.

'But through that sheer wall,' Mark marvelled, staring
ahead at the barrier of the mountains, 'surely we cannot go.'

'Yes, you will find there's a gate through, narrow but wide
enough, at the pass of Bwlch y Ddeufaen. We thread through
those hills, keep this high level three or four more miles, and
after that we begin to descend.'

'Towards the sea?'

'Towards the sea,' said Cadfael.

They came to the first decline, the first sheltered valley of
bushes and trees, and in the heart of it bubbled a spring that
became a lively brook, and accompanied them downhill gradually towards the coast. They had long left behind the
rivulets that flowed eastward towards the Conwy; here the
streams sprang sparkling into short, precipitous lives, and
made headlong for the sea. And down with this most diminutive of its kind went the track, raised to a firm level

above the water, at the edge of the cleft of trees. The descent became more gradual, the brook turned somewhat away from the path, and suddenly the view opened wide before them, and there indeed was the sea.

Immediately below them a village lay in its patterned fields, beyond it narrow meadowland melting into salt flats and shingle, and then the wide expanse of sea, and beyond that again, distant but clear in the late afternoon light, the coast of Anglesey stretched out northward, to end in the tiny island of Ynys Lanog. From the shore towards which they moved the shallow water shimmered pale gold overlaid with aquamarine, almost as far as the eye could distinguish colour, for Lavan Sands extended the greater part of the way to the island shore, and only there in the distance did the sea darken into the pure, greenish blue of the deep channel. At the sight of this wonder about which he had dreamed and speculated all day long, Mark checked his horse for a moment, and sat staring with flushed cheeks and bright eyes, enchanted by the beauty and diversity of the world.

It happened that Cadfael turned his head to see where someone else had reined in at the same moment, perhaps in the same rapt delight. Between her two guardian canons Heledd had checked and sat staring before her, but her sights were raised beyond the crystal and gold of the shallows, beyond the cobalt channel to the distant shore of Anglesey, and her lips were austerely drawn, and her brows level and unrevealing. She looked towards her bridegroom's land, the man against whom she knew nothing, of whom she had heard nothing but good; she saw marriage advancing upon her all too rapidly, and there was such a baffled and resentful sadness in her face, and such an obstinate rejection of her fate, that Cadfael marvelled no one else felt her burning outrage, and turned in alarm to find the source of this intense disquiet.

Then as suddenly as she had halted she shook the rein, and set her horse to an impatient trot downhill, leaving her black-habited escort behind, and threaded a way deeper into the cavalcade to shake them off at least for a few rebellious moments.

Watching her vehement passage through the ranks of the prince's retinue, Cadfael absolved her of any deliberate intent in drawing close alongside Bledri's mount. He was simply there in her way, in a moment she would have passed by him. But there was intent enough in the opportunist alacrity with which Bledri reached a hand to her bridle, and checked her passage knee to knee with him, and in the intimate, assured smile he turned upon her as she yielded to the persuasion. There was, Cadfael thought, one instant when she almost shook him off, almost curled her lip with the tolerant mockery which was all she truly felt for him. Then with perverse deliberation she smiled at him, and consented to fall in beside him, in no hurry to free herself of the muscular hand that detained her. They rode on together in apparent amity, with matched pace and in easy talk together. The rear view of them suggested to Cadfael nothing more than a continuation of a somewhat malicious but enjoyable game on both parts, but when he turned his head cautiously to see what effect the incident had had upon the two canons of Saint Asaph it was all too plain that to them it implied something very different. If Meirion's drawn brows and rigid lips threatened storms towards Heledd and rage towards Bledri ap Rhys, equally they were stiff with apprehension of what must be going on behind the controlled but ominous rectitude of Morgant's fleshy countenance.

Ah, well! Two days more, and it should be over. They

would be safely in Bangor, the bridegroom would cross the strait to meet them, and Heledd would be rapt away to that mist-blue shore beyond the faint gold and ice-blue of Lavan Sands. And Canon Meirion could draw breath in peace at last.

They came down to the rim of the salt flats and turned westward, with the quivering plane of the shallows reflecting glittering light on their right hand, and the green of field and copse on the left, rising terrace beyond terrace into the hills. Once or twice they plashed through tenuous streams trickling down through the salt marshes to the sea. And within the hour they were riding alongside the high stockade of Owain's royal seat and tref of Aber, and the porters and guards at the gates had seen the shimmer of their colours nearing, and cried their coming within.

From all the buildings that lined the walls of the great court of Owain's maenol, from stables and armoury and hall, and the array of guest dwellings, the household came surging to welcome the prince home, and make his visitors welcome. Grooms ran to receive the horses, squires came with pitchers and horns. Hywel ab Owain, who had distributed his hospitable attentions punctiliously during the journey, moving from rider to rider with civilities as his father's representative, and no doubt taking due note of all the undercurrents that drew taut between them, with his father's interests in mind, was the first out of the saddle, and went straight to take the prince's bridle, in an elegant gesture of filial respect, before ceding the charge to the waiting groom, and going to kiss the hand of the lady who had come out from the timber hall to welcome her lord home. Not his own mother! The two young boys who came leaping down the steps from the hall door after her were hers, lithe dark imps of about ten and seven years, shrilling with excitement and with a flurry of dogs wreathing round their feet. Owain's wife was daughter to a prince of Arwystli, in central Wales, and her lively sons had her rich colouring. But an older youth, perhaps fifteen or sixteen, followed them more circumspectly down the steps, and came with authority and confidence straight to Owain, and was embraced with an affection there was no mistaking. This one had his father's fair hair deepened into pure gold, and his father's impressive male comeliness refined into a startling beauty. Tall, erect, with an athlete's grace of movement, he could not emerge into any company without being noticed, and even at a distance the brilliant northern blue of his eyes was as clear as if an inner sun shone through crystals of sapphire. Brother Mark saw him, and held his breath.

'*His* son?' he said in an awed whisper.

'But not hers,' said Cadfael. 'Another like Hywel.'

'There cannot be many such in this world,' said Mark, staring. Beauty in others he observed with a particular, ungrudging delight, having always felt himself to be the plainest and most insignificant of mortals.

'There is but one such, lad, as you know full well, for there is but one of any man that ever lived, black or fair, And yet,' owned Cadfael, reconsidering the uniqueness of the physical envelope if not of the inhabiting soul, 'we go close to duplicating this one, there at home in Shrewsbury. The boy's name is Rhun. You might look at our Brother Rhun, since Saint Winifred perfected him, and think one or the other a miraculous echo.'

Even to the name! And surely, thought Mark, recalling with pleasure the youngest of those who had been his brothers in Shrewsbury, this is how the pattern of a prince, the son of a prince, should look – and no less, a saint, the protégé of a saint. All radiance and clarity, all openness and serenity in the face. No wonder his father, recognising a prodigy, loves him better than all others.

'I wonder,' said Cadfael half to himself, unwittingly casting a shadow athwart Mark's contemplation of light, 'how *her* two will look upon him, when they're all grown.'

'It is impossible,' Mark said firmly, 'that they should ever wish him harm, even if land-greed and power-greed have sometimes turned brothers into enemies. This youth no one could hate.'

Close at his shoulder a cool, dry voice observed ruefully: 'Brother, I envy your certainty, but I would not for the world share it, the fall is too mortal. There is no one who cannot be hated, against whatever odds. Nor anyone who cannot be loved, against all reason.'

Cuhelyn had approached them unnoticed, threading a way through the stir of men and horses, hounds and servants and children. For all his black intensity, he was a very quiet man, unobtrusive in all his comings and goings. Cadfael turned in response to the unexpected observation, just in time to see the intent glance of the young man's shrewd eyes, presently fastened with a wry, indulgent warmth upon the boy Rhun, sharpen and chill as another figure passed between, and follow the transit with a fixity that suggested to Cadfael, at first, nothing more than detached interest, and in a matter of seconds froze into composed but indubitable hostility. Perhaps even more than hostility, a measure of restrained but implacable suspicion.

A young man of about Cuhelyn's years, and by no means unlike him in build and colouring, though thinner in feature and somewhat longer in the reach, had been standing a little apart, watching the bustle all round him, his arms folded and his shoulders leaned against the wall of the undercroft, as though this tumultuous arrival concerned him rather less than the rest of the household. From this detached stance he had moved suddenly, crossing between Cuhelyn and the linked pair, father and son, and cutting off the view of Rhun's radiant face. Something to be seen here certainly mattered to this young man, after all, someone had been sighted who meant more to him than clerics from Saint Asaph or the young noblemen of Owain's guard. Cadfael followed his vehement passage through the press, and saw him take one dismounting horseman by the sleeve. The very touch, the very encounter, that had drawn taut all the lines of Cuhelyn's countenance. Bledri ap Rhys swung about, face to face with the youth who accosted him, visibly recognised an acquaintance, and guardedly acknowledged him. No very exuberant welcome, but on both parts there was one momentary flash of warmth and awareness, before Bledri made his visage formally blank, and the boy accepted the suggestion, and began what seemed to be the most current of court civilities. No need, apparently, to pretend they did not know each other well enough, but every need to keep the acquaintance on merely courteous terms.

Cadfael looked along his shoulder, and briefly, at Cuhelyn's face, and asked simply: 'Gwion?'

'Gwion!'

'They were close? These two?'

'No. No closer than two must be who hold by the same lord.'

'That might be close enough for mischief,' said Cadfael bluntly. 'As you told me, your man has given his word not to attempt escape. He has not pledged himself to give up his allegiance beyond that.'

'Natural enough he should welcome the sight of another

liegeman,' said Cuhelyn steadily. 'His word he will keep. As for Bledri ap Rhys, the terms of his sojourn with us *I* will see kept.' He shook himself briefly, and took each of them by an arm. The prince and his wife and sons were climbing the steps into the hall, the closest of their household following without haste. 'Come, Brothers, and let me be your herald here. I'll bring you to your lodging, and show you the chapel. Use it as you find occasion, and the prince's chaplain will make himself known to you.'

In the privacy of the lodging allotted to them, backed into the shelter of the maenol wall, Brother Mark sat refreshed and thoughtful, looking back with wide grey eyes at all that had passed during this arrival in Aber. And at length he said: 'What most caused me to watch and wonder, was how like they were, those two – the young liegemen of Anarawd and of Cadwaladr. It is no mere matter of the same years, the same manner of body, the same make of face, it is the same passion within them. In Wales, Cadfael, this is another fashion of loyalty even than the bond the Normans hold by, or so it seems to me. They are on opposing sides, your Cuhelyn and this Gwion, and they could be brothers.'

'And as brothers should, and by times do not, they respect and like each other. Which would not prevent them from killing each other,' Cadfael admitted, 'if ever it came to a clash between their lords in the field.'

'That is what I feel to be so wrong,' said Mark earnestly. 'How could either young man look at the other, and not see himself? All the more now that they have lived together in the same court, and admitted affection?'

'They are like twins, the one born left-handed, the other right-handed, at once doubles and opposites. They could kill without malice, and die without malice. God forbid,' said Cadfael, 'it should ever come to that. But one thing is certain. Cuhelyn will be watching every moment his mirror image brushes sleeves with Bledri ap Rhys, and marking every word that passes between them, and every glance. For I think he knows somewhat more of Cadwaladr's chosen envoy than he has yet told us.'

At supper in Owain's hall there was good food and plenteous mead and ale, and harp music of the best. Hywel ab Owain sang, improvising upon the beauty of Gwynedd and the splendour of her history, and Cadfael's recalcitrant heart shed its habit for a half-hour, and followed the verses far into the mountains inland of Aber, and across the pale mirror of Lavan Sands to the royal burial-place of Llanfaes on Anglesey. In youth his adventurings had all looked eastward, now in his elder years eyes and heart turned westward. All heavens, all sanctuaries of the blessed lie to westward, in every legend and every imagination, at least for men of Celtic stock; a suitable meditation for old men. Yet here in the royal llys of Gwynedd Cadfael did not feel old.

Nor did it seem that his senses were in the least dulled or blunted, even as he rejoiced in his dreams, for he was sharp enough to detect the moment when Bledri ap Rhys slid an arm about Heledd's waist as she served him with mead. Nor did he miss the icy rigidity of Canon Meirion's face at the sight, or the deliberation with which Heledd, well aware of the same maledictory stare, forbore from freeing herself immediately, and said a smiling word in Bledri's ear, which might as well have been a curse as a compliment, though there was no doubt how her father interpreted it. Well, if the girl was playing with fire, whose fault was that? She had lived with her sire many loyal, loving years, he should have known her better, well enough to trust her. For Bledri ap Rhys she had no use at all but to take out her grievance on the father who was in such haste to get rid of her.

Nor did it appear, on reflection, that Bledri ap Rhys was seriously interested in Heledd. He made the gesture of admiration and courtship almost absentmindedly, as though by custom it was expected of him, and though he accompanied it with a smiling compliment, he let her go the moment she drew away, and his gaze went back to a certain young man sitting among the noblemen of the guard at a lower table. Gwion, the last obstinate hostage, who would not forswear his absolute fealty to Cadwaladr, sat silent among his peers, and enemies, some of whom, like Cuhelyn, had become his friends. Throughout the feast he kept his own counsel, and guarded his thoughts, and even his eyes. But whenever he looked up at the high table, it was upon Bledri ap Rhys that his glance rested, and twice at least Cadfael saw them exchange a brief and brilliant stare, such as allies might venture to convey worlds of meaning where open speech was impossible.

Those two will somehow get together in private, Cadfael thought, before this night is out. And for what purpose? It is not Bledri who so passionately seeks a meeting, though he has been at liberty and is suspect of having some secret matter to impart. No, it is Gwion who wants, demands, relies upon reaching Bledri's ear. It is Gwion who has some deep and urgent purpose that needs an ally to reach fulfilment. Gwion who has given his word not to leave Owain's easy captivity. As Bledri ap Rhys has not done.

Well, Cuhelyn had vouched for Gwion's good faith, and pledged a constant watch upon Bledri. But it seemed to Cadfael that the llys was large enough and complex enough to provide him with a difficult watch, if those two were resolved to elude him.

The lady had remained with her children in private, and had not dined in hall, and the prince also withdrew to his own apartments early, having been some days absent from his family. He took his most beloved son with him, and left Hywel to preside until his guests chose to retire. With every man now free to change his place, or go out to walk in the fresh air of the late evening, there was considerable movement in the hall, and in the noise of many conversations and the music of the harpers, in the smoke of the torches and the obscurity of the shadowy corners, who was to keep a steady eye upon one man among so many? Cadfael marked the departure of Gwion from among the young men of the household, but still Bledri ap Rhys sat in his modest place towards the foot of the high table, serenely enjoying his mead – but in moderation, Cadfael noted – and narrowly observing everything that passed about him. He appeared to be cautiously impressed by the strength and strict order of the royal household, and the numbers, discipline and confidence of the young men of the guard.

'I think,' said Brother Mark softly into Cadfael's ear, 'we might have the chapel to ourselves if we go now.'

It was about the hour of Compline. Brother Mark would not rest if he neglected the office. Cadfael rose and went with him, out from the doorway of the great hall into the cool and freshness of the night, and across the inner ward to the timber chapel against the outer wall. It was not yet fully dark nor very late, the determined drinkers still in hall would not end their gathering yet, but in the shadowy passages between the buildings of the maenol those who had duties about the place moved without haste, and quietly, going about their usual tasks in the easy languor of the end of a long and satisfactory day.

They were still some yards from the door of the chapel when a man emerged from it, and turned along the row of lodgings that lined the wall of the ward, to disappear into one of the narrow passages behind the great hall. He did not pass them close, and he might have been any one of the taller and elder of the frequenters of Owain's court. He was in no haste, but going tranquilly and a little wearily to his night's rest, yet Cadfael's mind was so persistently running upon Bledri ap Rhys that he was virtually certain of the man's identity, even in the deepening dusk.

He was quite certain when they entered the chapel, dimly lit by the rosy eye of the constant lamp on the altar, and beheld the shadowy outline of a man kneeling a little aside from the small pool of light. He was not immediately aware of them, or at least seemed not to be, though they had entered without any great care to preserve silence; and when they checked and hung back in stillness to avoid interrupting his prayers he gave no sign, but continued bowed and preoccupied, his face in shadow. At length he stirred, sighed and rose to his feet, and passing them by on his way out, without surprise, he gave them: 'Goodnight, Brothers!' in a low voice. The small red eye of the altar lamp drew his profile on the air clearly, but only for a moment; long enough, however, to show plainly the young, intense, brooding features of Gwion.

Compline was long over, and midnight past, and they were peacefully asleep in their small, shared lodging, when the alarm came. The first signs, sudden clamour at the main gate of the maenol, the muted thudding of hooves entering, the agitated exchange of voices between rider and guard, passed dreamlike and distant through Cadfael's senses without breaking his sleep, but Mark's younger ear, and mind hypersensitive to the excitement of the day, started him awake even before the murmur of voices rose into loud orders, and the men of the household began to gather in the ward, prompt but drowsy from the rushes of the hall and the many lodgings of the maenol. Then what was left of the night's repose was shattered brazenly by the blasting of a horn, and Cadfael rolled from his brychan on to his feet, wide-awake and braced for action.

'What's afoot?'

'Someone rode in. In a hurry! Only one horseman!'

'They would not rouse the court for a little thing,' said Cadfael, clawing on his sandals and making for the door. The horn blared again, echoes ricocheting between the buildings of the prince's llys, and blunting their sharp edges against walls. In the open ward the young men came thronging in arms to the call, and the hum of many voices, still pitched low in awe of the night, swelled into a wordless, muted bellowing like a stormy tide flowing. From every open doorway a thread of light from hastily kindled lamps and candles spilled into the dark, conjuring here and there a recognisable face out of the crowd. A jaded horse, hard-ridden, was being led with drooping head towards the stables, and his rider, heedless of the many hands that reached to arrest him and the many voices that questioned, was thrusting a way through the press towards the great hall. He had barely reached the foot of the steps when the door above him opened, and Owain in his furred bed-gown came out, large and dark against the light from within, the squire who had run to arouse him with news of the coming close at his shoulder.

'Here am I,' said the prince, loud and clear and wide

awake. 'Who's come wanting me?' As he moved forward to the edge of the steps the light from within fell upon the messenger's face, and Owain knew him. 'You, is it, Goronwy? From Bangor? What's your news?'

The messenger scarcely took time to bend his knee. He was known and trusted, and ceremony was waste of precious moments. 'My lord, early this evening one came with word from Carnarvon, and I have brought that word here to you as fast as horse can go. About Vespers they sighted ships westward off Abermenai, a great fleet in war order. The seamen say they are Danish ships from the kingdom of Dublin, come to raid Gwynedd and force your hand. And that Cadwaladr, your brother, is with them! He has brought them over to avenge and restore him, in your despite. The fealty he could not keep for love he has bought with promised gold.'

Chapter Five

ITHIN OWAIN'S writ the invasion of disorder might bring about momentary consternation, but could not hope to create disorder in its turn. His mind was too quick and resolute ever to entertain chaos. Before the muted roar of anger and resentment had circled the ward the captain of the prince's guard was at his elbow, awaiting his orders. They understood each other too well to need many words.

'This report is certain?' Owain asked.

'Certain, my lord. The messenger I had it from saw them himself from the dunes. Too distant then to be sure how many ships, but no question whence they come, and small doubt why. It was known he had fled to them. Why come back in such force but for a reckoning?'

'He shall have one,' said Owain composedly. 'How long before they come to land?'

'My lord, before morning surely. They were under sail, and the wind is steady from the west.'

For the length of a deep breath Owain considered. Perhaps a quarter of the horses in his stables had been ridden far, though not hard, the previous day, and as many of his armed men had made that journey, and sat merry in hall late into the night. And the ride that faced them now would be urgent and fast.

'Short time,' he said, musing, 'to raise even the half of Gwynedd, but we'll make sure of reserves, and collect every man available between here and Carnarvon as we go. Six couriers I want, one to go before us now, the others to carry my summons through the rest of Arlechwedd and Arfon. Call them to Carnarvon. We may not need them, but no harm in making certain.' His clerks accepted the expected word, and vanished with commendable calm to prepare the sealed writs the couriers would bear to the chieftains of two cantrefs before the night was over. 'Now, every man who bears arms,' said Owain, raising his voice to carry to the containing walls and echo back from them, 'get to your beds and take what rest you can. We muster at first light.'

Cadfael, listening on the edge of the crowd, approved. Let the couriers, by all means, ride out by night, but to move the disciplined host across country in the dark was waste of time that could better be used in conserving their energy. The fighting men of the household dispersed, if reluctantly; only the captain of Owain's bodyguard, having assured himself of his men's strict obedience, returned to his lord's side.

'Get the women out of our way,' said Owain over his shoulder. His wife and her ladies had remained above in the open doorway of the hall, silent but for an agitated whispering among the younger maids. They departed uneasily and with many a glance behind, rather curious and excited than alarmed, but they departed. The princess had as firm a hold over her own household as Owain over his fighting men. There remained the stewards and elder counsellors, and such menservants as might be needed for any service, from armoury, stables, stores, brewhouse and bakehouse. Armed men also had needs, beyond their brands and bows, and the addition of some hundreds to a garrison meant a supply train following.

Among the smaller group now gathered about the prince Cadfael noted Cuhelyn, by the look of him fresh from his bed, if not from sleep, for he had thrown on his clothes in haste, he who was wont to appear rather elegantly presented. And there was Hywel, alert and quiet at his father's side. And Gwion, attentive and still, standing a little apart, as Cadfael had first seen him, as though he held himself always aloof from the concerns of Owain and Gwynedd, however honourably he acknowledged them. And Canon Meirion and Canon Morgant, for once drawn together in contemplating a crisis which had nothing to do with Heledd, and held no direct threat against either of them. They were onlookers, too, not participators. Their business was to get the reluctant bride safely to Bangor and her bridegroom's arms, and there were no Danish ships as near as Bangor, nor likely to be. Heledd had been safely disposed of for the night with the princess's women, and no doubt was gossiping excitedly with them now over what might well seem to her an almost welcome diversion.

'So this,' said Owain into the comparative silence that waited on his decree, 'is the dire consequence Bledri ap Rhys had in mind. He knew, none so well, what my brother had planned. He gave me fair warning. Well, let him wait his turn, we have other work to do before morning. If he's secure in his bed, he'll keep.'

The chosen couriers to his vassal princes were reappearing cloaked for the night ride, and up from the stables the grooms came leading the horses saddled and ready for them. The leader came almost at a trot, led by the head groom, and the man was in some measured excitement, poured out in a breath before ever he came to a halt.

'My lord, there's a horse gone from the stables, and harness and gear with him! We checked again, wanting to provide you the best for the morning. A good, young roan, no white on him, and saddle-cloth, saddle, bridle and all belonging to him.'

'And the horse he rode here – Bledri ap Rhys? His own horse that he brought to Saint Asaph with him?' Hywel demanded sharply. 'A deep grey, dappled lighter down his flanks? Is he still there?'

'I know the one, my lord. No match for this roan. Still jaded from yesterday. He's still there. Whoever the thief was, he knew how to choose.'

'And meant good speed!' said Hywel, burning. 'He's gone, surely. He's gone to join Cadwaladr and his Irish Danes at Abermenai. How the devil did he ever get out of the gates? And with a horse!'

'Go, some of you, and question the watch,' Owain ordered, but without any great concern, and without turning to see who ran to do his bidding. The guards on all the gates of his maenol were men he could trust, as witness the fact that not one of them had come running here from his post, however acute the curiosity he might be feeling about the audible turmoil continuing out of his sight. Only here at the main gate, where the messenger from Bangor had entered, had any man stirred from his duty, and then only the officer of the guard. 'There's no way of locking a man in,' reflected Owain philosophically, 'if he has his vigour and is determined to get out. Any wall ever built can be climbed, for a high enough cause. And he is to the last degree my brother's man.' He turned again to the tired messenger. 'In the dark a wise traveller would keep to the roads. Did you meet with any man riding west as you rode east here to us?'

'No, my lord, never a one. Not since I crossed the Cegin, and those were men of our own, known to me, and in no hurry.'

'He'll be far out of reach now, but let's at least start Einion off on his tracks with my writ. Who knows? A horse can fall lame, ridden hard in the dark, a man can lose his way in lands not his own. We may halt him yet,' said Owain, and turned to meet the steward who had run to see how watch was kept on the postern gates of the llys. 'Well?'

'No man challenged, no man passed. They know him now by sight, stranger though he may be. However he broke loose, it was not by the gates.'

'I never thought it,' the prince agreed sombrely. 'They never yet kept any but a thorough watch. Well, send out the couriers, Hywel, and then come to me within, to my private chamber. Cuhelyn, come with us.' He looked round briefly as his messengers mounted. 'Gwion, this is no fault nor concern of yours. Go to your bed. And keep your parole in mind still. Or take it back,' he added drily, 'and bide under lock and key while we're absent.'

'I have given it,' said Gwion haughtily, 'I shall keep it.'

'And I accepted it,' said the prince, relenting, 'and trust to it. There, go, what is there for you to do here?'

What, indeed, Cadfael thought wryly, except grudge us all the freedom he has denied himself? And the instant thought came, that Bledri ap Rhys, that fiery advocate so forward to excuse his lord and threaten in his name, had given no parole, and had, almost certainly, had very private and urgent conference with Gwion in the chapel of the llys only a matter of hours ago, and was now away to rejoin Cadwaladr at

Abermenai, with much knowledge of Owain's movements and forces and defences. Gwion had never promised anything except not to escape. Within the walls he might move at will, perhaps his freedom extended even to the tref that lay outside the gate. For that he had pledged his own consent to detention. No one had promised as much for Bledri ap Rhys. And Gwion had made no pretence of his steely loyalty to Cadwaladr. Could he be blamed as recreant if he had helped his unexpected ally to break out and return to his prince? A nice point! Knowing, if only at second hand from Cuhelyn, Gwion's stubborn and ferocious loyalty, he might well have warned his captors over and over of the limits he set on his parole, and the fervour with which he would seize any opportunity of serving the master he so obstinately loved, even at this remove.

Gwion had turned, slowly and hesitantly, to accept his dismissal, but then halted, stood with bent head and irresolute step, and in a moment gathered himself abruptly, and strode away instead towards the chapel; from the open door the faint red spark drew him like a lodestone. And what had Gwion to pray for now? A successful landing for Cadwaladr's Danish mercenaries, and a rapid and bloodless accommodation between brothers rather than a disastrous war? Or some repair to his own peace of mind? Fiercely upright, he might consider even his loyalty a sin where some unavoidable infringement of his oath was concerned. A complicated mind, sensitive to any self-reproach, however venial the sin.

Cuhelyn, who perhaps understood him best, and most resembled him, had watched him go with a thoughtful frown, and even taken a couple of impulsive steps to follow him before thinking better of the notion, and turning back to Owain's side. Prince and captains and counsellors mounted the steps to the great hall and the private apartments, and vanished purposefully within. Cuhelyn followed without another glance behind, and Cadfael and Mark, and a few hovering servants and retainers, were left in an almost empty ward, and the silence came down after clamour, and the dark stillness after a turmoil of movement. Everything was known and understood, everything was in hand, and would be dealt with competently.

'And there is no part in it for us,' Brother Mark said quietly at Cadfael's shoulder.

'None, except to saddle up tomorrow and ride on to Bangor.'

'Yes, that I must,' Mark agreed. There was a curious note of unease and regret in his voice, as if he found it almost a dereliction of his humanity to remove himself at this crisis in pursuit of his own errand, and leave all things here confounded and incomplete. 'I wonder, Cadfael . . . The watch on the gates, all the gates, were they thought enough? Do you suppose a watch was set on the man himself, even here within, or was it enough that the walls held him? No man stood guard over the door of his lodging, or followed him from hall to his bed?'

'From the chapel to his bed,' Cadfael amended, 'if any man had that charge. No, Mark, we watched him go. There was no one treading on his heels.' He looked across the ward, to the alley into which Bledri had vanished when he came from the chapel. 'Are we not taking too much for granted, all of us? The prince has more urgent matters on his hands, true, but should not someone confirm what we have all leaped to believe?'

Gwion emerged slowly and silently from the open doorway of the chapel, drawing the door to after him, so that the tiny gleam of red vanished. He came somewhat wearily across the ward, seemingly unaware of the two who stood motionless and mute in the shadows, until Cadfael stepped forward to intercept him, mildly seeking information from one who might be expected to be able to supply it: 'A moment! Do you know in which of the many lodgings here this Bledri ap Rhys slept overnight?' And as the young man halted abruptly, turning on him a startled and wary face: 'I saw you greet him yesterday when we rode in, I thought you might know. You must have been glad to have some talk with an old acquaintance while he was here.'

For some reason the protracted interval of silence was more eloquent than what was finally said in reply. It would have been natural enough to answer at once: 'Why do you want to know? What does it matter now?' seeing that lodging must be empty, if the man who had slept there had fled in the night. The pause made it plain that Gwion knew well enough who had walked in upon him in the chapel, and was well aware that they must have seen Bledri departing. He had time to think before he spoke, and what he said was: 'I *was* glad, to set eyes on a man of my own tribe. I have been here hostage more than half a year. They will have told you as much. The steward had given him one of the lodgings against the north wall. I can show you. But what difference does it make now? He's gone. Others may blame him,' he said haughtily, 'but not I. If I had been free, I would have done as he did. I never made secret of where my fealty lay. And lies still!'

'God forbid anyone should condemn a man for keeping faith,' agreed Cadfael equably. 'Did Bledri have his chamber to himself?'

'He did.' Gwion hoisted his shoulders, shrugging off an interest it seemed he did not understand, but accepted as meaning something to these wandering Benedictines if it meant nothing to him. 'There was none sharing it with him, to prevent his going, if that is what you mean.'

'I was wondering, rather,' said Cadfael deprecatingly, 'whether we are not assuming too much, just because a horse is missing. If his lodging was in a remote corner of the wards, with many a wall between, may he not have slept through this whole uproar, and be still snoring in all innocence? Since he lay alone, there was no one to wake him, if he proved so sound a sleeper.'

Gwion stood staring, eye to eye with him, his thick dark brows raised. 'Well, true enough, but for the horn call a man with enough drink in him might have slept through it all. I doubt it, but if you feel the need to see for yourself . . . It's not on my way, but I'll show you.' And without more words he set off into the passage between the rear of the great hall and the long timber range of the storehouse and armoury. They followed his brisk figure, shadowy in the dimness, through towards the long line of buildings in the shelter of the outer wall.

'The third door was his.' It stood just ajar, no gleam of light showing in the crack. 'Go in, Brothers, and see for yourselves. But by the look of it you'll find him gone, and all his gear with him.'

The range of small rooms was built in beneath the watch-platform along the outer wall, and shadowed deeply by its overhang. Cadfael had seen only one stairway to the platform, broad and easy of access but in full view of the main gate. Moreover, it would not be easy to descend on the outer side, unless with a long rope, for the fighting gallery projected outward from the wall, and there was a ditch below. Cadfael set a hand to the door and pushed it open upon darkness. His eyes, by this time accustomed to the night and such light as the clear but moonless sky provided, were at once blind again. There was no movement, and no sound within. He set the door wide, and advanced a step or two into the small chamber.

'We should have brought a torch,' said Mark, at his shoulder.

No need for that, it seemed, to show that the room was empty of life. But Gwion, tolerant of these exigent visitors, offered from the threshold: 'The brazier will be burning in the guard-house. I'll bring a light.'

Cadfael had made another step within, and all but stumbled as his foot tangled soundlessly with some shifting fold of soft material, as though a rumpled brychan had been swept from bed to floor. He stooped and felt forward into the rough weave of cloth, and found something of firmer texture within it. A fistful of sleeve rose to his grip, the warmth and odour of wool stirred on the air, and an articulated weight dangled and swung as he lifted it, solid within the cloth. He let it rest back again gently, and felt down the length of it to a thick hem, and beyond that, the smooth, lax touch of human flesh, cooling but not yet cold. A sleeve indeed, and an arm within it, and a large, sinewy hand at the end of the arm.

'Do that,' he said over his shoulder. 'Bring a light. We are going to need all the light we can get.'

'What is it? asked Mark, intent and still behind him.

'A dead man, by all the signs. A few hours dead. And unless he has grappled with someone who stood in the way of his flight, and left him here to tell the tale, who can this be but Bledri ap Rhys?'

Gwion came running with a torch, and set it in the sconce on the wall, meant only to hold a small lantern. In such confined rooms a torch would never normally be permitted, but this was crisis.

The sparse contents of the chamber sprang sharply outlined
from the dark, a rumpled bench bed against the rear wall, the
brychans spilled over and dangling to the floor, the impression of a long body still discernible indenting the cover of the
straw mattress. On a shelf beside the bed-head, convenient to
the guest's hand, a small saucer-lamp stood. Not quenched,
for it had burned out and left only a smear of oil and the
charred wick. Beneath the shelf, half-unfolded, lay a leather
saddle-roll, and dropped carelessly upon it a man's cotte and
chausses and shirt, and the rolled cloak he had not needed on
the journey. And in the corner his riding-boots, one over-
turned and displaced, as if a foot had kicked it aside.

And between the bed and the doorway, sprawled on his
back at Cadfael's feet, arms and legs flung wide, head
propped against the timber wall, as though a great blow had
lifted and hurled him backwards, Bledri ap Rhys lay with eyes
half-open, and lips drawn back from his large, even teeth in a
contorted grin. The skirts of his gown billowed about him in
disorder, the breast had fallen open wide as he fell, and
beneath it he was naked. In the flickering of the torch it was
hard to tell whether the darkened blotch on his left jaw and
cheek was shadow or bruise, but there was no mistaking the
gash over his heart, and the blood that had flowed from it
down into the folds of cloth under his side. The dagger that
had inflicted the wound had been as quickly withdrawn, and
drawn out the life after it.

Cadfael went down on his knees beside the body, and gently
turned back the breast of the woollen gown to reveal the
wound more clearly to the quivering light. Gwion, behind him
in the doorway and hesitant to enter, drew deep breath, and
let it out in a gusty sob that caused the flame to flicker wildly,
and what seemed a living shudder passed over the dead face.

'Be easy,' said Cadfael tolerantly, and leaned to close the half-open eyes. 'For he is easy enough now. Well I know, he was of your allegiance. And I am sorry!'

Mark stood quiet and still, staring down in undismayed compassion. 'I wonder had he wife and children,' he said at last. Cadfael marked the first focus of one fledgling priest's concern, and approved it. Christ's first instinct might have been much the same. Not: 'Unshriven, and in peril!' not even: 'When did he last confess and find absolution?' but: 'Who will care for his little ones?'

'Both!' said Gwion, very low. 'Wife and children he has. I know. I will deal.'

'The prince will give you leave freely,' said Cadfael. He rose from his knees, a little stiffly. 'We must go, all, and tell him what has befallen. We are within his writ and guests in his house, all, not least this man, and this is murder. Take the torch, Gwion, and go before, and I will close the door.'

Gwion obeyed this alien voice without question, though it had no authority over him but what he gave of his own free will. On the threshold he stumbled, for all he was holding the light. Mark took his arm until he had his balance again, and as courteously released him as soon as his step was secure. Gwion said no word, made no acknowledgement, as Mark needed none. He went before like a herald, torch in hand, straight to the steps of the great hall, and lit them steadily within.

'We were all in error, my lord,' said Cadfael, 'in supposing that Bledri ap Rhys had fled your hospitality. He did not go far, nor did he need a horse for the journey, though it is the longest a man can undertake. He is lying dead in the lodging where your steward housed him. From all we see there, he

96

never intended flight. I will not say he had slept. But he had certainly lain in his bed, and certainly put on his gown over his nakedness when he rose from it, to encounter whoever it may have been who walked in upon his rest. These two with me here have seen what I have seen, and will bear it out.'

'It is so,' said Brother Mark.

'It is so,' said Gwion.

Round Owain's council table in his private apartment, austerely furnished, the silence lasted long, every man among his captains frozen into stillness, waiting for the prince's reaction. Hywel, standing at his father's shoulder, in the act of laying a parchment before him, had halted with the leaf half-unrolled in his hands, his eyes wide and intent upon Cadfael's face.

Owain said consideringly, rather digesting than questioning the news thus suddenly laid before him: 'Dead. Well!' And in a moment more: 'And how did this man die?'

'By a dagger in the heart,' said Cadfael with certainty.

'From before? Face to face?'

'We have left him as we found him, my lord. Your own physician may see him just as we saw him. As I think,' said Cadfael, 'he was struck a great blow that hurled him back against the wall, so that he fell stunned. Certainly whoever struck him down faced him, this was confrontation, no assault from behind. And no weapon, not then. Someone lashed out with a fist, in great anger. But then he was stabbed as he lay. His blood has run down and gathered in the folds of his gown under his left side. There was no movement. He was out of his senses when he was stabbed. By someone!'

'The same someone?' wondered Owain.

'Who can tell? It is probable. It is not certain. But I doubt he would have lain helpless more than a matter of moments.'

Owain spread his hands upon the table before him, pushing aside the parchments scattered there. 'You are saying that Bledri ap Rhys has been murdered. Under my roof. In my charge, however he may have come there, friend or enemy, to all intent he was a guest in my house. This I will not abide.' He looked beyond Cadfael, at Gwion's sombre face. 'You need not fear that I will value my honest enemy's life at less than any man of my own,' he said in generous reassurance.

'My lord,' said Gwion, very low, 'that I never doubted.'

'If I must go after other matters now,' said Owain, 'yet he shall have justice, if by any means I can ensure it. Who last saw the man, living?'

'I saw him leave the chapel, late,' said Cadfael, 'and cross towards his own lodging. So did Brother Mark, who was with me. Beyond that I cannot say.'

'At that time,' said Gwion, his voice a little hoarse with constraint, 'I was in the chapel. I talked with him. I was glad to see a face I knew. But when he left I did not follow.'

'Enquiry shall be made,' said Owain, 'of all the servants of the house, who would be the last wakeful about the maenol. See to it, Hywel. If any had occasion to pass there, and saw either Bledri ap Rhys, or any man going or coming late about his door, bring the witness here. We muster at first light, but we have yet a few hours before dawn. If this thing can be resolved before I go to deal with my brother and his Danes, so much the better.'

Hywel departed on the word, laying his leaf of vellum down on the table, and plucking a couple of men out of the council to speed the search. There was to be no rest that night for the menservants, stewards and maids of Owain's court, none for the members of his bodyguard, or the young men who followed him in arms. Bledri ap Rhys had come to Saint Asaph intending mischief, threatening mischief, and the cost had fallen on his own head, but the echoes would spread outward like ripples from a stone flung into a pool, and scarify the lives of all here until murder was paid for.

'The dagger that was used,' said Owain, returning to his quest like a hawk stooping. 'It was not left in the wound?'

'It was not. Nor have I examined the wound so closely that I dare guess what manner of blade it had. Your own men, my lord, will be able to hazard that as well as I. Better,' said Cadfael, 'since even daggers change with years, and I am long out of the practice of arms.'

'And the bed, you say, had been slept in. At least lain in. And the man had made no preparation for riding, and left no sign he ever intended flight. It was not so vital a matter that I should set a man to watch him through the night. But there is yet another mystery here,' said the prince. 'For if he did not make away with one of our horses, who did? There is no question but the beast is gone.'

It was a point that Cadfael, in his preoccupation with Bledri's death, had not even considered. Somewhere at the back of his mind he had felt the nagging and elusive misgiving that something else would have to be investigated before the night was over, but in the brief instants when he ventured to turn and attempt to see it clearly, it had vanished from the corner of his eye. Suddenly confronted with the puzzle that had eluded him, he foresaw a lengthy and careful numbering of every soul in the maenol to find the one, the only one, lost without trace. Someone else would have to undertake that, for there could be no delay in the prince's dawn departure.

'It is in your hands, my lord,' he said, 'as are we all.'

Owain flattened a large and shapely hand upon the table before him. 'My course is set, and cannot be changed until

Cadwaladr's Dublin Danes are sent back to their own land with clipped ears, if it comes to that. And you, Brothers, have your own way to go, in less haste than my way, but not to be delayed, either. Your bishop is entitled to as strict service as princes expect. Let us by all means consider, in what time we have left, which among us may have done murder. Then, if it must be left behind for another time, yet it shall not be forgotten. Come, I'll see for myself how this ill matter looks, and then we'll have the dead cared for, and see due reparation made to his kin. He was no man of mine, but he did me no wrong, and such right as I may I'll do to him.'

They rejoined the gathering in the council chamber the better part of an hour later. By then the body of Bledri ap Rhys was decently bestowed in the chapel, in the charge of the prince's chaplain, and there was no more to be learned from the sparse furnishings of the room where he had died. No weapon remained to speak, even the flow of his blood was meagre, and left small trace behind, the stab wound being neat, narrow and precise. It is not difficult to make a clean and exact job of stabbing to the heart a man already laid senseless to your hand. Bledri could scarcely have felt death remove him from the world.

'He was not a man to be greatly loved, I fancy,' Owain said as they crossed once more to the hall. 'Many here must have resented him, for he came arrogantly enough. It might take no more than a quarrelsome encounter, after that, to make a man lash out on impulse. But to kill? Would any man of mine take it so far, when I had made him my guest?'

'It would need a very angry man,' Cadfael owned, 'to go so far in your despite. But it takes only an instant to strike, and less than an instant to forget all caution. He had made himself

100

a number of enemies, even in the short time we all rode together.' Names were to be suppressed at all cost, but he was thinking of the blackly murderous glare of Canon Meirion, beholding Bledri's familiarity with his daughter, and the consequent threat to a career the good canon had no intention of risking.

'An open quarrel would be no mystery,' said Owain. 'That I could have resolved. Even if it came to a death, a blood price would have paid it, the blame would not have been all one way. He did provoke hatred. But to follow him to his bedchamber and hale him out of his bed? It is a very different matter.'

They passed through the hall and entered the council chamber. Every eye turned upon them as they came in. Mark and Gwion had waited with the rest. They stood close together, silent, as though the very fact of discovering a death together had linked them in a continuing fellowship that set them apart from the captains round the council table. Hywel was back before his father, and had brought with him one of the kitchen servants, a shaggy dark boy a little puffy with sleep, but bright-eyed again with reviving wakefulness now that he knew of a sudden death, and had something, however small, to impart concerning it.

'My lord,' said Hywel, 'Meurig here is the latest I could find to pass by the lodgings where Bledri ap Rhys was housed. He will tell you what he saw. He has not yet told it, we waited for you.'

The boy spoke up boldly enough. It seemed to Cadfael that he was not altogether convinced of the importance of what he had to say, though it pleased him well enough to be here declaring it. Its significance he was content to leave to the princes.

101

'My lord, it was past midnight before I finished my work, and went through the passage there to my bed. There was no one about then, I was among the last. I did not see a soul until I came by the third door in that range, where they tell me now this Bledri ap Rhys was lodged. There was a man standing in the doorway, looking into the room, with the latch in his hand. When he heard me coming he closed the door, and went away along the alley.'

'In haste?' asked Owain sharply. 'Furtively? In the dark he could well slip away unrecognised.'

'No, my lord, no such matter. Simply, he drew the door to, and walked away. I thought nothing of it. And he took no care not to be seen. He said a goodnight to me as he went. As though he had been seeing a guest safe to his bed – one none too steady on his feet, or too sure of his way, it might be.'

'And you answered him?'

'Surely, my lord.'

'Now name him,' said Owain, 'for I think you knew him well enough to call him by name then.'

'My lord, I did. Every man in your court of Aber has got to know him and value him by now, though he came as a stranger when first the lord Hywel brought him from Deheubarth. It was Cuhelyn.'

A sharp, indrawn breath hissed round the table. All heads turned, and all eyes fixed upon Cuhelyn, who sat apparently unmoved at finding himself suddenly the centre of marked and loaded attention. His thick dark brows had risen in mild surprise, even a trace of amusement.

'That is true,' he said simply. 'That I could have told you, but for all I knew or know now there could have been others there after me. As certainly there was one. The last to see him, living, no question. But that was not I.'

102

'Yet you offered us no word of this,' the prince pointed out quietly. 'Why not?'

'True, I did none too well there. It came a little too close home for comfort,' said Cuhelyn. 'I opened my mouth once to say it, and shut it again with nothing said. For sober truth is that I did have the man's death in mind, and for all I never touched him nor went in to him, when Brother Cadfael told us he lay dead, I felt the finger of guilt cold on my neck. But for solitude, and chance, and this lad coming along when most he was needed, yes, I might have been Bledri's murderer. But I am not, thanks be to God!'

'Why did you go there, and at that hour?' asked Owain, giving no sign whether he believed or disbelieved.

'I went there to confront him. To kill him in single combat. Why at that hour? Because the hatred had taken hours to come to the boil within me, and only then had I reached the length of killing. Also, I think, because I wished to make it clear past doubt that no other man was drawn into my quarrel, and no other could be accused even of knowing what I did.' Cuhelyn's level voice remained quiet and composed still, but his face had tightened until pale lines stood clear over the cheekbones and round the lean, strong angle of his jaw.

Hywel said softly, filling and easing the pause: 'A one-armed man against a seasoned warrior with two?'

Cuhelyn looked down indifferently at the silver circlet that secured the linen cover over the stump of his left arm. 'One arm or two, the end would have been the same. But when I opened his door, there he lay fast asleep. I heard his breathing, long and placid. Is it fair dealing to startle a man out of his sleep and challenge him to the death? And while I stood there in the doorway, Meurig here came along. And I drew the door closed again, and went away, and left Bledri sleeping.

103

Not that I gave up my purpose,' he said, rearing his head fiercely. 'Had he been living when the morning came, my lord, I meant to challenge him openly of his mortal offence, and call him to battle for his life. And if you gave me countenance, to kill him.'

Owain was staring upon him steadily, and visibly probing the mind that fashioned this bitter speech and gave it such passionate force. With unshaken calm he said: 'So far as is known to me, the man had done me no grave offence.'

'Not to you, my lord, beyond his arrogance. But to me, the worst possible. He made one among the eight that set upon us from ambush, and killed my prince at my side. When Anarawd was murdered, and this hand was lopped, Bledri ap Rhys was there in arms. Until he came into the bishop's hall I did not know his name. His face I have never forgotten. Nor never could have forgotten, until I had got Anarawd's price out of him in blood. But someone else has done that for me. And I am free of him.'

'Say to me again,' Owain commanded, when Cuhelyn had made an end of this declaration, 'that you left the man living, and have no guilt in his death.'

'I did so leave him. I never touched him, his death is no guilt of mine. If you bid me, I will swear it on the altar.'

'For this while,' said the prince gravely,'I am forced to leave this matter unresolved until I come back from Abermenai with a more urgent matter settled and done. But I still need to know who did the thing you did not do, for not all here have your true quarrel against Bledri ap Rhys. And as I for my part take your word, there may be many who still doubt you. If you give your word to return with me, and abide what further may be found out, till all are satisfied, then come with me. I need you as I may need every good man.'

'As God sees me,' said Cuhelyn. 'I will not leave you, for any reason, until you bid me go. And the happier, if you never do so bid me.'

The last and most unexpected word of a night of the unexpected lay with Owain's steward, who entered the council chamber just as the prince was rising to dismiss his officers, sufficiently briefed for the dawn departure. Provision was already made for the rites due to the dead. Gwion would remain at Aber, according to his oath, and had pledged his services to send word to Bledri's wife in Ceredigion, and conduct such necessary duties for the dead man as she demanded. A melancholy duty, but better from a man of the same allegiance. The morning muster was planned with precision, and order given for the proper provision due to the bishop of Lichfield's envoy on his way to Bangor, while the prince's force pursued the more direct road to Carnarvon, the old road that had linked the great forts by which an alien people had kept their footing in Wales, long ago. Latin names still clung to the places they had inhabited, though only priests and scholars used them now; the Welsh knew them by other names. It was all prepared, to the last detail. Except that somehow the missing horse had been lost yet again, slipping through the cracks between greater concerns into limbo. Until Goronwy ab Einion came in with the result of a long and devious enquiry into the total household within the llys.

'My lord, the lord Hywel set me a puzzle, to find the one person who should be here, and is not. Our own household of retainers and servants I thought well to leave aside, why should any among them take to his heels? My lord, the princess's waiting woman knows the roll of her maids perfectly, and any guests who are women are her charge. There is one girl who came in your train yesterday, my lord, who is gone from the place allotted to her. She came here with her father, a canon of Saint Asaph, and a second canon of that diocese travelled with them. We have not disturbed the father as yet. I waited for your word. But there is no question, the young woman is gone. No one has seen her since the gates were closed.'

'God's wounds!' swore Owain, between laughter and exasperation. 'It was true what they told me! The dark lass that would not be a nun in England— God keep her, why should she, a black Welshwoman as ever was!— and said yes to Ieuan ab Ifor as a blessed relief by comparison – do you tell me she has stolen a horse and made off into the night before the guard shut us in? The devil!' he said, snapping his fingers. 'What is the child's name?'

'Her name is Heledd,' said Brother Cadfael.

Chapter Six

O QUESTION, Heledd was gone. No hostess here, with duties and status, but perhaps the least among the arriving guests, she had held herself aloof from the princess's waiting-woman, keeping her own counsel and, as it seemed, waiting her own chance. No more reconciled to the prospect of marriage with the unknown bridegroom from Anglesey than to a conventual cell among strangers in England, Heledd had slipped through the gates of Aber before they closed at night, and gone to look for some future of her own choosing. But how had she abstracted also a horse, saddled and bridled, and a choice and fleet horse into the bargain?

The last that anyone had seen of her was when she left the hall with an empty pitcher, barely halfway through the prince's feast, leaving all the nobility busy at table, and her father still blackly scowling after her as she swung the screen curtain closed behind her. Perhaps she had truly intended to refill the pitcher and return to resume replenishing the Welsh drinking horns, if only to vex Canon Meirion. But no one had seen her since that moment. And when the first light came, and the prince's force began to muster in the wards, and the bustle and clamour, however purposeful and moderate, would certainly bring out all the household, who was to tell the good canon that his daughter had taken flight in the darkness from the cloister, from marriage, and from her sire's very imperfect love and care for her?

Such an unavoidable task Owain chose not to delegate. When the light from the east tipped the outer wall of the maenol, and the ward began to fill with horse and groom and man-at-arms and archer roused and ready, he sent to summon the two canons of Saint Asaph to the gatehouse, where he waited with one shrewd eye on the ranks mustering and mounting, and one on a sky and light that promised good weather for riding. No one had forestalled him with the bad news; so much was plain from Canon Meirion's serene, assured face as he strode across the ward with a civil good-morning already forming on his lips, and a gracious benediction ready to follow it as soon as the prince should mount and ride. At his back, shorter-legged and more portly and selfconscious of bearing, Canon Morgant hugged his ponderous dignity about him, and kept a noncommittal countenance.

It was not Owain's way to beat about bushes. Time was short, business urgent, and what mattered was to make such provision as was now possible to repair what had gone awry, both with threats from an obdurate brother and peril to a lost daughter.

'There is news in the night,' said the prince briskly, as soon as the two clerics drew close, 'that will not please your reverences, and does not please me.'

Cadfael, watching from beside the gate, could detect no disquiet in Canon Meirion's face at this opening. No doubt he thought it referred only to the threat of the Danish fleet, and possibly the flight of Bledri ap Rhys, for the two clerics had gone to their beds before that supposed flight changed to a death. But either would come rather as a relief and satisfaction to him, seeing that Bledri and Heledd between them had given him cause to tremble for his future career, with Canon Morgant storing up behind his austere forehead every unbecoming look and wanton word to report back to his bishop. By his present bearing, Meirion knew of nothing worse, nothing in the world to disturb his complacency now, if Bledri was either fled or dead.

'My lord,' he began benignly, 'we were present to hear of the threat to your coast. It will surely be put off without harm . . .'

'Not that!' said Owain bluntly. 'This concerns yourself. Sir, your daughter has fled in the night. Sorry I am to say it, and to leave you to deal with the case in my absence, but there's no help. I have given orders to the captain of my garrison here to give you every aid in searching for her. Stay as long as you need to stay, make use of my men and my stables as best serves. I and all who ride with me will be keeping a watch and asking news of her westward direct to Carnarvon. So, I trust, will Deacon Mark and Brother Cadfael on their ride to Bangor. Between us we should cover the country to westward. You ask and search round Aber and eastward, and south if need be, though I think she would not venture the mountains alone. I will return to the search as soon as I may.'

He had proceeded thus far uninterrupted only because Canon Meirion had been struck mute and amazed at the very first utterance, and stood staring with round eyes and parted lips, paling until the peaks of his sharp cheekbones stood out white under the straining skin. Utter consternation stopped the breath in his throat.

'My daughter!' he repeated slowly at last, the words shaped almost without sound. And then in a hoarse wheeze: 'Gone? My daughter loose alone, and these sea-raiders abroad in the land?'

At least, thought brother Cadfael approvingly, if she could be here to hear it, she would know that he has some real care for her. His first outcry is for her safety, for once his own advancement is forgotten. If only for a moment!

'Half the width of Wales from here,' said Owain stoutly, 'and I'll see to it they come no nearer. She heard the messenger, she knows better than to ride into their arms. This girl you bred is no fool.'

'But headstrong!' Meirion lamented, his voice recovered and loud with anguish. 'Who knows what risk she might not venture? And if she has fled me now, she will still hide from me. This I never foresaw, that she could feel so driven and so beset.'

'I say again,' said Owain firmly, 'use my garrison, my stables, my men as you will, send out after news of her, for surely she cannot be far. As for the ways to westward, we will watch for her as we go. But go we must. You well know the need.'

Meirion drew himself back a little, erect at his tallest, and shook his broad shoulders.

'Go with God, my lord, you can do no other. My girl's life is but one, and many depend upon you. She shall be my care. I dread I have not served her turn lately as well as I have served my own, or she would never have left me so.'

And he turned, with a hasty reverence, and strode away towards the hall, so precipitately that Cadfael could see him clambering fiercely into his boots and marching down to the stable to saddle his horse, and away to question everyone in

110

the village outside the walls, in search of the dark daughter he had gone to some pains to despatch into distance, and now was all afire to recover. And after him, still silent, stonily expressionless, potentially disapproving, went Canon Morgant, a black recording angel.

They were more than a mile along the coastal track towards Bangor before Brother Mark broke his deep and thoughtful silence. They had parted from the prince's force on leaving Aber, Owain bearing south-west to take the most direct road to Carnarvon, while Cadfael and Mark kept to the shore, with the shining, pallid plain of the shallows over Lavan Sands reflecting the morning light on their right hand, and the peaks of Fryri soaring one above another on their left, beyond the narrow green lowlands of the coast. Over the deep channel beyond the sands, the shores of Anglesey were bright in sunlight.

'Did he know,' Mark wondered aloud suddenly, 'that the man was dead?'

'He? Meirion? Who can tell? He was there among the rest of us when the groom cried out that a horse was missing, and Bledri was held to have taken him and made off to his master. So much he knew. He was not with us when we looked for and found the man dead, nor present in the prince's counsel. If the pair of them were safe in their beds they cannot have heard the news until this morning. Does it signify? Dead or fled, the man was out of Meirion's way, and could scandalise Morgant no longer. Small wonder he took it so calmly.'

'That is not what I meant,' said Mark. 'Did he know of his own knowledge? Before ever another soul knew it?' And as Cadfael was silent, he pursued hesitantly: 'You had not considered it?'

'It had crossed my mind,' Cadfael admitted. 'You think him capable of killing?'

'Not in cool blood, not by stealth. But his blood is not cool, but all too readily heated. There are some who bluster and bellow, and rid their bile that way. Not he! He contains it, and it boils within him. It is likelier far to burst forth in action than in noise. Yes, I think him capable of killing. And if he did confront Bledri ap Rhys, he would meet only with provocation and disdain there. Enough to make for a violent end.'

'And could he go from that ending straight to his bed, in such unnerving company, and keep his countenance? Even sleep?'

'Who says that he slept? He had only to be still and quiet. There was nothing to keep Canon Morgant wakeful.'

'I return you another question,' said Cadfael. 'Would Cuhelyn lie? He was not ashamed of his purpose. Why, then, should he lie about it when it came to light?'

'The prince believes him,' said Mark, thoughtfully frowning.

'And you?'

'Any man may lie, not even for very grave reason. Even Cuhelyn may. But I do not think he would lie to Owain. Or to Hywel. He has given his second fealty, as absolute as the first. But there is another question to be asked concerning Cuhelyn. No, there are two. Had he told anyone what he knew about Bledri ap Rhys? And if he would not lie to Hywel, who had salved him and brought him to an honourable service, would he lie *for* him? For if he did tell anyone that he recognised Bledri as one among his prince's murderers, it would be Hywel. Who had no better reason to love the perpetrators of that ambush than had Cuhelyn himself.'

'Or any man who went with Hywel to drive Cadwaladr out

of Ceredigion for Anarawd's sake,' agreed Cadfael resignedly, 'or any who took bitter offence at hearing Bledri so insolent on Cadwaladr's behalf in hall that night, spitting his threats into Owain's face. True, a man is dead who was well-hated, living, and took no keep to be anything better than hated. In a crowded court where his very presence was an affront, is it any wonder if he came by a short ending? But the prince will not let it rest.'

'And we can do nothing,' said Mark, and sighed. 'We cannot even look for the girl until I have discharged my errand.'

'We can ask,' said Cadfael.

And ask they did, at every hamlet and dwelling along the way, whether a young woman had not ridden past by this road, a dark Welsh girl on a young roan, all of one colour. A horse from the prince's stables would not go unremarked, especially with a lone girl in the saddle. But the day wore on, and the sky clouded gently and cleared again, and they drew into Bangor by mid-afternoon; but no one could give them word of Heledd, Meirion's daughter.

Bishop Meurig of Bangor received them as soon as they had threaded their way through the streets of the town to his cathedral enclave, and announced themselves to his archdeacon. It seemed that here everything was to be done briskly and briefly, with small respect to the planned and public ceremony Bishop Gilbert had preferred. For here they were by many miles nearer to the threat of Danish raiders, and very sensibly taking such precautions as were possible to cope with them if they should penetrate so far. Moreover, Meurig was native Welsh, at home here, and had no need of the cautious dispositions Gilbert felt necessary to secure his position. It might be true that he had proved at first a disappointment to his prince, by succumbing to Norman pressure and submitting to Canterbury, but stoutly Welsh he remained, and his resistance, if diverted, must still be proceeding by more subtle ways. At least he did not seem to Cadfael, when they were admitted to his presence in private, the kind of man to compromise his Welshness and his adherence to the ways of the Celtic Church without a long and doughty rearguard action.

The bishop was not at all like his fellow of Saint Asaph. Instead of the tall, dignified Gilbert, selfconsciously patrician and austere without, and uneasily insecure within, here was a small, round, bustling cleric in his forties, voluble of speech but very much to the point, rapid of movement and a little dishevelled and shaggy, with a sharp eye and a cheerfully bouncing manner, like a boisterous but businesslike hound on a scent. His pleasure in the very fact of their coming on such an errand was made very plain, and outweighed even his delight in the breviary Mark had brought him, though clearly he had an eye for a handsome script, and turned the leaves with lovingly delicate movements of thick, strong fingers.

'You will have heard already, Brothers, of the threat to our shores, so you will understand that here we are looking to our defences. God grant the Norsemen never get ashore, or no further than the shore, but if they should, we have a town to keep, and churchmen must turn to like the rest. For that reason we observe at present little state or ceremony, but I trust you will be my guests for a day or two before you need return with my letters and compliments to your bishop.'

It was for Mark to respond to this invitation, which was offered warmly enough, but with a vaguely preoccupied look in the bishop's shrewd eyes. At least a part of his mind was away scanning the waterfront of his town, where the brief mudflat between the tides gave place to the narrowing neck of

114

the strait. Fifteen miles or more to the western end at Abermenai, but the smaller shallow-draught ships, oared by twenty rowers, could cover that distance rapidly. A pity the Welsh had never really taken to the seas! And Bishop Meurig had his flock to consider, and no amenable temper to let them suffer anything his vigour could prevent. He would not be sorry to pack his visitors from England off back to Lichfield, and have his hands free. Hands that looked quite capable of turning to the sword or the bow whenever the need arose.

'My lord,' said Brother Mark, after a brief thoughtful hesitation, 'I think we should leave tomorrow, if that does not cause you too much inconvenience. Much as I would like to linger, I have pledged myself to a prompt return. And even beyond that, the party with which we rode from Saint Asaph included a young woman who should have come here to Bangor with us, under Owain Gwynedd's protection, but now, bereft of that protection, since the prince perforce has hurried on to Carnarvon, she has unwisely ridden out from Aber alone, and somewhere has lost her way. They are seeking for her from Aber. But since we have come as far as Bangor, if I may justify the delay even of one day, or two, I should like to spend them searching for her in these parts also. If you will grant me leave to make use of so short a delay, we will spend it for the lady's benefit, and you, I know, will be making use of every moment for the better keep of your own people.'

A good speech, Cadfael approved, one that gives nothing away of what lies behind Heledd's flight, thereby sparing her reputation and this good prelate's very proper concern. He interpreted it carefully, improvising a little where memory faltered, since Mark had allowed him no pause between the lines. The bishop nodded instant comprehension, and demanded practically: 'Did the lady know of this threat from Dublin?'

'No,' said Mark, 'the messenger from Carnarvon came only later. She cannot have known.'

'And she is somewhere abroad between Aber and here, and alone? I wish I had more men to send out after her,' said Meurig, frowning, 'but we have already sent on to Carnarvon all the fighting men who can be spared, to join the prince there. Such as are left we may need here.'

'We do not know,' Cadfael said, 'which way she rode. She may be well behind us to the east, for all we know, and safe enough. But if we can do no more, we can divide on the ride back, and enquire everywhere after her.'

'And if she has by now heard of the peril,' Mark added eagerly, 'and very wisely looks for safe shelter, are there in these regions any houses of religious women, where she might take refuge?'

This also Cadfael translated, though he could have given a general answer to it himself, without troubling the bishop. The Church in Wales had never run to nunneries, as even conventual life for men had never been on the same monastic pattern as in England. Instead of the orderly, well-regulated house of sisters, with a recognised authority and a rule, here there might arise, in the most remote and solitary wilderness, a small wattled oratory, with a single, simple saint living within it, a saint in the old dispensation, without benefit of Pope or canonisation, who grew a few vegetables and herbs for her food, and gathered berries and wild fruit, and came to loving terms with the small beasts of the warren, so that they ran to hide in her skirts when they were hunted, and neither huntsmen nor horn could urge on the hounds to do the lady affront, or her little visitors harm. Though Cadfael had to admit, on reflection, that the Dublin Danes might not observe a proper respect to such unaccustomed evidences of sanctity.

The bishop shook his head. 'Our holy women do not gather in communities, like yours, but set up their cells in the wilds, alone. Such anchoresses would not settle near a town. More likely far to withdraw into the mountains. There is one we know of here, who has her hermitage by this same Menai water, some miles west from here, beyond the narrows. But as soon as we heard of this threat from the sea I sent to warn her, and bring her in here to shelter. And she had the good sense to come, and make no demur about it. God is the first and best defence of lone women, but I see no virtue in leaving all to him. I want no martyrs within my domain, and sanctity is small protection.'

'Then her cell is left empty,' said Mark, and sighed. 'But if this girl should have ridden so far, and failed to find a friend at need, where next might she turn?'

'Inland, surely, into the cover of woodland. I know of no defensible holding close by, but these raiders, if they land, would not go far from their ships. Any house in Arfon would take a girl in. Though the nearest and themselves most at risk,' he added simply, 'may well have drawn off into the hills themselves. Your fellow here knows how lightly we can vanish at need.'

'I doubt she can have gone far ahead of us,' said Cadfael, pondering possibilities. 'And for all we know she may have her own plans, and know very well where to run. At least we can ask wherever we touch on the way back.' There was always the chance, too, that Canon Meirion had already found his daughter, closer to the royal seat at Aber.

'I can have prayers said for her safety,' said the bishop briskly, 'but I have sheep of my own to fold, and cannot,

117

however willingly I would, go searching after one stray. At least, Brothers, rest this night over, before you take to the roads again, and may you ride safely and get good word of the young woman you seek.'

Bishop Meurig might be preoccupied with guarding his extended household, but he did not let that interfere with his hospitality. His table was well-supplied, his meat and mead ample and well-prepared, and he did not let his guests depart next morning without rising at dawn to see them off. It was a limpid, moist morning, after some fitful showers in the night, and the sun came up glistening and radiant, gilding the shallows to eastward.

'Go with God!' said the bishop, solid and square in the gateway of his precinct, as though he would hold it single-handed against all comers. His complimentary letters were already bestowed in Mark's saddle-roll, together with a small flask of gilded glass filled with the cordial he made from his own honey, and Cadfael carried before him a basket with a day's supply of food for six men rather than two. 'Come safely back to your bishop, on whom be God's blessing, and to your convent, Brother Cadfael, where his grace surely prevails. I trust some day we may meet again.'

Of the peril now threatening he certainly went in no awe. When they looked back from the street he was bustling purposefully across the open court, head foremost and lowered, like a small, determined bull not yet belligerent but certainly not to be trifled with.

They had emerged from the edges of the town on to the highroad, when Mark reined in, and sat his horse mute and thoughtful, looking first back along the road towards Aber, and then westward towards the invisible sinuous curves of the narrow strait that separated Anglesey from Arfon. Cadfael drew in beside him, and waited, knowing what was on his friend's mind.

'Could she have passed beyond this point? Ought we not to go on westward? She left Aber hours before us. How long, I wonder, before she got word of the coming of the Danes?'

'If she rode through the night,' said Cadfael, 'she was not likely to hear of it until morning, there would be no one abroad to warn her. By morning she could be well to the west, and if she intended by her flight to evade her marriage, she would not come near Bangor, for there she was to meet her husband. Yes, you are right, she might by this be well to westward, and into danger. Nor am I sure she would turn back even if she knew of it.'

'Then what are we waiting for?' demanded Mark simply, and turned his horse towards the west.

At the church of Saint Deiniol, several miles south-west from Bangor and perhaps two miles from the strait, they got word of her at last. She must have kept to the old, direct road, the same Owain and his host would take, but hours ahead of them. The only puzzle was why it had taken her so long to reach that point, for when they enquired of the priest there was no hesitation, but yes, she had lighted down here to ask directions only late the previous evening, about Vespers.

'A young woman on a light roan, and all alone. She asked her way to the cell of Nonna. Due west from here it lies, in the trees near the water. I offered her shelter for the night, but she said she would go to the holy woman.'

'She would find the cell deserted,' said Cadfael. 'Bishop Meurig feared for the anchoress, and sent to bring her into Bangor. From which direction did the girl ride in?'

'Down out of the forests, from the south. I did not know,' said the priest, distressed, 'that she would find the place empty. I wonder, poor child, what she would do? There would still be time enough for her to find refuge in Bangor.'

'That I doubt she would do,' said Cadfael. 'If she came to the cell only so late, she might well bide the night over there, rather than risk moving by darkness.' He looked at Mark, in no doubt already what that young man would be thinking. On this journey Mark had the governance, not for the world would Cadfael have robbed him of it by word or act.

'We will go and look for her at the hermitage,' said Mark firmly, 'and if she is not there, we will separate and try whatever tracks seem most likely to offer her refuge. In these lowland pastures there must be homesteads she may have tried.'

'Many will have taken advice,' the priest suggested, shaking his head dubiously. 'In a few weeks they would have been moving their herds and flocks into the uplands, even without this threat. Some may have moved early, rather than risk being plundered.'

'We can but make the assay,' said Mark stoutly. 'If need be, we'll take to the hills ourselves in search of her.'

And forthwith he made a brisk reverence to their informant, and wheeled his horse and set off due west, straight as an arrow. The priest of Saint Deiniol looked after him with raised brows and an expression half amused and half solicitous, and shook his head doubtfully.

'Would that young man be seeking the girl out of the goodness of his heart? Or for himself?'

'Even for that young man,' Cadfael said cautiously, 'I would not presume to say anything is impossible. But it comes as near as makes no matter. Any creature in peril of death or harm, be it man, woman, plough horse, or Saint Melangell's hare, could draw him through moss or quicksand. I knew I should never get him back to Shrewsbury while Heledd was astray.'

'You are turning back here yourself?' the priest demanded drily.

'Small chance! If he is bound to her, fellow-voyager to his fellow, so am I to him. I'll get him home!'

'Well, even if his concern for her is purer than dew,' said the priest with conviction, 'he had best take heed to his vows when he does find her. For she's a bonny black maid as ever I saw. I was glad of my evening years when I dared bid her shelter the night over in my house. And thankful when she would not. And that lad is at the best of the morning, tonsure or no tonsure.'

'The more reason I should go after him,' agreed Cadfael. 'And my thanks to you for the good word. For all the good words! I'll see them strictly delivered when I overtake him.'

'Saint Nonna,' said Cadfael didactically, threading the woodland belt that spread more than a mile inland from the strait, 'was the mother of Saint David. She has many sacred wells about the country, that give healing, especially to the eyes, even to curing blindness. This holy woman must have chosen to name herself after the saint.'

Brother Mark pursued his determined way along the narrow ride, and said nothing. On either hand the trees glittered in moist sunlight after the early morning showers, mixed woodland sufficiently open to let in the radiance of early afternoon, sufficiently close to be ridden in single file, and all just coming into the first full leaf, young and fresh and full of birds. Every Spring is the only Spring, a perpetual astonishment. It bursts upon a man every year, thought Cadfael, contemplating it with delight in spite of all anxieties, as though it had never happened before, but had just been shown by God how to do it, and tried, and found the impossible possible.

Ahead of him in the worn grass of the ride Mark had halted, staring ahead. Between the trees, here thinning, open light shone before them, at a little distance still, but now not very far, and shimmering with reflected gleams from water. They were nearing the strait. And on Mark's left hand a narrow footway twined in among the trees to a low-roofed hut some yards aside from the path.

'This is the place.'

'And she was here,' said Cadfael. The wet grass, unshaken on either side by any wind, had retained the soft dew of rain that dimmed its new green to a silver grey, but through it a horse had certainly passed, leaving his darker trail, and brushing before him the tips of new growth, for the passage to the cell was very narrow. The ride in which they had halted was in regular use, they had not thought to examine it as they rode. But here between the encroaching bushes a horse had certainly passed since the rain. And not inward, but outward. A few young shoots had been broken at the tip, leaning towards the open ride, and the longer grasses darkened by hooves clearly showed the direction in which they had been brushed in passing. 'And is gone,' said Cadfael, 'since the morning.'

They dismounted, and approached the cell on foot. Built little and low, and one room only, for a woman who had almost no needs at all, beyond her small stone-built altar against one wall, and her plain straw pallet against another, and her small cleared space of garden behind for vegetables and herbs. Her door was drawn to, but had no lock to be seen without, and no bar within, only a latch that any wayfarer could lift and enter. The place was empty now. Nonna had obeyed the bishop's expressed wish, and allowed herself to be escorted into shelter in Bangor, how willingly there was no knowing. If she had had a guest here in her absence, the guest too was gone. But in a patch of clear turf between the trees the grass had been grazed, and hooves had ranged on a long tether, leaving their traces before the rain fell, for drops still hung on the grasses, unshaken. And in one place the beast had left his droppings, fresh and moist still, but already cold.

'She passed the night here,' said Cadfael, 'and with the morning she left. After the rain she left. Which way, who knows! She came to Llandeiniolen from inland, out of the hills and through the forest, so the priest said. Had she some place of refuge in mind up there, some kinsman of Meirion's who might take her in? And did she find that place, too, already deserted, and think of the anchoress as her next hope? It would account for why it took her so long to get here. But as for where she is gone now, how can we tell?'

'She knows by now of the danger from the sea,' said Mark. 'Surely she would not go on westward into such a peril? But back towards Bangor and her marriage? She has already risked much to evade it. Would she make her way back to Aber, and her father? That would not deliver her from this marriage, if she is so set against it.'

'She would not do it,' said Cadfael, 'in any case. Strange as it may be, she loves her father as much as she hates him. The one is the reflection of the other. She hates him because her love is far stronger than any love he has for her, because he is so ready and willing to give her up, to put her away by any means possible, so that she may no longer cast a cloud over his reputation and his advancement. Very clearly she declared herself once, as I remember.'

'As I remember also,' said Mark.

'Nevertheless, she will do nothing to harm him. The veil she refused. This marriage she accepted only for his sake, as the lesser evil. But when chance offered, she fled that, too, and chose rather to remove herself from blocking his light than to let others scheme to remove her. She has taken her own life into her own hands, prepared to face her own risks and pay her own debts, leaving him free. She will not now go back on that resolve.'

'But he is not free,' said Mark, putting a finger regretfully on the centre of the convoluted core of pain in this seemingly simple relationship of sire and daughter. 'He is aware of her now in absence as he never was when she waited on him dutifully every day, present and visible. He will have no peace until he knows she is safe.'

'So,' said Cadfael, 'we had better set about finding her.'

Out on the ride, Cadfael looked back through the screen of trees towards the sparks of quivering water beyond which lay the Anglesey shore. A slight breeze had arisen, and fluttered the bright green leaves into a scintillating curtain, but still the fleeting reflections of water flashed brighter still through the folds. And something else, something that appeared and vanished as the branches revealed and hid it again, but remained constant in the same place, only seeming to rock up and down as if afloat and undulating with a tide. A fragment of bright colour, vermilion, changing shape with the movement of its frame of leaves.

'Wait!' said Cadfael, halting. 'What is that?'

Not a red that was to be found in nature, certainly not in the late Spring, when the earth indulges itself only with delicate tones of pale gold and faint purple and white against the virgin green. This red had a hard, impenetrable solidity about it. Cadfael dismounted, and turned back towards it, threading the trees in cover until he came to a raised spot where he could lie warily invisible himself, but see clear through the edge of the woodland three hundred paces or more down to the strait. A green level of pasture and a few fields, one dwelling, no doubt forsaken now, and then the silver-blue glitter of the water, here almost at its narrowest, but still half a mile wide. And beyond, the rich, fertile plain of Anglesey, the cornfield of Wales. The tide was flowing, the stretch of shingle and sand under the opposite coast half exposed. And riding to anchor, close inshore below the bank of trees in which Cadfael stood, a long, lean boat, dragon-headed fore and aft, dipped and rose gently on the tide, central sail lowered, oars shipped, a cluster of vermilion shields draped along its low flank. A lithe serpent of a ship, its mast lowered aft from its steppings, clearing the gaunt body for action, while it swayed gently to its mooring like a sleeping lizard, graceful and harmless. Two of its crew, big, fair-headed, one with plaited braids either side his neck, idled on its narrow rear deck, above the oarsmen's benches. One, naked, swam lazily in mid-strait. But Cadfael counted what he took to be oarports in the third strake of the hull, twelve of them in this steerboard side. Twelve pairs of oars, twenty-four rowers, and more crew beside these three left on guard. The rest could not be far.

Brother Mark had tethered the horses, and made his way down to Cadfael's shoulder. He saw what Cadfael had seen, and asked no questions.

'That,' said Cadfael, low-voiced, 'is a Danish keel from Dublin!'

125

Chapter Seven

HERE WAS NOT a word more said between them. By consent they turned and made their way back in haste to the horses, and led them away inland by the woodland track, until they were far enough from the shore to mount and ride. If Heledd, after her night in the hermitage, had seen the coming of this foraging boat with its formidable complement of warriors, small wonder she had made haste to remove herself from their vicinity. And small doubt but she would withdraw inland as quickly and as far as she could, and once at a sufficient distance she would make for the shelter of a town. That, at least, was what any girl in her right senses would do. Here she was midway between Bangor and Carnarvon. Which way would she take?

'One ship alone,' said Mark at last, where the path widened and made it possible for two to ride abreast. 'Is that good sense? Might they not be opposed, even captured?'

'So they might at this moment,' Cadfael agreed, 'but there's no one here to attempt it. They came by night past Carnarvon, be sure, and by night they'll slip out again. This will be one of the smallest and the fastest in their fleet; with more than twenty armed rowers aboard there's nothing we have could keep them in sight. You saw the building of her,

127

she can be rowed either way, and turn in a flash. The only risk they take is while the most of the company are ashore, foraging, and that they'll do by rushes, fast ashore and fast afloat again.'

'But why send one small ship out alone? As I have heard tell,' said Mark, 'they raid in force, and take slaves as well as plunder. That they cannot do by risking a single vessel.'

'This time,' said Cadfael, considering, 'it's no such matter. If Cadwaladr has brought them over, then he's promised them a fat fee for their services. They're here to persuade Owain he would be wise to restore his brother to his lands, and they expect to get well paid for doing it, and if it can be done cheaply by the threat of their presence, without the loss of a man in battle, that's what they'll prefer, and Cadwaladr will have no objection, provided the result is the same. Say he gets his way and returns to his lands, he has still to live beside his brother for the future, why make relations between them blacker than they need be? No, there'll be no random burning and killing, and no call to take bondmen, not unless the bargain turns sour.'

'Then why this foray by a single ship so far along the strait?' Mark demanded reasonably.

'The Danes have to feed their force, and it's not their way to carry their own provisions when they're heading for a land they can just as well live off at no cost. They know the Welsh well enough by now to know we live light and travel light, and can shift our families and our stock into the mountains at a few hours' notice. Yonder little ship has wasted no time in making inland from Abermenai as soon as it touched shore, to reach such hamlets as were late in hearing the news, or slow in rounding up their cattle. They'll be off back to their fellows tonight with a load of good carcases amidships, and whatever store of flour and grain they've been able to lay their hands on. And somewhere along these woods and fields they're about that very business this moment.'

'And if they meet with a solitary girl?' Mark challenged. 'Would they refrain from doing unnecessary offence even then?'

'I would not speak for any man, Dane or Welsh or Norman, in such a case,' Cadfael admitted. 'If she were a princess of Gwynedd, why, she'd be worth far more intact and well treated than violated or misused. And if Heledd was not born royal, yet she has a tongue of her own, and can very well make it plain that she is under Owain's protection, and they'll be answerable to him if they do her offence. But even so . . .'

They had reached a place where the woodland track divided, one branch bearing still inland but inclining to the west, the other bearing more directly east.

'We are nearer Carnarvon than Bangor,' Cadfael reckoned, halting where the roads divided. 'But would she know it? What now, Mark? East or west?'

'We had best separate,' Mark said, frowning over so blind a decision. 'She cannot be very far. She would have to keep in cover. If the ship must return this night, she might find a place to hide safely until they are gone. Do you take one way, and I the other.'

'We cannot afford to lose touch,' Cadfael warned seriously. 'If we part here it must be only for some hours, and here we must meet again. We are not free to do altogether as we choose. Go towards Carnarvon, and if you find her, see her safely there. But if not, make your way back here by dusk, and so will I. And if I find her by this lefthand way, I'll get her into shelter wherever I may, if it means turning back to Bangor. And at Bangor I'll wait for you, if you fail of meeting

129

me here by sunset. And if I fail you, follow and find me there.'

A makeshift affair, but the best they could do, with so limited a time, and an inescapable duty waiting. She had left the cell by the shore only that morning, she would have had to observe caution and keep within the woodland ways, where a horse must go slowly. No, she could not be far. And at this distance from the strait, surely she would keep to a used path, and not wind a laborious way deep in cover. They might yet find and bring her here by nightfall, or conduct her into safety somewhere, rendezvous here free of her, and be off thankfully back to England.

Mark looked at the light and the slight decline of the sun from the zenith. 'We have four hours or more,' he said, and turned his horse westward briskly, and was off.

Cadfael's track turned east on a level traverse for perhaps half a mile, occasionally emerging from woodland into open pasture, and affording glimpses of the strait through the scattered trees below. Then it turned inland and began to climb, though the gradient here was not great, for this belt of land on the mainland side partook to some extent of the rich fertility of the island before it reared aloft into the mountains. He went softly, listening, and halting now and again to listen more intently, but there was so sign of life but for the birds, very busy about their Spring occupations and undisturbed by the turmoil among men. The cattle and sheep had been driven up higher into the hills, into guarded folds; the raiders would find only the few stragglers here, and perhaps would venture no further along the strait. The news must be ahead of them now wherever they touched, they would have made their most profitable captures already. If Heledd had turned this way, she might be safe enough from any further danger.

He had crossed an open meadow and entered a higher belt
of woodland, bushy and dappled with sunbeams on his left
hand, deepening into forest on his right, when a grass snake,
like a small flash of silver-green lightning, shot across the path
almost under his horse's hooves to vanish in deeper grass on
the other side, and the beast shied for an instant, and let out a
muted bellow of alarm. Somewhere off to the right, among
the trees, and at no great distance, another horse replied,
raising an excited whinny of recognition. Cadfael halted to
listen intently, hoping for another call to allow him to take a
more precise reading of the direction, but the sound was not
repeated. Probably whoever was in refuge there, well aside
from the path, had rushed to soothe and cajole his beast into
silence. A horse's neighing could carry all too far along this
rising hillside.

Cadfael dismounted, and led his beast in among the trees,
taking a winding line towards where he thought the other
voyager must be, and halting at every turn to listen again, and
presently, when he was already deep among thick growth, he
caught the sudden rustling of shaken boughs ahead, quickly
stilled. His own movements, however cautious, had certainly
been heard. Someone there in close concealment was waiting
for him in ambush.

'Heledd!' said Cadfael clearly.

Silence seemed to become even more silent.

'Heledd? Here am I, Brother Cadfael. You can be easy,
here are no Dublin Danes. Come forth and show yourself.'

And forth she came, thrusting through the bushes to meet
him, Heledd indeed, with a naked dagger ready in her hand,
though for the moment she might well have forgotten that she
held it. Her gown was creased and soiled a little with the
debris of bushes, one cheek was lightly smeared with green

131

from bedding down in moss and grasses, and the mane of her hair was loose round her shoulders, here in shadow quite black, a midnight cloud. But her clear oval face was fiercely composed, just easing from its roused readiness to do battle, and her eyes, enormous in shade, were purple-black. Behind her among the trees he heard her horse shift and stamp, uneasy here in these unknown solitudes.

'It *is* you,' she said, and let the hand that held the knife slip down to her side with a great, gusty sigh. 'How did you find me? And where is Deacon Mark? I thought you would be off home before now.'

'So we would,' agreed Cadfael, highly relieved to find her in such positive possession of herself, 'but for you running off into the night. Mark is a mile or more from us on the road to Carnarvon, looking for you. We parted where the roads forked. It was guesswork which way you would take. We came seeking you at Nonna's cell. The priest told us he'd directed you there.'

'Then you've seen the ship,' said Heledd, and hoisted her shoulders in resignation at the unavoidable. 'I should have been well aloft into the hills by now to look for my mother's cousins up among the sheep-huts, the ones I hoped to find still in their lowland homestead, if my horse had not fallen a little lame. I thought best to get into cover and rest him until nightfall. And now we are two,' she said, and her smile flashed in shadow with recovering confidence, 'three if we can find your little deacon. And now which way should we make? Come with me over the hills, and you can find a safe way back to the Dee. For I am not going back to my father,' she warned, with a formidable flash of her dark eyes. 'He's rid of me, as he wanted. I mean him no ill, but I have not escaped them all only to go back and be married off to some man I have never seen, nor to dwindle away in a nunnery. You may tell him, or leave word with someone else to let him know, that I am safe with my mother's kinsmen, and he can be content.'

'You are going into the first safe shelter we can find,' said Cadfael firmly, moved to a degree of indignation he could not have felt if he had found her distressed and in fear. 'Afterwards, once this trouble is over, you may have your life and do what you will with it.' It seemed to him, even as he said it, that she was capable of doing with it something original and even admirable, and if it had to be in the world's despite, that would not stop her. 'Can your beast go?'

'I can lead him, and we shall see.'

Cadfael took thought for a moment. They were midway between Bangor and Carnarvon here, but once returned to the westward track by which Mark had set out, the road was more direct to Carnarvon, and by taking it they would eventually rejoin Mark. Whether he had gone on into the town, or turned back to return to the crossroads meeting place by dusk, along that pathway they would meet him. And in a city filled with Owain's fighting men there would be no danger. A force hired to threaten would not be so mad as to provoke the entire armies of Gwynedd. A little looting, perhaps, pleasant sport carrying off a few stray cattle and a few stray villagers, but they were not such fools as to bring out Owain's total strength against them in anger.

'Bring him out to the path,' said Cadfael. 'You may ride mine, and I'll walk yours.'

There was nothing in the glittering look she gave him to reassure him that she would do as he said, and nothing to disquiet him with doubts. She hesitated only an instant, in which the silence of the windless afternoon seemed

133

phenomenally intense, then she turned and parted the branches behind her, and vanished, shattering the silence with the rustling and thrashing of her passage through deep cover. In a few moments he heard the horse whinny softly, and then the stirring of the bushes as girl and horse turned to thread a more open course back to him. And then, astonishingly high, wild and outraged, he heard her scream.

The instinctive leap forward he made to go to her never gained him so much as a couple of paces. From either side the bushes thrashed, and hands reached to clutch him by cowl and habit, pin his arms and bring him up erect but helpless, straining against a grip he could not break, but which, curiously, made no move to do him any harm beyond holding him prisoner. Suddenly the tiny open glade was boiling with large, bare-armed, fair-haired, leather-girt men, and out of the thicket facing him erupted an even larger man, a young giant, head and shoulders above Cadfael's sturdy middle height, laughing so loudly that the hitherto silent woods rang and re-echoed with his mirth, and clutching in his arms a raging Heledd, kicking and struggling with all her might, but making small impression. The one hand she had free had already scored its nails down her captor's cheek, and was tugging and tearing in his long flaxen hair, until he turned and stooped his head and took her wrist in his teeth and held it. Large, even, white teeth that had shone as he laughed, and now barely dented Heledd's smooth skin. It was astonishment, neither fear nor pain, that caused her suddenly to lie still in his arms, crooked fingers gradually unfolding in bewilderment. But when he released her to laugh again, she recovered her rage, and struck out at him furiously, pounding her fist vainly against his broad breast.

Behind him came a grinning boy about fifteen years old,

leading Heledd's horse, which went a little tenderly on one foreleg. At sight of a second such prize tethered and shifting uneasily in the fringe of the trees, the boy let out a whoop of pleasure. Indeed, the entire mood of the marauding company seemed good-humoured and ebullient rather than menacing. There were not so many of them as at first they had seemed, by reason of their size and their exuberantly animal presence. Two, barrel-chested and moustached, with hair in straw-coloured braids down either cheek, held Cadfael pinioned by the arms. A third had taken the roan's bridle, and was fondling the long blazed brow and creamy mane. But somewhere out on the open ride there were others, Cadfael heard them moving and talking as they waited. The marvel was that men so massive could move so softly to close round their quarry. The horses, calling to each other, had alerted the returning foragers, and led them to this unexpected gain. A monastic, a girl, by her mount and dress a girl of quality, and two good horses.

The young giant was surveying his gains very practically over Heledd's unavailing struggles, and Cadfael noted that though he was casually rough with his captive, he was not brutal. And it seemed that Heledd had realised as much, and gradually abandoned her resistance, knowing it vain, and surprised into quietness by the fact that there was no retaliation.

'*Saeson*?' demanded the giant, eyeing Cadfael with curiosity. He already knew that Heledd was Welsh enough, she had been reviling him in the language until she ran out of breath.

'Welsh!' said Cadfael. 'Like the lady. She is daughter to a canon of Saint Asaph, and under the protection of Owain Gwynedd.'

'He keeps wildcats?' said the young man, and laughed again, and set her down on her feet in one lithe movement, but

135

kept a fast hold on the girdle of her gown, twisted in his large fist to tighten and secure it. 'And he'll want this one back without a hair missing? But the lady slipped her leash, seemingly, or what's she doing here with no bodyguard but a monk of the Benedictines?' He spoke a loose mixture of Erse, Danish and Welsh, very well able to make himself understood in these parts. Not all the centuries of fitful contact between Dublin and Wales had been by way of invasion and rapine, a good many marriages had been made between the princedoms, and a fair measure of honest commerce been profitable to both parties. Probably this youth had a measure of Norman French in his tongue, no less. Even Latin, for very likely Irish monks had had him in school. He was plainly a young man of consequence. Also, happily, of a very open and cheerful humour, by no means inclined to waste what might turn out a valuable asset. 'Bring the man,' said the young fellow, returning briskly to business, 'and keep him fast. Owain has a respect for the black habit, even if the Celtic clas suits him best. If it comes to bargaining, holiness fetches a good price. I'll see to the girl.'

They sprang to obey him, as light of heart, it seemed, as their leader, and all in high content with their foraging. When they emerged with their captives into the open ride, the two horses led along behind them, it was easy to see what reason they had for being in high feather. There were four more of them waiting there, all afoot, and burdened with two long poles loaded down with slaughtered carcases and slung sacks, the plunder of scattered folds, stray corners of grazing, and even the forest itself, for there was venison among the booty. A fifth man had improvised a wooden yoke for his shoulders, to carry two balanced wineskins. This must be one of at least two shore parties, Cadfael judged, for the little ship carried

twelve pairs of oars aside from other crew. It was guesswork
how many the Danish force would muster in full, but they
would not go short for a day or so.

He went where he was propelled, not entirely out of the
sensible realisation that he was no match at all for one of the
brawny warriors who held him, let alone two, not even
because, though he might break away himself, he could do
nothing to take Heledd with him. Wherever they were bound,
useful hostages, he might still be able to afford her some
protection and companionship. He had already given up any
idea that she was likely to come to any great harm. He had
done no more than confirm something already understood
when he urged that she was valuable; and this was not total
war, but a commercial expedition, to achieve the highest
profit at the least expenditure.

There was some redistribution of the booty they had
amassed, Heledd's lame horse being called into service to
carry a part of the load. They were notably brisk and neat in
their movements, balancing the weight and halting short of
overburdening a valuable beast. Among themselves they fell
back into their own Norse tongue, though the likelihood was
that all these young, vigorous warriors had been born in the
kingdom of Dublin, and their fathers before them, and had a
broad understanding of the Celtic languages that surrounded
their enclave, and dealt freely with them in war and peace. At
the end of this day of raiding they had an eye to the sun, and
but for this foray after the alarm the horses had sounded, they
were losing no time.

Cadfael had wondered how their leader would dispose of
the one sound horse, and fully expected he would claim the
privilege of riding for himself. Instead, the young man
ordered the boy into the saddle, the lightest weight among

them, and swung Heledd up before him and into arms even at fifteen years brawny enough to make her struggles ineffective once her hands were securely bound by her own girdle. But she had understood by this time that resistance would be both useless and undignified, and suffered herself to be settled against the boy's broad chest without deigning to struggle. By the set of her face she would be waiting for the first chance of escape, and keeping all her wits and strength in reserve until the moment offered. She had fallen silent, shutting lips and teeth upon anger or fear, and keeping a taut, brooding dignity, but what was brewing behind that still face there was no knowing.

'Brother,' said the young man, turning briskly upon Cadfael, still pinned between his guards, 'if you value the lass, you may walk beside her without a hand on you. But I warn you, Torsten will be close behind, and he can throw a lance to split a sapling at fifty paces, so best keep station.' He was grinning as he issued the warning, already assured that Cadfael had no intention of making off and leaving the girl in captivity. 'Forward now, and fast,' he said cheerfully, and set the pace, and the entire party fell into file down the ride, and so did Cadfael, close alongside his own roan horse, with a hand at the rider's stirrup-leather. If Heledd needed the fragile reassurance of his presence, she had it; but Cadfael doubted the need. She had made no move since she was hoisted aloft, except to stir and settle more comfortably on her perch, and the very tension of her face had softened into a thoughtful stillness. Every time Cadfael raised his eyes to take a fresh look at her he found her more at ease in this unforeseen situation. And every time, her eyes were dwelling in speculation upon the fair head that topped all the rest, stalking before them with erected crest and long blond locks stirring in the light breeze.

Downhill at a brisk pace, through woodland and pasture, until the first silvery glints of water winked at them through the last belt of trees. The sun was dipping gently towards the west, gilding the ripples drawn by the breeze along the surface, when they emerged upon the shore of the strait, and the crewmen left on guard launched a shout of welcome, and brought the dragon-ship inshore to take them aboard.

Brother Mark, returning empty-handed from his foray westward to keep the rendezvous at the crossroads before sunset, heard the passing of a company of men, swift and quiet though they were, crossing his track some little way ahead, going downhill towards the shore. He halted in cover until they had passed, and then followed cautiously in the same direction, intending only to make sure they were safely out of sight and earshot before he pushed on to the meeting place. It so happened that the line he followed downhill among the trees inclined towards the course of their open ride, and brought him rapidly closer, so that he drew back and halted again, this time catching glimpses of them between the branches of bushes now almost in full summer leaf. A tall youth, flaxen fair, his head floating past like a blown primrose but high as a three-year spruce, a led horse, loaded, two men with a pole slung on their shoulders, and animal carcases swinging to their stride. Then, unmistakably, he saw Heledd and the boy pass by, a pair entwined and afloat six feet from the ground, the horse beneath them only implied by the rhythm of their passing, for the branches swung impenetrable between at that moment, leaving to view only a trudging tonsure beside them, russet brown almost wholly salted with grey. A very small clue to the man who wore it, but all Mark needed to know Brother Cadfael.

So he had found her, and these much less welcome strangers had found them both, before they could slip away thankfully into some safe refuge. And there was nothing Mark could do about it but follow them, far enough at least to see where they were taken, and how they were handled, and then make sure that the news was carried where there were those who could take their loss into account, and make plans for their recovery.

He dismounted and left his horse tethered, the better to move swiftly and silently among the trees. But the shout that presently came echoing up from the ship caused him to discard caution and emerge into the open, hurrying downhill to find a spot from which he could see the waters of the strait, and the steersman bringing his craft close in beneath the grassy bank, at a spot where it was child's play to leap aboard over the low rim into the rowers' benches in the waist of the vessel. Mark saw the tide of fierce, fair men flow inboard, coaxing the loaded packhorse after them, and stowing their booty under the tiny foredeck and in the well between the benches. In with them went Cadfael, perforce, and yet it seemed to Mark that he went blithely where he was persuaded. Small chance to avoid, but another man would have been a shade less apt and adroit about it.

The boy on horseback had kept his firm hold of Heledd until the flaxen-haired young giant, having seen his men embarked, reached up and hoisted her in his arms, as lightly as if she had been a child, and leaped down with her between the rowers' benches, and setting her down there on her feet, stretched up again to the bridle of Cadfael's horse, and coaxed him aboard with a soft-spoken cajolery that came up strangely to Mark's ears. The boy followed, and instantly the steersman pushed off strongly from the bank, the knot of men busy bestowing their plunder dissolved into expert order at the oars, and the lean little dragon-ship surged out into midstream. She was in lunging motion before Mark had recovered his wits, sliding like a snake southwestward towards Carnarvon and Abermenai, where doubtless her companions were now in harbour or moored in the roads outside the dunes. She did not have to turn, even, being double-ended. Her speed could get her out of trouble in any direction; even if she was sighted off the town Owain had nothing that could catch her. The rapidity with which she dwindled silently into a thin, dark fleck upon the water left Mark breathless and amazed.

He turned to make his way back to where his horse was tethered, and set out in resolute haste westward towards Carnarvon.

Plumped aboard into the narrow well between the benches, and there as briskly abandoned, Cadfael took a moment to lean back against the boards of the narrow after-deck and consider their situation. Relations between captors and captives seemed already to have found a viable level, at surprisingly little cost in time or passion. Resistance was impracticable. Discretion recommended acceptance to the prisoners, and made it possible for their keepers to be about the more immediate business of getting their booty safely back to camp, without any stricter enforcement than a rapidly moving vessel and a mile or so of water on either side provided. No one laid hand on Cadfael once they were embarked. No one paid any further attention to Heledd, braced back defensively into the stern-post, where the young

Dane had hoisted her, with knees drawn up and skirts hugged about her in embracing arms. No one feared that she would leap overboard and strike out for Anglesey; the Welsh were not known as notable swimmers. No one had any interest in doing either of them affront or injury; they were simple assets to be retained intact for future use.

To test it further, Cadfael made his way the length of the well amidships, between the stowed loot of flesh and provisions, paying curious attention to the details of the lithe, long craft, and not one oarsman checked in the steady heave and stretch of his stroke, or turned a glance to note the movement at his shoulder. A vessel shaped for speed, lean as a greyhound, perhaps eighteen paces long and no more than three or four wide. Cadfael reckoned ten strakes a side, six feet deep amidships, the single mast lowered aft. He noted the clenched rivets that held the strakes together. Clincher-built, shallow of draught, light of weight for its strength and speed, the two ends identical for instant manoeuvring, an ideal craft for beaching close inshore in the dunes of Abermenai. No use for shipping more bulky freight; they would have brought cargo hulls for that, slower, more dependent on sail, and shipping only a few rowers to get them out of trouble in a calm. Square-rigged, as all craft still were in these northern waters. The two-masted, lateen-rigged ships of the unforgotten midland sea were still unknown to these Norse seafarers.

He had been too deeply absorbed in these observations to realise that he himself was being observed just as shrewdly and curiously by a pair of brilliant ice-blue eyes, from under thick golden brows quizzically cocked. The young captain of this raiding party had missed nothing, and clearly knew how to read this appraisal of his craft. He dropped suddenly from the steersman's side to meet Cadfael in the well.

'You know ships?' he demanded, interested and surprised at so unlikely a preoccupation in a Benedictine brother.

'I did once. It's a long time now since I ventured on water.'

'You know the sea?' the young man pursued, shining with pleased curiosity.

'Not this sea. Time was when I knew the middle sea and the eastern shores well enough. I came late to the cloister,' he explained, beholding the blue eyes dilate and glitter in delighted astonishment, a deeper spark of pleasure and recognition warming within them.

'Brother, you put up your own price,' said the young Dane heartily. 'I would keep you to know better. Seafaring monks are rare beasts, I never came by one before. How do they call you?'

'My name is Cadfael, a Welsh-born brother of the abbey of Shrewsbury.'

'A name for a name is fair dealing. I am Turcaill, son of Turcaill, kinsman to Otir, who leads this venture.'

'And you know what's in dispute here? Between two Welsh princes? Why put your own breast between their blades?' Cadfael reasoned mildly.

'For pay,' said Turcaill cheerfully. 'But even unpaid I would not stay behind when Otir puts to sea. It grows dull ashore. I'm no landsman, to squat on a farm year after year, and be content to watch the crops grow.'

No, that he certainly was not, nor of a temper to turn to cloister and cowl even when the adventures of his youth were over. Splendidly fleshed, glittering with animal energy, this was a man for marriage and sons, and the raising of yet more generations of adventurers, restless as the sea itself, and ready to cleave their way into any man's quarrel for gain, at the fair cost of staking their own lives.

He was away now, with a valedictory clap on Cadfael's

shoulder, steady of stride along the lunging keel, to swing himself up beside Heledd on the after-deck. The light, beginning to fade into twilight now, still showed Cadfael the disdainful set of Heledd's lips and the chill arching of her brows as she drew the hem of her skirt aside from the contamination even of an enemy touch, and turned her head away, refusing him the acknowledgement of a glance.

Turcaill laughed, no way displeased, sat down beside her, and took out bread from a pouch at his belt. He broke it in his big, smooth young hands, and offered her the half, and she refused it. Unoffended, still laughing, he took her right hand by force, folded his offering into the palm, and shut her left hand hard over it. She could not prevent, and would not compromise her mute disdain by a vain struggle. But when he forthwith got up and left her so, without a glance behind, to do as she pleased with his gift, she neither hurled it into the darkening water of the strait nor bit into its crust by way of acceptance, but sat as he had left her, cradling it between her palms and gazing after his oblivious flaxen head with a narrow and calculating stare, the significance of which Cadfael could not read, but which at once intrigued and disquieted him.

In the onset of night, in a dusk through which they slid silently and swiftly in midstream, only faint glimmers of phosphorescence gilding the dip of the oars, they passed by the shore-lights of Owain's Carnarvon, and emerged into a broad basin shut off from the open sea only by twin rolling spits of sand-dunes, capped with a close growth of bushes and a scattering of trees. Along the water the shadowy shapes of ships loomed, some with stepped masts, some lean and low like Turcaill's little serpent. Spaced along the shore, the torches of the Danish outposts burned steadily in a still air, and higher towards the crest glowed the fires of an established camp.

Turcaill's rowers leaned to their last long stroke and shipped their oars, as the steersman brought the ship round in a smooth sweep to beach in the shallows. Over the side went the Danes, hoisting their plunder clear, and plashing up from the water to solid ground, to be met by their fellows on guard at the rim of the tide. And over the side went Heledd, plucked up lightly in Turcaill's arms, and this time making no resistance, since it would in any case have been unavailing, and she was chiefly concerned with preserving her dignity at this pass.

As for Cadfael himself, he had small choice but to follow, even if two of the rowers had not urged him over the side between them, and waded ashore with a firm grip on his shoulders. Whatever chances opened before him, there was no way he could break loose from this captivity until he could take Heledd with him. He plodded philosophically up the dunes and into the guarded perimeter of the camp, and went where he was led, well assured that the guardian circle had closed snugly behind him.

Chapter Eight

ADFAEL AWOKE TO the pearl-grey light of earliest dawn, the immense sweep of open sky above him, still sprinkled at the zenith with paling stars, and the instant recollection of his present situation. Everything that had passed had confirmed that they had little to fear from their captors, at least while they retained their bargaining value, and nothing to hope for in the way of escape, since the Danes were clearly sure of the efficiency of their precautions. The shore was well watched, the rim of the camp securely guarded. There was no need, within that pale, to keep a constant surveillance on a young girl and an elderly monastic. Let them wander at will, it would not get them out of the circle, and within it they could do no harm.

Cadfael recalled clearly that he had been fed, as generously as the young men of the guard who moved about him, and he was certain that Heledd, however casually housed here, had also been fed, and once left to her own devices, unobserved, would have had the good sense to eat what was provided. She was no such fool as to throw away her assets for spite when she had a fight on her hands.

He was lying, snugly enough, in the lee of a windbreak of hurdles, in a hollow of thick grass, his own cloak wrapped .

147

about him. He remembered Turcaill tossing it to him as it was
unrolled from his small belongings as the horse was unloaded.
Round him a dozen of the young Danish seamen snored at
ease. Cadfael arose and stretched, and shook the sand from
his habit. No one made any move to intercept him as he made
for the higher ground to look about him. The camp was alive,
the fires already lit, and the few horses, including his own,
watered and turned on to the greener sheltered levels to landward, where there was better pasture. Cadfael looked in that
direction, towards the familiar solidity of Wales, and made
his way unhindered through the midst of the camp to find a
high spot from which he could see beyond the perimeter of
Otir's base. From the south, and after a lengthy march round
the tidal bay that bit deep to southward, Owain must come if
he was ever to attack this strongpoint by land. By sea he
would be at a disadvantage, having nothing to match the
Norse longships. And Carnarvon seemed a long, long way
from this armed camp.

The few sturdy tents that housed the leaders of the expedition had been pitched in the centre of the camp. Cadfael
passed by them closely, and halted to mark the men who
moved about them. Two in particular bore the unmistakable
marks of authority, though curiously the pair of them
together struck a discordant note, as if their twin authorities
might somehow be at cross-purposes. The one was a man of
fifty years or more, thickset, barrel-chested, built like the bole
of a tree, and burned by the sun and the spray and the wind to
a reddish brown darker than the two braids of straw-coloured
hair that framed his broad countenance, and the long mous-
taches that hung lower than his jaw. He was bare-armed to the
shoulder but for leather bands about his forearms and thick
gold bracelets at his wrists.

'Otir!' said Heledd's voice softly in Cadfael's ear. She had come up behind him unnoticed, her steps silent in the drifting sand, her tone wary and intent. She had more here to contend with than a good-humoured youngster whose tolerant attitude might not always serve her turn. Turcaill was a mere subordinate here; this formidable man before them could overrule all other authorities. Or was it possible that even his power might suffer checks? Here was this second personage beside him, lofty of glance and imperious of gesture, by the look of him not a man to take orders tamely from any other being.

'And the other?' asked Cadfael, without turning his head.

'That is Cadwaladr. It was no lie, he has brought these long-haired barbarians into Wales to wrest back his rights from the Lord Owain. I know him, I have seen him before. The Dane I heard called by his name.'

A handsome man, this Cadwaladr, Cadfael reflected, approving the comeliness of the shape, if doubtful of the mind within. This man was not so tall as his brother, but tall enough to carry his firm and graceful flesh well, and he moved with a beautiful ease and power beside the squat and muscular Dane. His colouring was darker than Owain's, thick russet hair clustered in curls over a shapely head, and dark, haughty eyes well set beneath brows that almost met, and were a darker brown than his hair. He was shaven clean, but had acquired some of the clothing and adornments of his Dublin hosts during his stay with them, so that it would not have been immediately discernible that here was the Welsh prince who had brought this entire expedition across the sea to his own country's hurt. He had the reputation of being hasty, rash, wildly generous to friends, irreconcilably bitter against enemies. His face bore out everything that was said of him.

149

Nor was it hard to imagine how Owain could still love his troublesome brother, after many offences and repeated reconciliations.

'A fine figure of a man,' said Cadfael, contemplating this perilous presence warily.

'If he did as handsomely,' said Heledd.

The chieftains had withdrawn eastward towards the strait, the circle of their captains surrounding them. Cadfael turned his steps, instead, still southward, to get a view of the land approach by which Owain must come if he intended to shut the invaders into their sandy beachhead. Heledd fell in beside him, not, he judged, because she was in need of the comfort of his or any other company, but because she, too, was curious about the circumstances of their captivity, and felt that two minds might make more sense of them than one alone.

'How have you fared?' asked Cadfael, eyeing her closely as she walked beside him, and finding her composed, self-contained and resolute of lip and eye. 'Have they used you well, here where there are no women?'

She curled a tolerant lip and smiled. 'I needed none. If there's cause I can fend for myself, but as yet there's no cause. I have a tent to shelter me, the boy brings me food, and what else I want they let me go abroad and get for myself. Only if I go too near the eastern shore they turn me back. I have tried. I think they know I can swim.'

'You made no attempt when we were no more than a hundred yards offshore,' said Cadfael, with no implication of approval or disapproval.

'No,' she agreed, with a small, dark smile, and added not a word more.

'And even if we could steal back our horses,' he reflected

150

philosophically, 'we could not get out of this armed ring with them.'

'And mine is lame,' she agreed again, smiling her private smile.

He had had no opportunity, until now, to ask her how she had come by that horse in the first place, somehow stealing him away out of the prince's stables while the feast was at its height, and before any word was brought from Bangor to alert Owain to the threat from Ireland. He asked her now. 'How came it that you ever came into possession of this horse you call yours so briskly?'

'I found him,' said Heledd simply. 'Saddled, bridled, tethered among the trees not far from the gatehouse. Better than ever I expected, I took it for a good omen and was thankful I had not to go wandering through the night afoot. But I would have done it. I had no thought of it when I went out to refill the pitcher, but out in the courtyard I thought, why go back? There was nothing left in Llanelwy I could keep, and nothing in Bangor or Anglesey that I wanted. But there must be something for me, somewhere in the world. Why should I not go and find it, if no one else would get it for me? And while I was standing there in shadow by the wall, the guards on the gate were not marking me, and I slipped out behind their backs. I had nothing, I took nothing, I would have walked away so, and never complained. It was my choice. But in the trees I found this horse, saddled and bridled and ready for me, a gift from God that I could not refuse. If I have lost him now,' she said very solemnly, 'it may be he has brought me where I was meant to be.'

'A stage on your journey, it may be,' said Cadfael, concerned, 'but surely not the end. For here are you and I, hostages in a very questionable situation, and you I take to be a

151

lass who values her freedom highly. We have yet to get ourselves out of captivity, or wait here for Owain to do it for us.' He was revolving in some wonder what she had told him, and harking back to all that had happened in Aber. 'So there was this beast, made ready for riding and hidden away outside the enclave. And if heaven meant him for you, there was someone else who intended a very different outcome when he saddled him and led him out into the woods. Now it seems to me that Bledri ap Rhys did indeed mean to escape to his lord with word of all the prince's muster and strength. The means of flight was ready outside the gate for him. And yet he was found naked in his bedchamber, no way prepared for riding. You have set us a riddle. Did he go to his bed to wait until the llys was well asleep? And was killed before the favourable hour? And how did he purpose to leave the maenol, when every gate was guarded?'

Heledd was studying him intently along her shoulder, brows knitted together, only partially understanding, but hazarding very alert and intelligent guesses at what was still obscure to her. 'Do you tell me Bledri ap Rhys is dead? Killed, you said. That same night? The night I left the llys?'

'You did not know? It was after you were gone, so was the news that came from Bangor. No one has told you since?'

'I heard of the coming of the Danes, yes, that news was everywhere from the next morning. But I heard nothing of any death, never a word.'

No, it would not be news of crucial importance, like the invasion from Ireland, tref would not spread it to tref and maenol to maenol as Owain's couriers had spread word of the muster to Carnarvon. Heledd was frowning over the belated news, saddened by any man's death, especially one she had known briefly, even made use of, in her own fashion, to plague a father who wronged her affection.

'I am sorry,' she said. 'He had such life in him. A waste! Killed, you think, to prevent his going? One more warrior for Cadwaladr, and with knowledge of the prince's plans to make him even more welcome? Then *who*? Who could have found out, and made such dreadful shift to stop him?'

'That there's no knowing, nor will I hazard guesses where they serve no purpose. But soon or late, the prince will find him out. The man was in a sense his guest, he will not let the death go unavenged.'

'You foretell another death,' said Heledd, with forceful bitterness. 'What does that amend?'

And to that there was no answer that would not raise yet further questions, probing all the obscure corners of right and wrong. They walked on together, to a higher point near the southern rim of the armed camp, unhindered, though they were observed with brief, curious interest by many of the Danish warriors through whose lines they passed. On the hillock, clear of the sparse trees, they halted to survey the ground all about them.

Otir had chosen to make his landfall not on the sands to the north of the strait, where the coast of Anglesey extended into a broad expanse of dune and warren, none too safe in high tides, and terminating in a long bar of shifting sand and shingle, but to the south, where the enclosing peninsula of land stood higher and dryer, sheltered a deeper anchorage, and afforded a more defensible campsite, as well as more rapid access to the open sea in case of need. That it fronted more directly the strong base of Carnarvon, where Owain's forces were mustered in strength, had not deterred the invader. The shores of his chosen encampment were well manned, the landward approach compact enough to afford a formidable defence under assault, and a broad bay of tidal water separated it from the town. Several rivers drained into this bight, Cadfael recalled, but at low tide they would be mere meandering streaks of silver in a treacherous waste of sand, not lightly to be braved by an army. Owain would have to bring his forces far round to the south to approach his enemy on safe ground. With some six or seven miles of marching between himself and Owain, and with a secure ground base already gained, no doubt Cadwaladr felt himself almost invulnerable.

Except that the six or seven miles seemed to have shrunk to a single mile during the night. For when Cadfael topped the ridge of bushes, and emerged with a clear view well beyond the rim of the camp to southward, the open sea just glimmering with morning light on his right hand, the pallid shallow waters and naked sands of the bay to his left, he caught in the distance, spaced across the expanse of dune and field and scrubland, an unmistakable shimmer of arms and faint sparkle of coloured tents, a wall ensconced overnight. The early light picked out traces of movement like the quiver of a passing wind rippling a cornfield, as men passed purposefully to and fro about their unhurried business of fortifying their chosen position. Out of range of lance or bow, Owain had brought up his army under cover of darkness to seal off the top of this peninsula, and pen the Danish force within it. There was to be no time wasted. Thus forehead to forehead, like two rival rams measuring each other, one party or the other must open the business in hand without delay.

It was Owain who opened dealings, and before the morning was out, while the Danish chiefs were still debating the appearance of his host so close to their boundaries, and what action he might have in mind now that he was there. It was unlikely that they had any qualms about their own security, having swift access to the open sea at need, and ships the Welsh could not match, and doubtless, thought Cadfael, discreetly, drawn back from the knot of armed men gathered now on the knoll, they were also speculating as to how strong a garrison he had left to hold Carnarvon, and whether it would be worth staging a raid by water upon the town if the prince attempted any direct assault here. As yet they were not persuaded that he would risk any such costly action. They stood watching the distant lines narrowly, and waited. Let him speak first. If he was already minded to receive his brother into favour again, as he had done several times before, why make any move to frustrate so desirable a resolution?

It was mid-morning, and a pale sun high, when two horsemen were seen emerging from a slight dip in the sandy levels between the two hosts. Mere moving specks as yet, sometimes lost in hollows, then breasting the next rise, making steadily for the Danish lines. There were barely half a dozen dwellings in all that stretch of dune and warren, since there was little usable pasture and no good ploughland, and doubtless those few settlements had been evacuated in the night. Those two solitary figures were the sole inhabitants of a no-man's-land between armies, and as it appeared, charged with opening negotiations to prevent a pointless and costly collision. Otir waited for their nearer approach with a face wary but content, Cadwaladr with braced body and tense countenance, but foreseeing a victory. It was in the arrogant spread of his feet bestriding Welsh ground, and the lofty lift of his head and narrowing of his eyes to view the prince's envoys.

Still at the limit of the range of lance or arrow, the second rider halted and waited, screened by a thin belt of trees. The

155

other rode forward to within hailing distance, and there sat his horse, looking up at the watchful group on the hillock above him.

'My lords,' the hail came up to them clearly, 'Owain Gwynedd sends his envoy to deal with you on his behalf. A man of peace, unarmed, accredited by the prince. Will you receive him?'

'Let him come in,' said Otir. 'He shall be honourably received.'

The herald withdrew to a respectful distance. The second rider spurred forward towards the rim of the camp. As he drew near it became apparent that he was a small man, slender and young, and rode with more purpose than grace, as if he had dealt rather with farm horses than elegant mounts for princes and their ambassadors. Nearer still, and Cadfael, watching as ardently as any from the crest of the dunes, drew deep breath and let it out again in a great sigh. The rider wore the rusty black habit of the Benedictines, and showed the composed and intent young face of Brother Mark. A man of peace indeed, messenger of bishops and now of princes. No doubt in the world but he had begged this office for himself, none that he had urged upon the prince the practicality of making use of one whose motives could hardly be suspected, who had nothing to gain or lose but his own freedom, life and peace of mind, no axe to grind, no profit to make, no lord to placate in this world, Welsh, Danish, Irish or any other. A man whose humility could move like a charmed barrier between the excesses of other men's pride.

Brother Mark reached the edge of the camp, and the guards stood aside to let him pass. It was the young man Turcaill, twice Mark's modest size, who stepped forward hospitably to take his bridle, as he lighted down and set out briskly to climb the slight slope to where Otir and Cadwaladr waited to greet him.

In Otir's tent, crammed to the entrance with the chief among his forces, and every other man who could get a toehold close to the threshold, Brother Mark delivered himself of what he had come to say, partly on his own behalf, partly on behalf of Owain Gwynedd. Aware by instinct of the common assumption among these freebooters that they had rights in the counsels of their leaders, he let his voice ring out to reach the listeners crowding close outside the tent. Cadfael had made it his business to secure a foothold near enough to hear what passed, and no one had raised any objection to his presence. He was a hostage here, concerned after his own fashion as they were after theirs. Every man with a stake in the venture exercised his free right to guard his position.

'My lords,' said Brother Mark, taking his time to find the right words and give them their due emphasis, 'I have asked to undertake this embassage because I am not involved upon any part in this quarrel which brings you into Wales. I bear no arms, and I have nothing to gain, but you and I and every man here have much, all too much, to lose if this dispute ends in needless bloodshed. If I have heard many words of blame upon either side, here I use none. I say only that I deplore enmity and hatred between brothers as between peoples, and hold that all disputes should be resolved without the shedding of blood. And for the prince of Gwynedd, Owain ap Griffith ap Cynan, I say what he has instructed me to say. This quarrel holds good between two men only, and all others should hold back from a cause which is not theirs. Owain Gwynedd bids me say that if Cadwaladr his brother has a grievance, let him come and discuss it face to face, in guaranteed safety to come and to return.'

'And I am to take his word for that, without security?' Cadwaladr demanded. But by the guarded gleam in his eyes he was not displeased with this approach.

'As you know very well that you can,' said Mark simply.

Yes, he knew it. Every man there knew it. Ireland had had dealings with Owain Gwynedd many times before this, and not always by way of contention. He had kin over there who knew his value as well as it was known in Wales. Cadwaladr's face had a glossy look of contained pleasure, as though he found this first exchange more than encouraging. Owain had taken warning, seeing the strength of the invading force, and was preparing to be conciliatory.

'My brother is known for a man of his word,' he conceded graciously. 'He must not think that I am afraid to meet him face to face. Certainly I will go.'

'Wait a little, wait a little!' Otir shifted his formidable bulk on the bench where he sat listening. 'Not so fast! This issue may well have arisen between two men, but there are more of us in it now, invited in upon terms to which I hold, and to which I will hold you, my friend. If you are content to let go your assets on any man's word, without security, I am not willing to let go mine. If you leave here to enter Owain's camp and submit yourself to Owain's persuasion or Owain's compulsion, then I require a hostage for your safe return, not a hollow promise.'

'Keep me,' said Brother Mark simply. 'I am willing to remain as surety that Cadwaladr shall go and come without hindrance.'

'Were you so charged?' Otir demanded, with some suspicion of the efficacy of such an exchange.

'No. But I offer it. It is your right, if you fear treachery. The prince would not deny you.'

Otir eyed the slight figure before him with a cautious degree of approval, but remained sceptical. 'And does the prince place on you, Brother, an equal value with his own kinsman and enemy? I think I might be tempted to secure the one bird in hand, and let the other fly or founder.'

'I am in some sort Owain's guest,' said Mark steadily, 'and in some sort his courier. The value he sets on me is the value of his writ and his honour. I shall never be worth more than I am as you see me here.'

Otir let loose a great bellow of laughter, and struck his palms together. 'As good an answer as I need. Stay, then, Brother, and be welcome! You have a brother here already. Be free of my camp, as he is, but I warn you, never venture too near the rim. My guards have their orders What I have taken I keep, until it is fairly redeemed. When the lord Cadwaladr returns, you have due leave to go back to Owain, and give him such answer as we two here see fit.'

It was, Cadfael thought, a deliberate warning to Cadwaladr, as well as to Mark. There was no great trust between these two. If Otir required a surety that Cadwaladr would come back unmolested, it was certainly not simply out of concern for Cadwaladr's safety, but rather taking care of Otir's own bargain. The man was his investment, to be guarded with care, but never, never, to be wholly trusted. Once out of sight, who knew what use so rash a princeling would make of whatever advantage circumstances offered him?

Cadwaladr rose and stretched his admirable body with sleek, pleasurable assurance. Whatever reservations others might have, he had interpreted his brother's approach as wholly encouraging. The threat to the peace of Gwynedd had been shrewdly assessed, and Owain was ready to give ground,

159

by mere inches it might be, but sufficient to buy off chaos. And now all he, Cadwaladr, had to do was go to the meeting, behave himself seemly before other eyes, as he knew well how to do with grace, and in private surrender not one whit of his demands, and he would regain all, every yardland that had been taken from him, every man of his former following. There could be no other ending, when Owain spoke so softly and reasonably at the first advance.

'I go to my brother,' he said, grimly smiling, 'and what I bring back with me shall be to your gain as well as mine.'

Brother Mark sat with Cadfael in a hollow of the sand dunes overlooking the open sea, in the clear, almost shadowless light of afternoon. Before them the swathes of sand, sculptured by sea winds, went rolling down in waves of barren gold and coarse, tenacious grass to the water's edge. At a safe depth offshore seven of Otir's ships rode at anchor, four of them cargo hulls, squat and sturdy, capacious enough to accommodate a wealth of plunder if it came to wresting their price out of Gwynedd by force, the other three the largest of his longships. The smaller and faster vessels all lay within the mouth of the bay, where there was safe anchorage at need, and comfortable beaching inshore. Beyond the ships to westward the open, silvery water extended, mirroring a pallid, featureless blue sky, but dappled in several places by the veiled gold of shoals.

'I knew,' said Mark, 'that I should find you here. But I would have come, even without that inducement. I was on my way back to the meeting-place when they passed by. I saw you prisoners, you and the girl. The best I could do was make for Carnarvon, and carry that tale to Owain. He has your case well in mind. But what else he has in his mind, with this meeting he has sought, I do not know. It seems you have not fared so badly with these Danes. I find you in very good heart. I confess I feared for Heledd.'

'There was no need,' Cadfael said. 'It was plain we had our value for the prince, and he would not suffer us to go unransomed, one way or another. They do not waste their hostages. They have a reward promised, they are bent on earning it as cheaply as possible, they'll do nothing to bring out the whole of Gwynedd angry and in arms, not unless the whole venture turns sour on them. Heledd has been offered no affront.'

'And has she told you what possessed her to run from us at Aber, and how she contrived to leave the llys? And the horse she rode – for I saw it led along with the raiders, and that was good harness and gear from the prince's stable – how did she come by her horse?'

'She found it,' said Cadfael simply, 'saddled and bridled and tethered among the trees outside the walls, when she slipped out at the gate behind the backs of the guards. She says she would have fled afoot, if need had been, but there was the beast ready and waiting for her. And what do you make of that? For I am sure she speaks truth.'

Mark gave his mind to the question very gravely for some minutes. 'Bledri ap Rhys?' he hazarded dubiously. 'Did he indeed intend flight, and make certain of a mount while the gates were open, during the day? And some other, suspicious of his stubborn adherence to his lord, prevented the departure? But there was nothing to show that he ever thought of leaving. It seemed to me that the man was well content to be Owain's guest, and have Owain's hand cover him from harm.'

'There is but one man who knows the truth,' said Cadfael,

'and he has good reason to keep his mouth shut. But for all that, truth will out, or the prince will never let it rest. So I said to Heledd, and the girl says in reply: "You foretell another death. How does that amend anything?" '

'She says well,' agreed Mark sombrely. 'She has better sense than most princes and many priests. I have not yet seen her, here within the camp. Is she free to move as she pleases, within limits, like you?'

'You may see her this moment,' said Cadfael, 'if you please to turn your head, and look down to the right there, where the spit of sand juts out into the shallows yonder.'

Brother Mark turned his head obediently to follow where Cadfael pointed. The tongue of sand, tipped with a ridge of coarse blond grass to show that it was not quite submerged even at a normal high tide, thrust out into the shallows on their right like a thin wrist and hand, straining towards the longer arm that reached southward from the shores of Anglesey. There was soil enough on its highest point to support a few scrub bushes, and there a minute outcrop of rock stood up through the soft sand. Heledd was walking without haste along the stretched wrist towards this stony knuckle, at one point plashing ankle-deep through shallow water to reach it; and there she sat down on the rock, gazing out to sea, towards the invisible and unknown coast of Ireland. At this distance she appeared very fragile, very vulnerable, a small, slender, solitary figure. It might have been thought that she was withdrawing herself as far as possible from her captors, in a hapless defence against a fate she had no means of escaping in the body. Alone by the sea, with empty sky above her, and empty ocean before her, at least her mind sought a kind of freedom. Brother Cadfael found the picture deceptively appealing. Heledd was shrewdly aware of the strength, as well as the weakness, of her situation, and knew very well that she had little to fear, even had she been inclined to fear, which decidedly she was not. She knew, also, how far she could go in asserting her freedom of movement. She could not have approached the shores of the enclosed bay without being intercepted long before this. They knew she could swim. But this outer beach offered her no possibility of escape. Here she could wade through the shallows, and no one would lift a finger to prevent. She was hardly likely to strike out for Ireland, even if there had not been a flotilla of Danish ships offshore. She sat very still, her bare arms wreathed about her knees, gazing westward, but with head so alertly erect that even at this distance she seemed to be listening intently. Gulls wheeled and cried above her. The sea lay placid, sunlit, for the moment complacent as a cat. And Heledd waited and listened.

'Did ever creature seem more forlorn!' Brother Mark wondered, half aloud. 'Cadfael, I must speak with her as soon as may be. In Carnarvon I have seen her bridegroom. He came hotfoot from the island to join Owain, she should know that she is not forsaken. This Ieuan is a decent, stalwart man, and will put up a good fight for his bride. Even if Owain could be tempted to leave the girl to her fate here – and that is impossible! – Ieuan would never suffer it. If he had to venture for her with no forces but his own small following, I am sure he would never give up. Church and prince have offered her to him, and he is afire for her.'

'I do believe,' Cadfael said, 'that they have found her a good man, with all the advantages but one. A fatal lack! He is not of her choosing.'

'She might do very much worse. When she meets him, she may be wholly glad of him. And in this world,' Mark reflected ruefully, 'women, like men, must make the best of what they can get.'

'With thirty years and more behind her,' said Cadfael, 'she might be willing to settle for that. At eighteen – I doubt it!'

'If he comes in arms to carry her away – at eighteen that might weigh with her,' Mark observed, but not with entire conviction in his tone.

Cadfael had turned his head and was looking back towards the crest of the dunes, where a man's figure had just breasted the rise and was descending towards the beach. The long, generous stride, the exuberant thrust of the broad shoulders, the joyous carriage of the flaxen head, bright in the sun, would have given him a name even at a greater distance.

'I would not wager on the issue,' said Cadfael cautiously. 'And even so, he comes a little late, for someone else has already come in arms and carried her away. That issue, too, is still in doubt.'

The young man Turcaill erupted into Brother Mark's view only as he drew towards the spit of sand, and scorning to go the whole way to walk it dryshod, waded cheerfully through the shallows directly to where Heledd sat. Her back remained turned towards him, but doubtless her ears were pricked.

'Who is that?' demanded Mark, stiffening at the sight.

'That is one Turcaill, son of Turcaill, and if you saw us marched away to his ship, you must have seen that lofty head go by. It can hardly be missed, he tops the rest of us by the length of it.'

'That is the man who made her prisoner?' Mark was frowning down at Heledd's minute island, where still she maintained her pretence at being unaware of any intruder into her solitude.

'It was you said it. He came in arms and carried her away.'

164

'What does he want with her now?' Mark wondered, staring.

'No harm. He's subject to authority here, but even aside from that, no harm.' The young man had emerged in a brief flurry of spray beside Heledd's rock, and dropped with large, easy grace into the sand at her feet. She gave him no acknowledgement, unless it could be considered an acknowledgement that she turned a little away from him. Whatever they may have said to each other could not be heard at such a distance, and it was strange that Cadfael should suddenly feel certain that this was not the first time Heledd had sat there, nor the first time that Turcaill had coiled his long legs comfortably into the sand beside her.

'They have a small private war going on,' he said placidly. 'They both take pleasure in it. He loves to make her spit fire, and she delights in flouting him.'

A children's game, he thought, a lively battle that passes the time pleasantly for both of them, all the more pleasantly because neither of them need take it seriously. By the same token, neither need we take it seriously.

It occurred to him afterwards that he was breaking his own rule, and wagering on an issue that was still in doubt.

Chapter Nine

N THE ABANDONED farmstead where Owain had set up his headquarters, a mile from the edge of Otir's camp, Cadwaladr set forth the full tale of his grievances, with some discretion because he spoke in the presence not only of his brother, but of Hywel, against whom he felt perhaps the greatest and most bitter animosity, and of half a dozen of Owain's captains besides, men he did not want to alienate if he could keep their sympathy. But he was incapable of damping down his indignation throughout the lengthy tale, and the very reserve and tolerance with which they listened to him aggravated his burning resentment. By the end of it he was afire with his wrongs, and ready to proceed to what had been implied in every word, the threat of open warfare if his lands were not restored to him.

Owain sat for some minutes silent, contemplating his brother with a countenance Cadwaladr could not read. At length he stirred, without haste, and said calmly: 'You are under some misapprehension concerning the state of the case, and you have conveniently forgotten a small matter of a man's death, for which a price was exacted. You have

167

brought here these Danes of Dublin as a means of forcing my hand. Not even by a brother is my hand so easily forced. Now let me show you the reality. The boot is on the other foot now. It is no longer a matter of you saying to me: give me back all my lands, or I will let loose these barbarians on Gwynedd until you do. Now hear me saying to you: You brought this host here, now you get rid of them, and then you may – I say *may*! – be given back what was formerly yours.'

It was by no means what Cadwaladr had hoped for, but he was so sure of his fortune with such allies that he could not refrain from putting the best construction upon it. Owain meant more and better than he was yet prepared to say. Often before he had proved pliant towards his younger brother's offences, so he would again. In his own way he was already declaring an alliance to defy and expel the foreign invaders. It could not be otherwise.

'If you are ready to receive and join with me . . .' he had begun, for his high temper mildly and civilly, but Owain cut him off without mercy.

'I have declared no such intent. I tell you again, get rid of them, and only then shall I consider restoring you to your right in Ceredigion. Have I even said that I promise you anything? It rests with you, and not solely upon this present ground, whether you ever rule in Wales again. I promise you nothing, no help in sending these Danes back across the sea, no payment of any kind, no truce unless or until *I* choose to make truce with them. They are your problem, not mine. I may have, and reserve, my own quarrel with them for daring to invade my realm. But now any such consideration is in abeyance. Your quarrel with them, if you dismiss their help now, is your problem.'

Cadwaladr had flushed into angry crimson, his eyes hot with incredulous rage. 'What is this you are demanding of me? How do you expect me to deal with such a force? Unaided? What do you want me to do?'

'There is nothing simpler,' said Owain imperturbably. 'Keep the bargain you made with them. Pay them the fee you promised, or take the consequences.'

'And that is all you have to say to me?'

'That is all I have to say. But you may have time to think what further may be said between us if you show sense. Stay here overnight by all means,' said Owain, 'or return when you will. But you will get no more from me. While there's a Dane uninvited on Welsh ground.'

It was so plainly a dismissal, and Owain so unremittingly the prince rather than the brother, that Cadwaladr rose tamely and went out from the presence shocked and silent. But it was not in his nature to accept the possibility that his endeavours had all come to nothing. Within his brother's compact and well-planned camp he was received and acknowledged as both guest and kin, sacred and entitled to the ultimate in courtesy on the one ground, treated with easy familiarity on the other. Such usage only confirmed his native optimism and reassured his arrogant self-confidence. What he had heard was the surface that covered a very different reality. There were many among Owain's chiefs who kept a certain affection for this troublesome prince, however sorely that affection had been tried in the past, and however forthrightly they condemned the excesses to which his lofty temper drove him. How much greater, he reflected, at Owain's campaign table and in Owain's tent overnight, was the love his brother bore him. Time and again he had flouted it, and been chastened, even cast out of all grace, but only for a while. Time and again Owain had softened towards him, and taken him back brotherly into the former inescapable affection. So he would again. Why should this time be different?

He rose in the morning certain that he could manipulate his brother as surely as he had always done before. The blood that held them together could not be washed away by however monstrous a misdeed. For the sake of that blood, once the die was cast, Owain would do better than he had said, and stand by his brother to the hilt, against whatever odds.

All Cadwaladr had to do was cast the die that would force Owain's hand. The result was never in doubt. Once deeply embroiled, his brother would not desert him. A less sanguine man might have seen these calculations as providing only a somewhat suspect wager. Cadwaladr saw the end result as certainty.

There were some in the camp who had been his men before Hywel drove him out of Ceredigion. He reckoned their numbers, and felt a phalanx at his back. He would not be without advocates. But he used none of them at this juncture. In the middle of the morning he had his horse saddled, and rode out of Owain's encampment without taking any formal leave, as though to return to the Danes, and take up his bargaining with them with as little loss of cattle or gold or face as possible. Many saw him go with some half-reluctant sympathy. So, probably, did Owain himself, watching the solitary horseman withdraw across open country, until he vanished into one of the rolling hollows, to reappear on the further slope already shrunken to a tiny, anonymous figure alone in the encroaching waste of blown sand. It was something new in Cadwaladr to accept reproof, shoulder the burden laid on him, and go back without complaint to do the best he could with it. If he maintained this unexpected grace, it would be well worth a brother's while to salvage him, even now.

The reappearance of Cadwaladr, sighted before noon from the guard-lines covering Otir's landward approach, excited no surprise. He had been promised freedom to go and to return. The watch, captained by the man Torsten, he who was reputed to be able to split a sapling at fifty paces, sent word inward to Otir that his ally was returning, alone and unmolested, as he had been promised. No one had expected any other development; they waited only to hear what reception he had had, and what terms he was bringing back from the prince of Gwynedd.

Cadfael had been keeping a watchful eye on the approaches since morning, from a higher spot well within the lines, and at the news that Cadwaladr had been sighted across the dunes Heledd came curiously to see for herself, and Brother Mark with her.

'If his crest is high,' Cadfael said judicially, 'when he gets near enough for us to take note, then Owain has in some degree given way to him. Or else he believes he can prevail on him to give way with a little more persuasion. If there is one deadly sin this Cadwaladr will never fall by, it is surely despair.'

The lone horseman came on without haste into the sparse veil of trees on a ridge at some distance from the rim of the camp. Cadwaladr was as good a judge of the range of arrow or lance as most other men, for there he halted, and sat his horse in silence for some minutes. The first ripple of mild surprise passed through the ranks of Otir's warriors at this delay.

'What ails him?' wondered Mark at Cadfael's shoulder. 'He has his freedom to come and go. Owain has made no move to hold him, his Danes want him back. Whatever he brings with him. But it seems to me his crest is high enough. He may as well come in and deliver his news, if he has no cause to be ashamed of it.'

Instead, the distant rider sent a loud hail echoing over the folds of the dunes to those listening at the stockade. 'Send for Otir! I have a message to him from Gwynedd.'

'What can this be?' asked Heledd, puzzled. 'So he might well have, why else did he go to parley? Why deliver it in a bull's bellow from a hundred paces distance?'

Otir came surging over the ridge of the camp with a dozen of his chiefs at his heels, Turcaill among them. From the mouth of the stockade he sent back an answering shout: 'Here am I, Otir. Bring your message in with you, and welcome.' But if he was not by this time mulling over many misgivings and doubts in his own mind, Cadfael thought, he must be the only man present still sure of his grip on the expedition. And if he was, he chose for the moment to dissemble them, and wait for enlightenment.

'This is the message I bring you from Gwynedd,' Cadwaladr called, his voice deliberate, high and clear, to be heard by every man within the Danish lines. 'Be off back to Dublin, with all your host and all your ships! For Owain and Cadwaladr have made their peace, Cadwaladr will have his lands back, and has no more need of you. Take your dismissal, and go!'

And on the instant he wheeled his horse, and spurred back into the hollows of the dunes at a gallop, back towards the Welsh camp. A great howl of rage pursued him, and two or three opportunist arrows, fitted on uneasy suspicion, fell harmlessly into the sand behind him. Further pursuit was impossible, he had the wings of any horse the Danes could provide, and he was off back to his brother in all haste, to make good what he had dared to cry aloud. They watched him vanish and reappear twice in his flight, dipping and rising with the waves of the dunes, until he was a mere speck in the far distance.

'Is this possible?' marvelled Brother Mark, shocked and incredulous. 'Can he have turned the trick so lightly and easily? Would Owain countenance it?'

The clamour of anger and disbelief that had convulsed the Danish freebooters sank with ominous suddenness into the contained and far more formidable murmur of understanding and acceptance. Otir gathered his chiefs about him, turned his back on the act of treachery, and went striding solidly up the dunes to his tent, to take counsel what should follow. There was no wasting time on denunciation or threat, and there was nothing in his broad brown countenance to give away what was going on behind the copper forehead. Otir beheld things as they were, not as he would have wished them. He would never be hesitant in confronting realities.

'If there's one thing certain,' said Cadfael, watching him pass by, massive, self-contained and perilous, 'it is that there goes one who keeps his own bargains, bad or good, and will demand as much from those who deal with him. With or without Owain, Cadwaladr had better watch his every step, for Otir will have his price out of him, in goods or in blood.'

No such forebodings troubled Cadwaladr on his ride back to his brother's camp. When he was challenged at the outer guard he drew rein long enough to reassure the watch blithely: 'Let me by, for I am as Welsh as you, and this is where I belong. We have common cause now. I will be answerable to the prince for what I have done.'

To the prince they admitted, and indeed escorted him, unsure of what lay behind this return, and resolute that he should indeed make good his purpose to Owain before he spoke with any other. There were enough of his old associates among the muster, and he had a way of retaining devotion long after it was proven he deserved none. If he had brought the Danes here to threaten Gwynedd, he might now have conspired with them in some new and subtle measure to get his way. And Cadwaladr stalked into the presence in their midst with a slight, disdainful smile for their implied distrust, as always convinced by the arguments of his own sanguine mind, and sure of his dominance.

Owain swung about from the section of the stockade that his engineers were reinforcing, to stare and frown at sight of his brother, so unexpectedly returned. A frown as yet only of surprise and wonder, even concern that something unforeseen might have prevented Cadwaladr's freedom of movement.

'You back again? What new thing is this?'

'I am come to myself,' said Cadwaladr with assurance, 'and have returned where I belong. I am as Welsh as you, and as royal.'

'It is high time you remembered it,' said Owain shortly. 'And now you are here, what is it you intend?'

'I intend to see this land freed of Irishman and Dane, as I am instructed is your wish also. I am your brother. Your forces and mine are one force, must be one force. We have the same interests, the same needs, the same aims . . .'

Owain's frown had gathered and darkened on his brow into a thundercloud, as yet mute, but threatening. 'Speak plainly,' he said, 'I am in no mood to go roundabout. What have you done?'

'I have flung defiance at Otir and all his Danes!'
Cadwaladr was proud of his act, and assured he could make
it acceptable, and fuse into one the powers that would
enforce it. 'I have bidden them board and up sail and be off
home to Dublin, for you and I together are resolute to drive
them from our soil, and they had best accept their dismissal
and spare themselves a bloody encounter. I was at fault ever
to bring them here. If you will, yes, I repent of it. Between
you and me there is no need of such harsh argument. Now I
have dismissed and spurned their bought services. We will
rid ourselves of every last man of them. If we are at one,
they will not dare stand against us . . .'

He had progressed thus far in an ever-hastening torrent of
words, as if desperate to convince rather himself than
Owain. Misgivings had made their stealthy way into his
mind almost without his knowledge, by reason of the chill
stillness of his brother's face, and the grimly silent set of his
mouth below the unrelenting frown. Now the flow of
eloquence flagged and faltered, and though Cadwaladr drew
deep breath and took up the thread again, he could no
longer recover the former conviction. 'I have still a following, I will do my part. We cannot fail, they have no firm
foothold, they will be caged in their own defences, and swept
into the sea that brought them here.'

This time he let fall the very effort of speech. There was
even a silence, very eloquent to the several of Owain's men
who had ceased their work on the defences to listen with a
free tribesman's interest, and without any dissembling.
There was never born a Welshman who would not speak his
mind bluntly even to his prince.

'What is there,' Owain wondered aloud, to the sky above
him and the soil below, 'persuades this man still that my

175

words do not mean what they seem to mean in sane men's ears? Did I not say you get no more from me? Not a coin spent, not a man put at risk! This devilment of your own making, my brother, it was for you to unmake. So I said, so I meant and mean.'

'And I have gone far to do it!' Cadwaladr flared, flushing red to the brows. 'If you will do your part as heartily we are done with them. And who is put at risk? They dare not put it to the test of battle. They will withdraw while there's time.'

'And you believe I would have any part in such a betrayal? You made an agreement with these freebooters, now you break it as lightly as blown thistledown, and look to me to praise you for it? If your word and troth is so light, at least let me weight it with my black displeasure. If it were for that alone,' said Owain, abruptly blazing, 'I would not lift a finger to save you from your folly. But there is worse. Who is put at risk, indeed! Have you forgotten, or did you never condescend to understand, that your Danes hold two men of the Benedictine habit, one of them willing hostage for your good faith, which now all men see was not worth a bean, let alone a good man's liberty and life. Yet more, they also hold a girl, one who was in my retinue and in my care, even if she chose to venture to leave it and make shift alone. For all these three I stand responsible. And all these three you have abandoned to whatever fate your Otir may determine for his hostages, now that you have spited, cheated and imperilled him at the cost of your own honour. This is what you have done! Now I will undo such part of it as I can, and you may make such terms as you can with the allies you have cheated and discarded.'

And without pause for any rejoinder, even had his brother retained breath enough to speak, Owain flung away from

176

him to call to the nearest of his men: 'Send and saddle me my horse! Now, and hasten!'

Cadwaladr came to his senses with a violent convulsion, and sprang after him to catch him by the arm. 'What will you do? Are you mad? There's no choice now, you are committed as deep as I. You cannot let me fall!'

Owain plucked himself away from the unwelcome hold, thrusting his brother to arm's length in brief and bitter detestation. 'Leave me! Go or stay, do as you please, but keep out of my sight until I can bear the very look and touch of you. You have not spoken for me. If you have so represented the matter, you lied. If a hair of the young deacon's head has been harmed, you shall answer for it. If the girl has suffered any insult or hurt, you shall pay the price of it. Go, hide yourself, think on your own hard case, for you are no brother nor ally of mine; you must carry your own follies to their deserved ending.'

It was not more than two hours past noon when another solitary horseman was sighted from the camp on the dunes, riding fast and heading directly for the Danish perimeter. One man alone, coming with manifest purpose, and making no cautious halt out of range of weapons, but posting vehemently towards the guards, who stood watching his approach with eyes narrowed to weigh up his bearing and accoutrements, and guess at his intent. He wore no mail, and bore no visible arms.

'No harm in him,' said Torsten. 'What he wants he'll tell us, by the cut of him. Go tell Otir we have yet another visitor coming.'

It was Turcaill who carried the message, and delivered it as he interpreted it. 'A man of note by his beast and his harness. Fairer-headed then I am, he could be a man of our own, and big enough. My match, if I'm a judge. He might even top me. By this he's close. Shall we bring him in?'

Otir gave no more than a moment to considering it. 'Yes, let him come. A man who spurs straight in to me man to man is worth hearing.'

Turcaill went back jauntily to the guardpost, in time to see the horseman rein in at the gate, and light down empty-handed to speak for himself. 'Go tell Otir and his peers that Owain ap Griffith ap Cynan, prince of Gwynedd, asks admittance to speech with them.'

There had been very serious and very composed and deliberate consultation in Otir's inner circle of chieftains since Cadwaladr's defiance. They were not men of a temper to accept such treachery, and make the best of their way tamely out of the trap in which it had left them. But whatever they had discussed and contemplated in retaliation suddenly hung in abeyance when Turcaill, grinning and glowing with his astonishing embassage, walked in upon their counsels to announce:

'My lords, here on the threshold is Owain Gwynedd in his own royal person, asking speech with you.'

Otir had a sense of occasion that needed no prompting. The astonishment of this arrival he put by in an instant, and rose to stride to the open flap of his tent and bring in the guest with his own hand to the trestle table round which his captains were gathered.

'My lord prince, whatever your word, your self is welcome. Your line and your reputation are known to us, your forebears on your grandmother's side are close kin to kin of ours. If we have our dissensions, and have fought on opposing sides before now, and may again, that is no bar but we may meet in fair and open parley.'

'I expect no less,' said Owain. 'You I have no cause otherwise to love, since you are here upon my ground uninvited,
and for no good purpose towards me. I am not come to
exchange compliments with you, nor to complain of you,
but to set right what may be misunderstood between us.'

'Is there such misunderstanding?' asked Otir with dry
good humour. 'I had thought our situation must be clear
enough, for here I am, and here are you acknowledging
freely that here I have no right to be.'

'That, as at this moment,' said Owain, 'we may leave to
be resolved at another time. What may have misled you is
the visit my brother Cadwaladr paid you this morning.'

'Ah, that!' said Otir, and smiled. 'He is back in your
encampment, then?'

'He is back. He is back, and I am here, to tell you – I
could even say, to warn you – that he did not speak for me. I
knew nothing of his intent. I thought he had come back to
you just as he left you, still your ally, still hostile to me, still
a man of his word and bound to you. It was not with my will
or leave that he discarded you, and with you the sacred
worth of his word. I have not made peace with him, nor will
I make war with him against you. He has not won back the
lands I took from him, for good reason. The bargain he
made with you he must abide as best he may.'

They were steadily gazing at him, and from him to one
another, about the table, waiting to be enlightened, and
withholding judgement until the mists cleared.

'I am slow to see, then, the purpose of this visit,' said Otir
civilly, 'however much pleasure the company of Owain
Gwynedd gives me.'

'It is very simple,' said Owain. 'I am here to lay claim to
three hostages you hold in your camp. One of them, the

179

young deacon Mark, willingly remained to ensure the safe return of my brother, who has now made that return impossible, and left the boy to answer for it. The other two, the girl Heledd, a daughter of a canon of Saint Asaph, and the Benedictine Brother Cadfael of the abbey of Shrewsbury, were captured by this young warrior who conducted me in to you, when he raided for provisions far up the Menai. I came to ensure that no harm should come to any of these, by reason of Cadwaladr's abandonment of his agreement. They are no concern of his. They are all three under my protection. I am here to offer a fair ransom for them, no matter what may follow between your people and mine. My own responsibilities I will discharge honourably. Cadwaladr's are nothing to do with me. Exact from him what he owes you, not from any of these three innocent people.'

Otir did not openly say: 'So I intend!' but he smiled a tight and relishing smile that spoke just as clearly for him. 'You may well interest me,' he said, 'and I make no doubt we could agree upon a fair ransom, between us. But for this while you must hold me excused if I reserve all my assets. When I have given consideration to all things, then you shall know whether, and at what price, I am willing to sell your guests back to you.'

'At least, then,' said Owain, 'give me your pledge that they shall come back to me unharmed when I do recover them – whether by purchase or by capture.'

'I do not spoil what I may wish to sell,' agreed Otir. 'And when I collect what is due to me, it will be from the debtor. That I promise you.'

'And I take your word,' said Owain. 'Send to me when you will.'

'And there is no more to be said between us two?'

'As yet,' said Owain, 'there is nothing more. All your choices you have reserved. So do I reserve mine.'

Cadfael left the place where he had stood motionless and quiet, in the lee of the tent, and followed down through the mute ranks of the Danes as they drew aside to give the prince of Gwynedd clear passage back to his waiting horse. Owain mounted and rode, without haste now, more certain of his enemy than ever he had been since boyhood of his brother. When the fair head, uncovered to the sun, had twice dipped from sight and reappeared again, and was dwindling into a distant speck of pale gold in the distance, Cadfael turned back along the fold of the dunes, and went to look for Heledd and Mark. They would be together. Mark had taken upon himself, somewhat diffidently, the duty of keeping a guardian eye upon the girl's privacy. She might shake him off at will when she did not want him; when if ever she did want him, he would be within call. Cadfael had found it oddly touching how Heledd bore with this shy but resolute attendance, for she used Mark as an elder sister might, considerate of his dignity and careful never to open upon him the perilous weaponry she had at her disposal in dealing with other men, and sometimes had been known to indulge for her own pleasure no less than in hurt retaliation against her father. For there was no question but this Heledd, with her gown frayed at the sleeve and crumpled by sleeping in a scooped hollow of sand lined with grass, and her hair unbraided and loose about her shoulders in a mane of darkness burnished into blue highlights by the sun, and her feet as often as not bare in the warm sand and the cool shallows along the seaward shore, was perceptibly closer to pure beauty than she had ever been before, and could have wreaked havoc in most young men's lives here had she been so minded. Nor was it wholly in her own defence that she went about the camp so discreetly, suppressing her radiance, and avoided contact with her captors but for the young boy who waited on her needs and Turcaill, to whose teasing company she had become accustomed, and whose shafts she took passing pleasure in returning.

There was a bloom upon Heledd in these days of captivity, a summer gloss that was more than the sheen of the sun on her face. It seemed that now that she was a prisoner, however easy was her captivity within its strict limits, and had accepted her own helplessness, now that all action and all decisions were denied her she had abandoned all anxiety with them, and was content to live in the passing day and look no further. More content than she had been, Cadfael thought, since Bishop Gilbert came to Llanelwy, and set about reforming his clergy while her mother was on her deathbed. She might even have suffered the extreme bitterness of wondering whether her father was not looking forward to the death that would secure him his tenure. There was no such cloud upon her now, she radiated a warmth that seemed to have no cares left in the world. What she could not influence she had settled down to experience and survive, even to enjoy.

They were standing among the thin screen of trees on the ridge when Cadfael found them. They had seen Owain arrive, and they had climbed up here to watch him depart. Heledd was still staring wide-eyed and silent after the last glimpse of the prince's bright head, lost now in distance. Mark stood always a little apart from her, avoiding touch. She might treat him sisterly, but Cadfael wondered at times whether Mark felt himself in danger, and kept always a space between them. Who could ensure that his own feelings should always remain brotherly? The very concern he felt for her, thus suspended between an uncertain past and a still more questionable future, was a perilous pitfall.

'Owain will have none of it,' Cadfael announced practically. 'Cadwaladr lied, Owain has set the matter straight. His brother must work out his own salvation or damnation unaided.'

'How do you know so much?' asked Mark mildly.

'I took care to be close. Do you think a good Welshman would neglect his interests where the contrivances of his betters are concerned?'

'I had thought a good Welshman never acknowledged any betters,' said Mark, and smiled. 'You had your ear to the leather of the tent?'

'For your benefit no less. Owain has offered to buy us all three out of Otir's hold. And Otir, if he has held back from coming to terms at once, has promised us life and limb and this degree of freedom until he comes to a decision. We have nothing worse to fear.'

'I was not in any fear,' said Heledd, still gazing thoughtfully southward. 'Then what comes next, if Owain has left his brother to his fate?'

'Why, we sit back and wait, here where we are, until either Otir decides to accept his price for us, or Cadwaladr somehow scrapes together whatever fool sum in money and stock he promised his Danes.'

'And if Otir cannot wait, and decides to cut his fee by force out of Gwynedd?' Mark wondered.

'That he will not do, unless some fool starts the killing and forces his hand. I exact my dues, he said, from the debtor who owes them. And he means it, not now simply out of self-interest, but out of a very deep grudge against

183

Cadwaladr, who has cheated him. He will not bring Owain and all his power into combat if by any means he can avoid it and still get his profit. And he is as able to make his own dispositions,' said Cadfael shrewdly, 'as any other man, and for all I can see, better than most. Not only Owain and his brother are calling the shots here, Otir may well have a trick or two of his own up his sleeve.'

'I want no killing,' said Heledd peremptorily, as though she gave orders by right to all men presently in arms. 'Not for us, not for them. I would rather continue here prisoner than have any man brought to his death. And yet,' she said grieving, 'I know it cannot go on thus deadlocked, it must end somehow.'

It would end, Cadfael reflected, unless some unforeseen disaster intervened, in Otir's acceptance of Owain's ransom for his captives, most probably after Otir had dealt, in whatever fashion he saw fit, with Cadwaladr. That score would rank first in his mind, and be tackled first. He had no obligation now to his sometime ally, that compact had been broken once for all. Cadwaladr might go into exile, once he had paid his dues, or go on his knees to his brother and beg back his lands. Otir owed him nothing. And since he had all his following to pay, he would not refuse the additional profit of Owain's ransom. Heledd would go free, back to Owain's charge. And there was a man now in Owain's muster who was waiting to claim her on her return. A good man, so Mark said, presentable to the eye, well-thought of, a man of respectable lands, in good odour with the prince. She might do very much worse.

'There is no cause in the world,' said Mark, 'why it should not end for you in a life well worth the cherishing. This Ieuan whom you have never seen is wholly disposed to receive and love you, and he is worth your acceptance.'

'I do believe you,' she said, for her almost submissively. But her eyes were steady upon a far distance over the sea, where the light of air and the light of water melted into a shimmering mist, indissoluble and mysterious, everything beyond hidden in radiance. And Cadfael wondered suddenly if he was not, after all, imagining the conviction in Brother Mark's voice, and the womanly grace of resignation in Heledd's.

Chapter Ten

URCAILL CAME DOWN from conference in Otir's tent towards the shore of the sheltered bay, where his lithe little dragon-ship lay close inshore, its low sides mirrored in the still water of the shallows. The anchorage at the mouth of the Menai was separated from the broad sandy reaches of the bay to southward by a long spit of shingle, beyond which the water of two rivers and their tributaries wound its way to the strait and the open sea, in a winding course through the waste of sands. Turcaill stood to view the whole sweep of land and water, the long stretch of the bay extending more than two miles to the south, pale gold shoals and sinuous silver water, the green shore of Arfon beyond, rolling back into the distant hills. The tide was flowing, but it would be two hours or more yet before it reached its highest, and covered all but a narrow belt of salt marsh fringing the shore of the bay. By midnight it would be on the turn again, but full enough to float the little ship with its shallow draught close inshore. Inland of the saltings there would, if luck held, be scrub growth that would give cover to a few skilled and silent men moving inland. Nor would they have far to go. Owain's encampment must span the waist of the peninsula. Even at its narrowest point it might be as much

187

as a mile across, but he would have pickets on either shore. Fewer and less watchful, perhaps, on the bay shore, since attack by ship was unlikely that way. Otir's larger vessels would not attempt to thread the shoals. The Welsh would be concentrating their watch on the sea to westward.

Turcaill was whistling to himself, very softly and contentedly, as he scanned a sky just deepening into dusk. Two hours yet before they could set out, and with the evening clouds had gathered lightly over the heavens, a grey veil, not threatening rain, but promising cover against too bright a night. From his outer anchorage he would have to make a detour round the bar of shingle to the mouth of the river to reach the clear channel, but that would add only some quarter of an hour to the journey. Well before midnight, he decided blithely, we can embark.

He was still happily whistling when he turned back to return to the heart of the camp and consider on the details of his expedition. And there confronting him was Heledd, coming down from the ridge with her long, springy stride, the dark mane of her hair swaying about her shoulders in the breeze that had quickened with evening, bringing the covering of cloud. Every encounter between them was in some sense a confrontation, bringing with it a racing of the blood on both sides, curiously pleasurable.

'What are you doing here?' he asked, the whistle breaking off short. 'Were you thinking of escaping across the sands?' He was mocking her, as always.

'I followed you,' she said simply. 'Straight from Otir's tent, and off with you this way, and eyeing the sky and the tide and that snake-ship of yours. I was curious.'

'The first time ever you were curious about me or anything I did,' he said cheerfully. 'Why now?'

'Because suddenly I see you head-down on a hunt, and I cannot but wonder what mischief you're about this time.'

'No mischief,' said Turcaill. 'Why should there be?' He was regarding her, as they walked back slowly together, with somewhat narrower attention than he gave to their usual easy skirmishing, for it seemed to him that she was at least half serious in her probing, even in some way anxious. Here in her captivity, between two armed camps, a solitary woman might well scent mischief, the killing kind, in every move, and fear for her own people.

'I am not a fool,' said Heledd impatiently. 'I know as well as you do that Otir is not going to let Cadwaladr's treason go unavenged, nor let his fee slip through his fingers. He's no such man! All this day he and all his chiefs have had their heads together over the next move, and now suddenly you come bursting out shining with the awful delight you fool men feel in plunging headfirst into a fight, and you try to tell me there's nothing in the wind. *No mischief!*'

'None that need trouble you,' he assured her. 'Otir has no quarrel with Owain or any of Owain's host, they have cast off Cadwaladr to untie his own knots and pay his own debts, why should we want to provoke worse? If the promised price is paid, we shall be off to sea and trouble you no more.'

'A good riddance that will be,' said Heledd sharply. 'But why should I trust you and your fellows to manage things so well? It needs only one chance wounding or killing, and there'll be blazing warfare, and a great slaughter.'

'And since you are so sure I'm deep in this mischief you foresee . . .'

'The very instrument of it,' she said vehemently.

189

'Then can you not trust *me* to bring it to a good end?' He was laughing at her again, but with a degree of almost apprehensive delicacy.

'You least of all,' she said with vicious certainty. 'I know you, you have a lust after danger, there's nothing so foolhardy but you would dare it, and bring down everything in a bloody battle on all of us.'

'And you, being a good Welshwoman,' said Turcaill, wryly smiling, 'fear for your Gwynedd, and all those men of Owain's host camped there barely a mile from us.'

'I have a bridegroom among them,' she reminded him smartly, and set her teeth with a snap.

'So you have. I will not forget your bridegroom,' Turcaill promised, grinning. 'At every step I take, I will think on your Ieuan ab Ifor, and draw in my hand from any stroke that may bring him into peril of battle. There's no other consideration could so surely curb any rashness of mine as the need to see you married to a good, solid *uchelwr* from Anglesey. Will that content you?'

She had turned to look at him intently, her great eyes purple-black and unwaveringly earnest. 'So you are indeed bound on some mad foray for Otir! You have as good as said so.' And as he did not make any protest or attempt to deny it further: 'Make good what you have promised me, then. Take good care! Come back without hurt to any. I would not have even you come to harm.' And meeting the somewhat too bright intelligence of the blue eyes, she added with a toss of her head, but with a little too much haste for the disdainful dignity at which she aimed: 'Let alone my own countrymen.'

'And foremost of all your countrymen, Ieuan ab Ifor,' Turcaill agreed with a solemn face: but she had already turned her back on him and set off with erected head and vehement

190

stride towards the sheltered hollow where her own small tent was placed.

Cadfael arose from his chosen nest in the lee of the squat salt bushes wakeful and restless for no good reason, left Mark already sleeping, and dropped his cloak beside his friend, for the night was warm. It was at Mark's insistence that they lay always within call of Heledd's tent, though not so close as to offend her independent spirit. Cadfael had small doubt by this time of her safety within the Danish enclave. Otir had given his orders, and no man of his following was likely to take them lightly, even if their minds had not been firmly fixed upon more profitable plunder than one Welsh girl, however tempting. Adventurers, Cadfael had noted throughout his own early life of adventure, were eminently practical people, and knew the value of gold and possessions. Women came much lower down in the scale of desirable loot.

He looked towards where her low windbreak lay, and all was dark and silent there. She must be asleep. For no comprehensible reason, sleep eluded him. The sky bore a light covering of cloud, through which only a star here and there showed faintly. There was no wind, and tonight there would be no moon. The cloud might well thicken by morning, even bring rain. At this midnight hour the stillness was profound, even oppressive, the darkness over the dunes shading away both east and west into a very faint impression of lambent light from the sea, now almost at its fullest tide. Cadfael turned eastward, where the line of guards was more lightly manned, and he was less likely to excite any challenge by being up and about in the dead of night. There were no fires, except those turfed down in the heart of the camp to burn slowly till morning, and no torches to prick through the darkness. Otir's watchmen relied on their night eyes. So did Brother Cadfael. Shapes grew out of shapelessness gradually, even the curves and slopes of the dunes were dimly perceptible. It was strange how a man could be so solitary in the midst of thousands, as if solitude could be achieved at will, and how one to all intents and purposes a prisoner could feel himself freer than his captors, who went hampered by their numbers and chained by their discipline.

He had reached the crest of the ridge above the anchorage, where the lighter and faster Danish ships lay snugly between the open sea and the strait. A wavering line of elusive light, appearing and vanishing as he watched, lipped the shore, and there within its curve they lay, so many lean, long fishes just perceptible as darker flecks briefly outlined by the stroking of the tide. They quivered, but did not stir from their places. Except for one, the leanest and smallest. He saw it creep out from its anchorage so softly that for a moment he thought he was imagining the forward surge. Then he caught the dip of the oars, pinpricks of fire, gone almost before he could realise what they were. No sound came up to him from the distance, even in this nocturnal stillness and silence. The least and probably fastest of the dragon-ships was snaking out into the mouth of the Menai, heading eastward into the channel.

Another foraging expedition? If that was the intent, it would make good sense to take to the strait by night, and lie up somewhere well past Carnarvon to begin their forays ashore before dawn. The town would certainly have been left well garrisoned, but the shores beyond were still open to raiding, even if most of the inhabitants had removed their stock and all their portable goods into the hills. And what was there among the belongings of a good Welshman that was not portable? With ease they could abandon their homesteads if need arose, and rear them again when the danger was over. They had been doing it for centuries, and were good at it. Yet these nearest fields and settlements had already been looted once, and could not be expected to go on providing food for a small army. Cadfael would have expected rather that they would prefer combing the soft coast southward from the open sea, Owain's muster notwithstanding. Yet this small hunter set off silently into the strait. In that direction lay only the long passage of the Menai, or, alternatively, she could be meaning to round the bar of shingle and turn south into the bay by favour of this high tide. Unlikely, on the face of it, though so small a fish could find ample draught for some hours yet, until the tide was again well on the ebb towards its lowest. A larger craft, Cadfael reflected thoughtfully, would never venture there. Could that in itself be the reason why this one was chosen, and despatched alone? Then for what nocturnal purpose?'

'So they're gone,' said Heledd's voice behind him, very softly and sombrely.

She had come up at his shoulder soundlessly, barefoot in the sand still warm from the day's sunlight. She was looking down to the shore as he was, and her gaze followed the faintly luminous single stroke of the longship's wake, withdrawing rapidly eastward. Cadfael turned to look at her, where she stood composed and still, the cloud of her long hair about her.

'*So they're gone!* Had you wind of it beforehand? It does not surprise you!'

'No,' she said, 'it does not surprise me. Not that I know anything of what is in their minds, but there has been something brewing all day since Cadwaladr so spited them as he did. What they are planning for him I do not know, and what it may well mean for all the rest of us I dare not guess, but surely nothing good.'

193

'That is Turcaill's ship,' said Cadfael. It was already so far lost in the darkness that they could follow it now only with the mind's eye. But it would not yet have reached the end of the shingle bar.

'So it would be,' she said. 'If there's mischief afoot, he must be in it. There's nothing Otir could demand of him, however mad, but he would plunge into it headfirst, joyfully, with never a thought for the consequences.'

'And you have thought of the possible consequences,' Cadfael deduced reasonably, 'and do not like them.'

'No,' she said vehemently, 'I do not like them! There could be battle and slaughter if by some foul chance he kills a man of Owain's. It needs no more to start such a blaze.'

'And what makes you think he is going anywhere near Owain's men, to risk such a chance?'

'How should I know what the fool has in mind?' she said impatiently. 'What troubles me is what he may bring down on the rest of us.'

'I would not so readily score him down as a fool,' said Cadfael mildly. 'I would have reckoned him as shrewd in the wits as he is an able man of his hands. Whatever he's about, judge it when he returns, for it's my belief he'll come back successful.' He was careful not to add: 'So leave fretting over him!' She would have denied any such concern, though now with less ferocity than once she would have attempted. Best leave well alone. However she might hope to deceive others, Heledd was not the girl to be able to deceive herself.

And away there to the south in Owain's camp was the man she had never yet seen, Ieuan ab Ifor, not much past thirty, which is not all that old, well thought of by his prince, holder of good lands, and personable to the beholder's eye, possessed of every asset but one, and invisible and negligible without it. He was not the man she had chosen.

'Tomorrow will show,' said Heledd, with relentless practicality. 'We had best go get our sleep, and be ready for it.'

They had rounded the tip of the shingle bar, and kept well out in the main channel as they turned southward into the bay. Once well within, they could draw inshore and keep a watch on the coastline for the first outlying pickets of Owain's camp. Turcaill's boy Leif kneeled on the tiny foredeck, narrowing his eyes attentively upon the shore. He was fifteen years old, and spoke the Welsh of Gwynedd, for his mother had been snatched from this same north-western coast at twelve years old, on a passing Danish raid, and had married a Dane of the Dublin kingdom. But she had never forgotten her language, and had spoken it always with her son, from the time that he learned to speak at all. A half-naked boy in the high summer, Leif could go among the Welsh trefs and the fishing villages here and pass for one of their own, and his talent for acquiring information had brought in beforehand a useful harvest.

'Cadwaladr has kept touch always with those who hold by him,' Leif had reported cheerfully, 'and there are some among his brother's muster now would go with him if he attempted some act of his own. And I hear them say he has sent word south from Owain's camp to his men in Ceredigion. What word nobody knows, whether to come and join him in arms, or whether to be ready to put together money and cattle if he is forced to pay what he promised us. But if a messenger comes asking for him he'll think it no harm, rather to his gain.'

And there was more to be told, the fruit of much attentive listening. 'Owain will not have him close to him. He keeps a few of his own about him now, and has made his base at the southern edge of the camp, in the corner nearest the bay. There if news comes for him from his old lands, he can let the messenger in and Owain need not know. For he'll play one hand against the other however his vantage lies,' said Leif knowingly.

There was no arguing with that. Everyone who knew Cadwaladr knew it for truth. If the Danes had been slow to realise it, they knew it now. And Leif could be the messenger as well as any other. At fourteen a Welsh boy becomes a man, and is acknowledged as a man.

The ship drew in cautiously closer to shore. Outlines of dune and shingle and scattered bushes showed as denser or paler bulks in the dark, slipping by on their right hand. And presently the outer fringe of the Welsh camp became perceptible rather by the lingering intimations of humanity, the smoke of fires, the resinous odours of newly split wood in the lengths of stockade, even the mingled, murmurous sounds of such activity as persisted into the night, than by anything seen or clearly heard. The steersman brought his barque still closer, wary of the undulations of marsh grass beneath the placid surface of the shallows, until they should have passed the main body of the camp, and drawn along-side that southern corner where Cadwaladr was reputed to have set up his camp within the camp, drawing about him men of his old following, whose adherence to his brother remained less reliable than to their former prince. More than one fashion of messenger could make contact with him there, and other tidings reach him besides the gratifying news that his lavish generosity was still remembered by some, and himself still held in respect as lord and prince, to whom old fealty was due. He could still be reminded, not only of privileges, but of responsibilities owing, and debts unpaid.

The line of the shore receded from them, dipping westward, and closed with them again gradually as they slid past. The faint warmth and stir that was not quite sound, but only some primitive sensitivity to the presence of other human creatures, unseen, unheard, watchful and potentially hostile, fell behind then into the empty silence of the night.

'We are past,' said Turcaill softly into the steersman's ear. 'Lay us inshore.'

The oars dipped softly. The lithe little ship slid smoothly in among the tufted grasses, and touched bottom as gently as a feather lighting. Leif swung his legs over the side, and dropped into the shallows. There was firm sand under his bare feet, and the water reached barely halfway to his knee. He looked back along the line of the shore where they had passed, and even over the darkened camp there still hung a faint glow left over from the day.

'We're close. Wait till I bring word.'

He was gone, winding his way in through the salt grasses and the straggle of scrub to the lift of the dunes beyond, narrow here, and soon rising into rough pasture, and then into good fields. His slight shape melted into the soft, dense darkness.

He was back within a quarter of an hour, sliding out of the night as silently as a wisp of mist before they were prepared for his return, though they had waited without impatience, with ears pricked for any alien sound. Leif waded through the salt bush and the shallow water cold round his legs, and reached to hold by the ship's side and whisper in an excited hiss: 'I have found him! And close! He has a man of his own on the guard-post. Nothing simpler than to come to him in secret from this side. Here they expect no attack by land, he can go and come as he pleases, and so can some who would liefer do his bidding than Owain's.'

'You have not been within?' demanded Turcaill. 'Past the guard?'

'No need! Someone else found the way there not a moment ahead of me, coming from the south. I was in the bushes, close enough to hear him challenged. He had but to open his mouth, whoever he is, and he was welcome within. And I saw where he was led. He's fast within Cadwaladr's tent with him now, and even the guard sent back to his watch. There's none inside there now but Cadwaladr and his visitor, and only one guard between us and the pair of them.'

'Are you sure Cadwaladr is there?' demanded Torsten, low-voiced. 'You cannot have seen him.'

'I heard his voice. I waited on the man from the time we left Dublin,' said the boy firmly. 'Do you think I do not know the sound of him by now?'

'And you heard what was said? This other – did he name him?'

'No name! "You!" he said, loud and clear, but no name. But he was surprised and glad, more than glad of him. You may take the pair of them, once the guard is silenced, and let the man himself tell you his name.'

'We came for one,' said Turcaill, 'and with one we'll go back. And no killing! Owain is out of this quarrel, but he'll be in fast enough if we do murder on one of his men.'

'But won't stir for his brother?' marvelled Leif, half under his breath.

'What should he fear for his brother? Not a scratch upon Cadwaladr, bear in mind! If he pays his proper ransom he gets his leave to go, as whole as when he hired us. Owain knows it better than any. No need to have it said.

Over with you, then, and we'll be out with the tide.'

Their plans had been made beforehand; and if they had taken no count of this unexpected traveller from the south, they could very simply be adapted to accommodate him. Two men alone together in a tent conveniently close to the rim of the camp offered an easy target, once the guard was put out of action. Cadwaladr's own man, in his confidence and in whatever schemes he had in mind, must take his chance of rough handling, but need come to no permanent harm.

'I will take care of the guard,' said Torsten, first to slip over the side to where Leif waited. Five more of Turcaill's oarsmen followed their leader into the salt marsh and across the sandy beach. The night received them silently and indifferently, and Leif went before, retracing his own path from cover to sparse cover towards the perimeter of the camp. In the shelter of a straggling cluster of low trees he halted, peering ahead between the branches. The line of the defences was perceptible ahead merely as a more solid and rigid darkness where every other shadow was sinuous and elusive. But Cadwaladr's liegeman could be seen against the gap which was the gate he guarded, as he paced back and forth across it, head and shoulders clear against the sky. A big man, and armed, but casual in his movements, expecting no alarm. Torsten watched the leisurely patrol for some minutes, marked its extent, and slipped sidelong among the trees to be behind its furthest eastward point, where bushes approached to within a few yards of the stockade, and a man could draw close without being heard or seen.

The guard was whistling softly to himself as he turned in the soft sand, and Torsten's sinewy left arm took him hard around body and arms, and the right clamped a palm hard over his mouth and cut off the whistle abruptly. He groped frantically upward to try and grip the arm that was gagging him, but could not reach high enough, and his struggles to kick viciously backward cost him his balance and did no harm to Torsten, who swung him off his feet and dropped bodily over him into the sand, holding him face-down. By that time Turcaill was beside them, ready to thrust a fold of woollen cloth into the man's mouth as soon as he was allowed to raise himself, and empty it splutteringly of sand and grass. They wound him head and shoulders in his own cloak, and bound him fast hand and foot. There they bestowed him safely enough, if none too comfortably, among the bushes, and turned their attention to the rim of the camp. There had been no outcry, and there was no stirring within the fences. Somewhere about the prince's tents there would be men wakeful and alert, but here at the remotest corner, deliberately chosen by Cadwaladr for his own purposes, there was no one at hand to turn back retribution from him.

Only Turcaill and Torsten and two others followed Leif as he padded softly in through the unguarded gate, and along the stockade towards the remembered spot where he had caught the unmistakable, authoritative tones of Cadwaladr's voice, raised in astonished pleasure as he recognised his midnight visitor. The lines of the camp ended here, in stillness and silence, the invaders moved as shadows among shadows. Leif pointed, and said no word. There was no need. Even in a military camp Cadwaladr would have his rank heeded and his comforts attended to. The tent was ample, proof against wind and weather, and no doubt as well supplied within. At the edges of the flap that shielded its entrance fine lines of light showed, and on the still air of the night lowered voices made a level, confidential murmur, too soft for words. The messenger from the south was still there with his prince, their

200

heads together over tidings brought and plans to be hatched.

Turcaill set his hand to the tent-flap, and waited until Torsten, with his drawn dagger in his hand, had circled the tent to find a rear seam where the skins were sewn together. Thin leather thongs or greased cord, either could be cut with a sharp enough blade. The light within, by the steady way it burned and its low source, must be a simple wick in a small dish of oil, set perhaps on a stool or a trestle. Bodies moving outside would show no outline, while Torsten as he selected his place, could sense rather than see the vague bulks of the two within. Close indeed, attentive, absorbed, expecting no interruption.

Turcaill whipped aside the tent-flap and plunged within so fast, and with two others so hard on his heels, that Cadwaladr had no time to do more than leap to his feet in indignant alarm, his mouth open to vent his outrage, before there was a drawn dagger at his throat, and princely anger at being rudely interrupted changed instantly into frozen understanding and devout and quivering stillness. He was a foolhardy man, but of excellently quick perceptions, and his foolhardiness did not extend so far as to argue with a naked blade when his own hands were empty. It was the man who sat beside him on the well-furnished brychan who sprang to the attack, lunging upward at Turcaill's throat. But behind him Torsten's knife had sliced down the leather thongs that bound the skins of the tent together, and a great hand took the stranger by the hair, and dragged him backwards. Before he could rise again he was swathed in the coverings of the bed and held fast by Turcaill's men.

Cadwaladr stood motionless and silent, well aware of the steel just pricking his throat. His fine black eyes were glittering with fury, his teeth set with the effort of restraint, but he made no move as the companion he had welcomed with pleasure was trussed into helplessness, in spite of his struggles, and disposed of almost tenderly on his lord's bed.

'Make no sound,' said Turcaill, 'and come to no harm. Cry out, and my hand may slip. There is a little matter of business Otir wishes to discuss with you.'

'This you will rue!' said Cadwaladr though his teeth.

'So I may,' Turcaill agreed accommodatingly, 'but not yet. I would offer you the choice between walking or being dragged, but there's no putting any trust in you.' And to his two oarsmen he said: 'Secure him!' and drew back his hand to sheathe the dagger he held.

Cadwaladr was not quick enough to seize the one instant when he might have cried out loudly and raised a dozen men to his aid. As the steel was withdrawn he did open his mouth to call on his own, but a rug from the brychan was flung over his head, and a broad hand clamped it smotheringly into his open mouth. The only sound that emerged was a strangled moan, instantly crushed. He lashed out then with fists and feet, but the harsh woollen cloth was wound tightly about him, and bound fast.

Outside the tent Leif stood sentinel with pricked ears, and wide eyes sweeping the dark spaces of the camp for any movement that might threaten their enterprise, but all was still. If Cadwaladr had desired and ordered private and undisturbed converse with his visitor, he had done Turcaill's work for him very thoroughly. No one stirred. In the copse where they had left the guard the last of their party came looming out of the dark to join them, and laughed softly at sight of the burden they carried between them, slung by the ropes that pinioned him.

'The guard?' asked Turcaill in a whisper.

'Well alive, and muttering curses. And we'd best be aboard before they find he's missing and come looking for him.'

'And the other one?' Leif ventured to ask softly, as they wound their way back from cover to cover towards the beach and the saltings. 'What have you done with him?'

'Left him to his rest,' said Turcaill.

'You said no killing!'

'And there's been none. Not a scratch on him, you can be easy. Owain has no cause for feud against us more than he had from the moment we set foot on his soil.'

'And we still don't know,' marvelled Leif, padding steadily along beside him into the moist fringe left by the receding tide, 'who the other one was, and what he was doing there. You may yet wish you'd secured him while you could.'

'We came for one, and we're taking back one. All we wanted and needed,' said Turcaill.

The crew left aboard reached to hoist Cadwaladr over into the well between the benches, and help their fellows after. The steersman leaned upon his heavy steerboard, the inshore rowers thrust off with their oars, poling the little ship quite lightly and smoothly back along the furrow she had ploughed in the sand, until she rode clear and lifted joyously into the ebb of the tide.

Before dawn they delivered their prize, with some pride, to an Otir who had just roused from sleep, but came bright-eyed and content to the encounter. Cadwaladr emerged from his stifling wrappings flushed and tousled and viciously enraged, but containing his bitter fury within an embattled silence.

'Had you trouble by the way?' asked Otir, eyeing his prisoner with shrewd satisfaction. Unmarked, unblooded, extracted from among his followers without trampling his formidable brother's toes, or harming any other soul. A mission very neatly accomplished, and one that should be made to show a profit.

'None,' said Turcaill. 'The man had prepared his own fall, withdrawing himself so to the very rim, and planting a man of his own on guard. Not for nothing! I fancy he has been looking for word from his old lands, and made shift to keep a door open. For I doubt he'll get any sympathy from Owain, or expects any.'

At that Cadwaladr did open his mouth, unlocking his set teeth with an effort, for it was doubtful if he himself quite believed what he was about to say. 'You misread the strength of the Welsh blood-tie. Brother will hold by brother. You have brought Owain down on you with all his host, and so you will discover.'

'As brother held by brother when you came hiring Dublin men to threaten *your* brother with warfare,' said Otir, and laughed briefly and harshly.

'You will see,' said Cadwaladr hotly, 'what Owain will venture for my sake.'

'So we shall, and so will you. I doubt you'll find less comfort in it than we shall. He has given both you and me fair notice that your quarrel is not his quarrel, and you must pay your own score. And so you shall,' said Otir with glossy satisfaction, 'before you set foot again outside this camp. I have you, and I'll keep you until you pay me what you promised. Every coin, every calf, or the equal in goods we will have out of you. That done, you may go free, back to your lands or beggarly into the world again, as Owain pleases. And I warn you, never again look to Dublin for help, we know now the worth of your word. And that being so,' he said, thoughtfully plying his massive jowls in a muscular fist, 'we'll make sure of you, now that we have you!' He turned upon Turcaill, who stood by watching this encounter with detached interest, his own part already done. 'Give him in charge to Torsten to keep, but see him tethered. We know all too well his word and oath are no bond to him, so we may rightly use other means. Put chains on him, and see him watched and kept close.'

'You dare not!' Cadwaladr spat on a hissing breath, and made a convulsive movement to launch himself against his judge, but ready hands plucked him back with insulting ease, and held him writhing and sweating between his grinning guards. In the face of such casual and indifferent usage his boiling rage seemed hardly more than a turbulent child's tantrum, and burned itself out inevitably into the cold realisation that he was helpless, and must resign himself to the reversion of his fortunes, for he could do nothing to change it.

'Pay what you owe us, and go,' said Otir with bleak simplicity. And to Torsten: 'Take him away!'

Chapter Eleven

WO MEN OF Cuhelyn's company, making the complete rounds of the southern rim of the encampment, found the remotest gate unguarded in the early hours of the morning, and reported as much to their captain. If he had been any other than Cuhelyn this early check upon the defences would not have been ordered in the first place. To him the presence within Owain's camp of Cadwaladr, tolerated if not accepted, was deep offence, not only for the sake of Anarawd dead, but also for the sake of Owain living. Nor had Cadwaladr's proceedings within the camp been any alleviation of the suspicion and detestation in which Cuhelyn bore him. Retirement into this remote corner might have been interpreted by others as showing a certain sensitivity to the vexation the sight of him must cause his brother. Cuhelyn knew him better, an arrogant creature blind to other men's needs and feelings. And never to be trusted, since all his acts were reckless and unpredictable. So Cuhelyn had made it his business, with nothing said to any other, to keep a close eve upon Cadwaladr's movements, and the behaviour of those who gathered about him. Where they mustered, there was need of vigilance.

The defection of a guard brought Cuhelyn to the gate in

haste, before the lines were astir. They found the missing man lying unhurt but wound up like a roll of woollen cloth among the bushes not far from the fence. He had contrived to loosen the cord that bound his hands, though not yet enough to free them, and had worked the folds of cloth partly loose from his mouth. The muffled grunts that were all he could utter were enough to locate him as soon as the searchers reached the trees. Released, he came stiffly to his feet, and reported from swollen lips what had befallen him in the night.

'Danes – five at least— They came up from the bay. There was a boy could be Welsh showed them the way . . .'

'Danes!' Cuhelyn echoed, between wonder and enlightenment. He had expected devilment of some kind from Cadwaladr, was it now possible that this meant devilment aimed against Cadwaladr, instead? The thought gave him some sour amusement, but he did not yet quite believe in it. This could still be mischief of another kind, Dane and Welshman regretting their severance and compounding their differences secretly to act together in Owain's despite.

He set off in haste to Cadwaladr's tent, and walked in without ceremony. A rising breeze blew in his face, flapping the severed skins behind the brychan. The swaddled figure on the bed heaved and strained, uttering small animal sounds. This second bound victim confounded all possible notions that might account for the first. Why should a party of Danes, having made its way clandestinely here to Cadwaladr, next proceed to bind and silence him, and then leave him here to be found and set free as inevitably as the sun rises? If they came to enter into renewed conspiracy with him, if they came to secure him hostage for what he owed them, either way it made no sense. So Cuhelyn was reflecting bewilderedly as he untied the ropes that pinioned arms and legs, plucking the knots

208

loose with grim patience with his single hand, and unwound the twisted rugs from about the heaving body. A hand scored by the rope came up gropingly as it was freed, and plucked back the last folds from a shock head of disordered dark hair, and a face Cuhelyn knew well.

Not Cadwaladr's imperious countenance, but the younger, thinner, more intense and sensitive face of Cuhelyn's mirror twin, Gwion, the last hostage from Ceredigion.

They came to Owain's headquarters together, the one not so much shepherding the other as deigning to walk behind him, the other stalking ahead to make it plain to all viewers that he was not being driven, but going in vehement earnest where he wished to go. The air between them vibrated with the animosity that had never existed between them until this moment, and by its very intensity and pain could not endure long. Owain saw it in the stiff set of their bodies and the arduous blankness of their faces when they entered his presence and stood side by side before him, awaiting his judgement.

Two dark, stern, passionate young men, the one a shade taller and leaner, the other a shade sturdier and with colouring of a less vivid darkness, but seen thus shoulder to shoulder, quivering with tension, they might indeed have been twin brothers. The glaring difference was that one of them was lopped of half a limb, and that by an act of blazing treachery on the part of the lord the other served and worshipped. But that was not what held them counterpoised in this intensity of anger and hostility, so strange to both of them, and causing them both such indignant pain.

Owain looked from the one grim face to the other, and asked neutrally of both: 'What does this mean?'

'It means,' said Cuhelyn, unlocking his set teeth, 'that this man's word is worth no more than his master's. I found him trussed up and gagged in Cadwaladr's tent. The why and how he must tell you, for I know nothing more. But Cadwaladr is gone, and this man left, and the guard who kept the lines there says that Danes came up from the bay in the night, and left him, too, bound among the bushes to open a way within. If all this to-do has a meaning, he must deliver it, not I. But I know, and so do you, my lord, better than any, that he gave his oath not to attempt flight from Aber, and he has broken his oath and befouled his bond.'

'Scarcely to his own gain,' said Owain, and forbore to smile, eyeing Gwion's face marked by the harsh folds of the brychan, his black hair tangled and erected, and the swollen lips bruised by the gag. And to the young man so grimly silent and defiantly braced he said mildly: 'And how do you say, Gwion? Are you forsworn? Dishonoured, with your oath in the mire?'

The misshapen lips parted, and shook for a moment with the recoil from tension. So low as to be barely audible, Gwion said remorselessly: 'Yes.'

It was Cuhelyn who twisted a little aside, and averted his eyes. Gwion fixed his black gaze on Owain's face, and drew deeper breath, having freely owned to the worst.

'And why did you so, Gwion? I have known you some while now. Read me your riddle. Truly I left you work to do in Aber, in the matter of Bledri ap Rhys dead. Truly I had your parole. So much we all know. Now tell me how it came that you so belied yourself as to abandon your troth.'

'Let it lie!' said Gwion, quivering. 'I did it! Let me pay for it.'

'Nevertheless, tell it!' said Owain with formidable quietness. 'For I will know!'

'You think I will use excuses in my own defence,' said Gwion. His voice had steadied and firmed into a calm of utter detachment, indifferent to whatever might happen to him. He began gropingly, as if he himself had never until now probed the complexities of his own behaviour, and was afraid of what he might find. 'No, what I have done I have done, I do not excuse it, it *is* shameful. But I saw shame every way, and no choice but to accept and bear the lesser shame. No, wait. This is not for me to say. Let me tell it as I did it. You left it to me to send back Bledri's body to his wife for burial, and to convey to her the news of how he died. I thought I might without offence do her the grace of facing her, and bringing him to her myself, intending a return to my captivity – if I can so call that easy condition I had with you, my lord. So I went to her in Ceredigion, and there we buried Bledri. And there we talked of what Cadwaladr your brother had done, bringing a Danish fleet to enforce his right, and I came to see that both for you and for him, and for all Gwynedd and Wales, the best that could be was that you two should be brought together, and together send the Danes empty-handed back to Dublin. The thought did not come from me,' he said meticulously. 'It came from the old, wise men who have outlived wars and come to reason. I was, I am, Cadwaladr's man, I can be no other. But when they had shown me that for his very sake there must be peace made between you two brothers, then I saw as they saw. And I made cause with such of his old captains as I could in such haste, and gathered a force loyal to him, but intent on the reconciliation I also desired to see. And I broke my oath,' said Gwion with brutal vehemence. 'Whether our fine plans had succeeded or failed, I tell you openly, I would have fought for him. Against the Danes, joyfully. What business had they making such a bargain?

211

Against you, my lord Owain, with a very heavy heart, but if it came to it, I would have done it. For he is my lord, and I serve no other. So I did not go back to Aber. I brought a hundred good fighting men of my own mind to deliver to Cadwaladr, whatever use it might be his intent to make of them.'

'And you found him in my camp,' said Owain, and smiled. 'And half of your design seemed to be already done for you, and our peace made.'

'So I thought and hoped.'

'And did you find it so? For you have talked with him, have you not, Gwion? Before the Danes came up from the bay, and took him with them a prisoner, and left you behind? Was he of your mind?

A brief contortion shook Gwion's dark face. 'They came, and they have taken him. I know no more than that. Now I have told you, and I am in your hands. He is my lord, and if you will have me to fight under you I will yet be of service to him, but if you deny me that, you have the right. I thought on him beleaguered, and my heart could not stand it. Nevertheless, as I have given him my fealty, so now I have given for him even my honour, and I know all too well I am utterly the worse by its loss. Do as you see fit.'

'Do you tell me,' said Owain, studying him narrowly, 'that he had no time to tell you how things stand between us two? If I will have you to fight under me, you say! Why, so I might, and not the worst man ever I had under my banner, if I had fighting in mind, but while I can get what I aim at without fighting, I have no such matter in mind. What makes you think I may be about to sound the onset?'

'The Danes have taken your brother!' protested Gwion, stammering and suddenly at a loss. 'Surely you mean to rescue him?'

'I have no such intent,' said Owain bluntly. 'I will not lift a finger to pluck him out of their hands.'

'What, when they have snatched him hostage because he has made his peace with you?'

'They have snatched him hostage,' said Owain, 'for the two thousand marks he promised them if they would come and hammer me into giving him back the lands he forfeited.'

'No matter, no matter what it is they hold against him, though that cannot be the whole! He is your brother, and in enemy hands, he is in peril of his life! You cannot leave him so!'

'He is in no peril at all of the least harm,' said Owain, 'if he pays what he owes. As he will. They will keep him as tenderly as their own babes, and turn him loose without a scratch on him when they have loaded his cattle and goods and gear to the worth he promised them. They do not want outright war any more than I do, provided they get their dues. And they know that if they maim or kill my brother, then they *will* have to deal with me. We understand each other, the Danes and I. But put my men into the field to pull him out of the mire he chose for himself? No! Not a man, not a blade, not a bow!'

'This I cannot believe!' said Gwion, staring wide-eyed.

'Tell him, Cuhelyn, how this contention stands,' said Owain, leaning back with a sigh from such irreconcilable and innocent loyalty.

'My lord Owain offered his brother parley, without prejudice,' said Cuhelyn shortly, 'and told him he must get rid of his Danes before there could be any question of his lands being given back to him. And there was but one way to send them home, and that was to pay what he had promised. The quarrel was his, and he must resolve it. But Cadwaladr believed he knew better, and if he forced my lord's hand, my lord would have to join with him, to drive the Danes out by battle. And he would have to pay nothing! So he delivered defiance to Otir, and bade him be off back to Dublin, for that Owain and Cadwaladr had made their peace, and would drive them into the sea if they did not up anchor and go. In which,' said Cuhelyn through his teeth, and with his eyes fierce and steady and defiant upon Owain, who after all was brother to this devious man, and might recoil from too plain speaking, 'he lied. There was no such peace, and no such alliance. He lied, and he broke a solemn compact, and looked to be praised and approved for it! Worse, by such a cheat he left in peril three hostages, two monks and a girl taken by the Danes. Over them my lord has spread his hand, offering a fair price for their ransom. But for Cadwaladr he will not lift a finger. And now you know,' he said fiercely, 'why the Danes have sent by night to fetch him away, and why they have dealt fairly by you, who have committed no offence against them. They have shed no blood, harmed no man of my lord's following. From Cadwaladr they have a debt to collect. For even to Danes a prince of the Welsh people should keep his word.'

All this he delivered in a steady, deliberate voice, and yet at a white heat of outrage that kept Gwion silent to the end.

'All that Cuhelyn tells you is truth,' said Owain.

Gwion opened stiff lips to say hollowly: 'I do believe it. Nevertheless, he is still your brother and my lord. I know him rash and impulsive. He acts without thought. I cannot therefore abjure my fealty, if you can renounce your blood.'

'That,' said Owain with princely patience, 'I have not done. Let him keep his word to those he brought in to recover his right for him, and deliver my Welsh soil from an unwanted invader, and he is my brother as before. But I would have him clean of malice and false dealing, and I will not put my seal to those things he has done which dishonour him.'

'I can make no such stipulation,' said Gwion with a wry and painful smile, 'nor set any such limit to my allegiance. I am forsworn myself, even in this his fellow. I go with him wherever he goes, even into hell.'

'You are in my mercy,' said Owain, 'and I have not hell in mind for you or him.'

'Yet you will not help him now! Oh, my lord,' pleaded Gwion hotly, 'consider what men will say of you, if you leave a brother in the hands of his enemies.'

'Barely a week ago,' said Owain with arduous patience, 'these Danes were his friends and comrades in arms. If he had not mistaken me and cheated them out of their price they would be so still. If I pass over his treachery to them, I will not pass over his gross and foolish misreading of me. I do not like being taken for a man who will look kindly on oath-breakers, and men who go back shamefully on bargains freely made.'

'You condemn me no less than him,' said Gwion, writhing.

'You at least I understand. Your treason comes of too immovable a loyalty. It does you no credit,' said Owain, wearying of forbearance, 'but it will not turn away your friends from you.'

'I am in your mercy, then. What will you do with me?'

'Nothing,' said the prince. 'Stay or go, as you please. We will feed and house you as we did at Aber, if you want to stay, and wait out his fortune. If not, go when and where you please. You are his man, not mine. No one will hinder you.'

'And you no longer ask for my submission?'

'I no longer value it,' said Owain, and rose with a motion of his hand to dismiss them both from his presence.

*　　*　　*

They went out together, as they had entered, but once out of the farmstead Cuhelyn turned away, and would have departed brusquely and without a word, if Gwion had not caught him by the arm.

'He damns me with his mercy! He could have had my life, or loaded me with the chains I have earned. Do you, too, avert your eyes from me? Had it been otherwise, had it been Owain himself, or Hywel, beleaguered among enemies, would not you have set your fealty to him above even your word, and gone to him forsworn if need were?'

Cuhelyn had pulled up as abruptly as he had turned away. His face was set. 'No. I have never given my fealty but to lords absolute in honour themselves, and demanding as much of those who serve them. Had I done as you have done, and brought the dishonour as a gift to Hywel, he would have struck me down and cast me out. Cadwaladr, I make no doubt, welcomed and was glad of you.'

'It was a hard thing to do,' said Gwion with the solemnity of despair. 'Harder than dying.'

But Cuhelyn had already plucked himself free, with fastidious care, and was striding away through the camp just stirring into life with the morning light.

Among Owain's men Gwion felt himself an exile and an outcast, even though they accepted his presence in their midst without demur, and took no pains to avoid or exclude him. Here he had no function. His hands and skills did not belong to this lord, and to his own lord he could not come. He passed through the lines withdrawn and mute, and from a hillock within the northern perimeter of the encampment he stood for a long time peering towards the distant dunes where Cadwaladr was a prisoner, a hostage for two thousand marks' worth in stock and money and goods, the hire of a Danish fleet.

Within his vision the fields in the distance gave way to the first undulations of sand, and the scattered trees dwindled into clusters of bushes and scrub. Somewhere beyond, perhaps even in chains after his recapture, Cadwaladr brooded and waited for help which his brother coldly withheld. No matter what the offence, not the breaking of his pledged word, not even the murder of Anarawd, if indeed such guilt touched him, nothing could justify for Gwion Owain's abandonment of his brother. His own breach of faith in leaving Aber Gwion saw as unforgivable, and had no blame for those who condemned it, but there was nothing Cadwaladr had done or could do that would have turned his devout vassal from revering and following him. Once given and accepted, fealty was for life.

And he could do nothing! True, he had leave to depart if he so wished, and also true, he had a company of a hundred good fighting men bivouacked not many miles away, but what was that against the numbers the Danes must have, and the defences they had secured? An ill-considered attempt to storm their camp and free Cadwaladr might only cost him his life, or, more likely, cause the Danes to up anchor and put to sea, where they could not be matched, and take their prisoner away with them, back to Ireland, out of reach of any rescue.

The distant prospect afforded him no enlightenment, and no glimmer of a way forward towards the liberation of his lord. It grieved him that Cadwaladr, who had already lost so much, should be forced to pay out what remained to him in treasury and stock to buy his liberty, without even the certainty that he might recover his lost lands, for which the sum demanded of him had been promised in the first place. Even if Owain was right, and the Danes intended him no harm

217

provided the debt was paid, the humiliation of captivity and submission would gnaw like an ulcer in that proud spirit. Gwion grudged Otir and his men every mark of their fee. It might be said that Cadwaladr should never have invoked alien aid against a brother, but such impetuous and flawed impulses had always threatened Cadwaladr's wisdom, and men who loved him had borne with them as with the perilous cantrips of a valiant and foolhardy child, and made the best of the resultant chaos. It was not kind or just to withdraw now, when most it was needed, the indulgence which had never before failed him.

Gwion moved on along the ridge, still straining his eyes towards the north. A fringe of trees crowned the crest, squat and warped by the salt air, and leaning inland from the prevailing wind. And there beyond their uneven line, still and sturdy and himself rooted as a tree, a man stood and stared towards the unseen Danish force as Gwion was staring. A man perhaps in his middle thirties, square-built and muscular, the first fine salting of grey in his brown hair, his eyes, over-shadowed beneath thick black brows, fixed darkly upon the sand-moulded curves of the naked horizon. He went unarmed, and bare of breast and arms in the sunlight of the morning, a powerful body formidably still in his concentration on distance. Though he heard Gwion's step in the dry grass beneath the trees, and it was plain that he must have heard it, he did not turn his head or stir from his fixed surveillance for some moments, until Gwion stood within touch of him. Even then he stirred and turned about only slowly and indifferently.

'I know,' he said, as though they had been aware of each other for a long time. 'Gazing will bring it no nearer.'

It was Gwion's own thought, worded very aptly, and it

took the breath out of him for a moment. Warily he asked: 'You, too? What stake have you over there among the Danes?'

'A wife,' said the other man, with a brief, dry force that needed no more words to express the enormity of his deprivation.

'A wife!' echoed Gwion uncomprehendingly. 'By what strange chance . . .' What was it Cuhelyn had said, of three hostages left in peril after Cadwaladr's defection and defiance, two monks and a girl taken by the Danes? Two monks and a girl had set out from Aber in Owain's retinue. To fall victim in the first place to Cadwaladr's mercenaries, and then to be left to pay the price of Cadwaladr's betrayal, if the minds of the Danes ran to vengeance? Oh, the account was growing long, and Owain's obduracy became ever easier to understand. But Cadwaladr had not thought, he never thought before, he acted first and regretted afterwards, as by now he must be regretting everything he had done since he made the first fatal mistake of fleeing to the kingdom of Dublin for redress.

Yes, the girl – Gwion remembered the girl. A black-browed beauty, tall, slender, and mute, serving wine and mead about the prince's table without a smile, except occasionally the malicious and grieving smile with which she plagued the cleric they said was her father, reminding him on what thin ice he walked, and how she could shatter it under him if she so pleased. That story had been whispered around the llys from ostler to maid to armourer to page, and come early to the ears of the last hostage from Ceredigion, who alone could observe all these goings-on with an indifferent eye, since Gwynedd was not home to him, and Owain was not his lord, nor Gilbert of Saint Asaph his bishop. The same girl? She had been on her way, he recalled, to match with a man of Anglesey in Owain's service.

'You are that Ieuan ab Ifor,' he said, 'who was to marry the canon's daughter.'

'I am that same,' said Ieuan, bending thick black brows at him. 'And who are you, who know my name and what I'm doing here? I have not seen you among the prince's liegemen until now.'

'For reason enough. I am not his liegeman. I am Gwion, the last of the hostages he brought from Ceredigion. My allegiance was and is to Cadwaladr,' said Gwion starkly, and watched the slow fire kindle and glow in the sharp eyes that watched him. 'For good or ill, I am his man, but I would far rather it should be for good.'

'It is his doing,' said Ieuan, smouldering, 'that Meirion's daughter is left captive among these sea-pirates. Such good as ever came from him you may measure within the cup of an acorn, and like an acorn feed it to the pigs. He brings barbarian raiders into Gwynedd, and then goes back on his bargain, and takes to his heels into safety, leaving innocent hostages to bear the brunt of Otir's rage. He has been as dire a curse to his own best kin as he was to Anarawd, whom he had done to death.'

'Take heed not to go too far in his dispraise,' said Gwion, but in weariness and grief rather than indignation, 'for I may not hear him miscalled.'

'Oh, be easy! God knows I cannot hold it against any man that he stands by his prince, but God send you a better prince to stand by. You may forgive him all, no matter how he shames you, but do not ask me to forgive him for abandoning my bride to whatever fate the Danes keep for her.'

'The prince has declared her in his protection,' said Gwion, 'as I have heard only an hour ago. He has offered fair ransom for her and for the two monks who came from England,

and warned to the value he sets on her safe-keeping.'

'The prince is here,' said Ieuan grimly, 'and she is there, and they have lost their grip on the one they would liefer have in hold. Other captives may find themselves serving in his place.'

'No,' said Gwion, 'you mistake. Whatever rancour you may have against him, be content! This past night they have sent a ship into the bay, and put men ashore to break their way into the camp to his tent. They have taken Cadwaladr prisoner back with them, to pay his own ransom or suffer his own fate. No need for another victim, they have the chosen one fast in their hands.'

Ieuan's rough brows, the most expressive thing about him, knotted abruptly into a ruled line of suspicion and disbelief, and then, confronted by Gwion's unwavering gaze, released their black tension into open bewilderment and wonder.

'You are deceived, that cannot be . . .'

'It is truth.'

'How do you know it? Who has told you?'

'There was no need for any man to tell me,' said Gwion. 'I was there with him when they came. I saw it. Four of Otir's Danes burst in by night. Him they took, me they left bound and muted, as they had left the guard who kept the gate. Here I have still the grazes of the cords with which they tied me. See!'

They had scored his wrist deep in his efforts to break free; there was no mistaking rope-burns. Ieuan beheld them with a long, silent stare, assessing and accepting.

'So that is why you said to me: "You, too?" Now I know without asking what stake you have over there among the Danes. Hold me excused if I say plainly that your grief is no grief to me. What may fall upon him he has brought down on his own head. But what has my girl done to deserve the peril in which he left her? If his capture delivers her, I am right glad of it.'

Since there was no arguing with that, Gwion was silent.

'If I had but a dozen of my own mind,' Ieuan pursued, rather to himself than to any other, 'I would bring her off myself, against every Dane Dublin can ship over into Gwynedd. She is mine, and I will have her.'

'And you have not even seen her yet,' said Gwion, shaken by the sudden convulsion of passion in a man so contained and still.

'Ah, but I have seen her. I have been within a stone-throw of their stockade undetected, and can do as much again. I saw her within there, on a crest of the dunes, looking south, looking for the deliverance no one sends her. She is more than they told me. As lissome and bright as steel, and moves like a fawn. I would venture for her alone, but that I dread to be her death before ever I could break through to her.'

'I would as much for my lord,' said Gwion, grown quiet and intent, for this bold and fervent lover had started a vein of hope within him. 'If Cadwaladr is nothing to you, and your Heledd hardly more to me, yet if we put our heads and our forces together we may both benefit. Two is better than one alone.'

'But still no more than two,' said Ieuan. But he was listening.

'Two is but the beginning. Two now may be more in a few days. Even if they break my lord into paying his ransom, it will take some days to bring in and load his cattle, and put together what remains in silver coin.' He drew closer, his voice lowered to be heard only by Ieuan, if any other should pass by. 'I did not come here alone. From Ceredigion I have collected and led some hundred men who still hold by Cadwaladr. Oh, not for the purpose we have in mind at this

222

moment. I was certain that there would be peace made between brothers, and they would combine to drive out the Danes, and I brought my lord at least a fair following to fight for him side by side with those who fight for Owain. I would not have him go free and living only by his brother's grace, but at the head of a company of his own men. I came ahead of them to carry him the news, only to find that Owain has abandoned him. And now the Danes have taken him.'

Ieuan's face had resumed its impassive calm, but behind the wide brow and distant gaze a sharp mind was busy with the calculation of chances hitherto unforeseen. 'How far distant are your hundred men?'

'Two days' march. I left my horse, and a groom who rode with me, a mile south and came alone to find Cadwaladr. Now Owain has cast me free of him into the world to stay or go, I can return within the hour to where I left my man, and send him to bring the company as fast as men afoot can march.'

'There are some within here,' said Ieuan, 'would welcome a venture. A few I can persuade, some will need no persuasion.' He rubbed large, powerful hands together softly, and shut the fingers hard on an invisible weapon. 'You and I, Gwion, will talk further of this. And before this day is out, should you not be on your way?'

Chapter Twelve

T WAS WELL past noon when Torsten again produced his prisoner, chained and humbled and choked with spleen, before Otir. Cadwaladr's handsome lips were grimly set, and his black eyes burning with rage all the more bitter for being under iron control. For all his protestations, he knew as well as any that Owain would not now relent from the position he had taken up. The time for empty hopes was past, and reality had engulfed him and brought him to bay. There was no point in holding out, since eventual submission was inevitable.

'He has a word for you,' said Torsten, grinning. 'He has no appetite for living in chains.'

'Let him speak for himself,' said Otir.

'I will pay you your two thousand marks,' said Cadwaladr. His voice came thinly through gritted teeth, but he had himself well in hand. 'You leave me no choice, since my brother uses me unbrotherly.' And he added, testing such shallows as were left to him in this flood of misfortune: 'You will have to allow me a few days at liberty to have such a mass of goods and gear collected together, for it cannot all be in silver.'

That brought a gust of throaty laughter from Torsten, and an emphatic jerk of the head from Otir. 'Oh, no, my friend! I am not such a fool as to trust you yet again. You do not stir one step out of here, nor shed your fetters, until my ships are loading and ready for sea.'

'How, then, do you propose I should effect this matter of ransom?' demanded Cadwaladr with a savage snarl. 'Do you expect my stewards to render up my cattle to you, and my purse, simply at your orders?'

'I will use an agent I can trust,' said Otir, unperturbed now by any flash of anger or defiance from a man so completely in his power. 'If, that is, he will act for you even in this affair. That he approves it we already know, you better than any of us. What you will do, before I let you loose even within my guard, is to render up your small seal – I know you have it about you, you would not stir without it – and give me a message so worded that your brother will know it could come only from you. I will deal with a man I can trust, no matter how things stand between us, friend or enemy. Owain Gwynedd, if he will not buy you out of bondage, will not stint to welcome the news that you intend to pay your debts honourably, nor refuse you his aid to see due reparation made. Owain Gwynedd shall do the accounting between you and me.'

'He will not do it!' flared Cadwaladr, stung. 'Why should he believe that I have given you my seal of my own will, when you could as well have stripped me and taken it from me? No matter what message I might send, how can he trust, how can he be sure that I send it of my own free will, and not wrung from me with your dagger at my throat, under the threat of death?'

'He knows me by now well enough,' said Otir drily, 'to know that I am not so foolish as to destroy what can and shall be profitable to me. But if you doubt it, very well, we will send him one he will trust, and the man shall take due orders from you in your very person, and bear witness to Owain that he has so taken them, and that he saw you whole and in your right mind. Owain will know truth by the bearer of it. I doubt he can take pleasure in the sight of you, not yet. But he'll so far prove your brother as to put together your price in haste, once he knows you've chosen to honour your debts. He wants me gone, and go I will when I have what I came for, and he may have you back and welcome.'

'You have not such a man in your muster,' said Cadwaladr with a curling lip. 'Why should he trust any man of yours?'

'Ah, but I have! No man of mine, nor of Owain's, nor of yours, his service falls within quite another writ. One that offered himself freely as guarantor for your safe return when you left here to go and parley with your brother. Yes, and one that you left to his fate and my better sense when you tossed your defiance in my face and turned tail for your life back to a brother who despised you for it.' Otir watched the prince's dark face flame into scarlet, and took dour satisfaction in having stung him.

'Hostage for you he was, out of goodwill, and now you are returned indeed, though in every manner of illwill, and I have no longer any claim to keep him here. And he's the man shall go as your envoy to Owain, and in your name bid him plunder such means and valuables as you have left, and bring your ransom here.' He turned to Torsten, who had stood waiting in high and obvious content through these exchanges. 'Go and find that young deacon from Lichfield, the bishop's lad, Mark, and ask him to come here to me.'

Mark was with Brother Cadfael when the word reached him, gathering dry and fallen twigs for their fire from among the

227

stunted trees along the ridge. He straightened up with his load gathered into the fold of a wide sleeve, and stared at the messenger in mild surprise, but without any trace of alarm. In these few days of nominal captivity he had never felt himself a captive, or in any danger or distress, but neither had he ever supposed that he was of any particular interest or consequence to his captors beyond what bargaining value his small body might have.

Like a curious child he asked, wide-eyed: 'What can your captain want with me?'

'No harm,' said Cadfael. 'For all I can see, these Irish Danes have more of the Irish than the Dane in them after all this time. Otir strikes me as Christian as most that habit in England or Wales, and a good deal more Christian than some.'

'He has a thing for you to do,' said Torsten, goodnaturedly grinning, 'that comes as a benefit to us all. Come and hear it for yourself.'

Mark piled his gathered fuel close to the hearth they had made for themselves of stones in their sheltered hollow of sand, and followed Torsten curiously to Otir's open tent. At the sight of Cadwaladr, rigidly erect in his chains and taut as a bowstring, Mark checked and drew breath, astonished. It was the first intimation he had had that the turbulent fugitive was back within the encampment, and to see him here fettered and at bay was baffling. He looked from captive to captor, and saw Otir grimly smiling and obviously in high content. Fortune was busy overturning all things for sport.

'You sent for me,' said Mark simply. 'I am here.'

Otir surveyed with an indulgent eye and some surprisingly gentle amusement this slight youth, who spoke here for a Church that Welsh and Irish and the Danes of Dublin all alike acknowledged. Some day, when a few more years had passed, he might even have to call this boy 'Father'! 'Brother' he might call him already.

'As you see,' said Otir, 'the lord Cadwaladr, for whom you stood guarantor that he should go and come again without hindrance, has come back to us. His return sets you free to leave us. If you will do an errand for him to his brother Owain Gwynedd, you will be doing a good deed for him and for us all.'

'You must tell me what that is,' said Mark. 'But I have not felt myself deprived of my freedom here. I have no complaint.'

'The lord Cadwaladr will tell you himself,' said Otir, and his satisfied smile broadened. 'He has declared himself ready to pay the two thousand marks he promised to us for coming to Abermenai with him. He desires to send word to his brother how this is to be done. He will tell you.'

Mark regarded with some doubt Cadwaladr's set face and darkly smouldering eyes. 'Is this true?'

'It is.' The voice was strong and clear, if it grated a little. Since there was no help for it, Cadwaladr accepted necessity, if not with grace, at least with the recovered remnant of his dignity. 'I am required to pay for my freedom. Very well, I choose to pay.'

'It is truly your own choice?' Mark wondered doubtfully.

'It is. Beyond what you see, I am not threatened. But I am not free until the ransom is paid, and the ships loaded for sea, and therefore I cannot go myself to see my cattle rounded up and driven, nor draw on my treasury for the balance. I want my brother to manage all for me, and as quickly as may be. I will send him my authority by you, and my seal by way of proof.'

'If it is what you wish,' said Mark, 'yes, I will bear your message.'

229

'It is what I wish. If you tell him you had it from my own lips, he will believe you.' His lips at that moment were drawn thin with the hard-learned effort to keep the bitterness and fury caged within, but his mind was made up. There could be revenges later, there could be another repayment to be made in requital of this one, but now what he needed was his freedom. He slid out his private seal from a pocket in his sleeve, and held it out, not to Otir, who sat watching with a glittering grin, but to Mark. 'Take my brother this, tell him you had it from my hand, and ask him to hasten what I need.'

'I will, faithfully,' said Mark.

'Then ask him for my sake to send to Llanbadarn, to Rhodri Fychan, who was my steward, and will be my steward again if ever I regain what is mine. What is left of my treasury he will know where to find, and at my orders, witnessed by my seal, he will deliver it over. If the sum is not enough, what is lacking must be made up in cattle. Rhodri knows where my stock are bestowed in safe charge. There are still herds kept for me, more than enough. Two thousand marks is the sum. Ask my brother to make haste.'

'I will,' said Mark simply, and began by himself making all haste. It was he who took an ambassador's leave of them, rather than acknowledging his own dismissal from Otir's presence. A brisk reverence and a brief farewell, and he was already on his way, and for some reason the space within the tent and about it looked curiously empty by the removal of his small, slight figure.

He went on foot; the distance was barely more than a mile. Within the halfhour he would be delivering his message to Owain Gwynedd, and setting in motion the events which were to restore Cadwaladr his freedom, if not his lands, and remove from Gwynedd the threat of war, and the oppressive presence of an alien army.

The only pause he made before leaving was to impart to Cadfael the errand on which he was sent.

Brother Cadfael came very thoughtfully to where Heledd was stirring the sleeping fire in the stone hearth, to prepare food for the evening meal. His mind was full of what he had just learned, but he could not help remarking how well this vagrant life in a military camp suited her. She had taken the sun graciously, her skin was a golden bronze, with an olive bloom upon it, suave and infinitely becoming to her dark hair and eyes, and the rich red of her mouth. She had never in her life been so free as she was now in her captivity. The gloss of it was about her like cloth of gold, and it mattered not at all that her sleeve was torn, and the hem of her gown soiled and frayed.

'There's news that could be good for us all,' said Cadfael, watching her neat movements with pleasure. 'Not only did Turcaill come back safely from his midnight foray, it seems he brought back Cadwaladr with him.'

'I know,' said Heledd, and stilled her busy hands for a moment, and stared into the fire and smiled. 'I saw them come back, before dawn.'

'And you never said word?' But no, she would not, not yet, not to anyone. That would be to reveal more than she was yet ready to reveal. How could she say that she had risen before the sun, to watch for the little ship's safe return? 'I've scarcely seen you today. No harm had come of whatever they were up to, that was all that mattered. Why, what follows? How is it so good for us all?'

'Why, the man has come to his senses, and agreed to pay

231

these Danes what he promised them. Mark has just been sent off to commission Owain, in his brother's name, and with his brother's seal for surety, to collect and pay his ransom. Otir will take it and go, and leave Gwynedd in peace.'

Now she had indeed turned to pay due attention to what he was saying, with raised brows and sharply arrested hands. 'He has given in? Already? He will pay?'

'I have it from Mark, and Mark is already on his way. Nothing could be surer.'

'And they will go!' she said, a mere murmur within her still lips. She drew up her knees and folded her arms about them, and sat gazing before her, neither smiling nor frowning, only coolly and resolutely assessing these changed prospects for good and evil. 'How long, do you think, Cadfael, it will take to bring cattle up here by the drove roads from Ceredigion?'

'Three days at the least,' said Cadfael, and watched her put away that factor in the methodical recesses of her mind, to be kept in the reckoning.

'Three days at the most, then,' she said, 'for Owain will make all haste to be rid of them.'

'And you will be glad to be free,' said Cadfael, probing gently into regions where truth had at least two faces, and he could not be sure which one was turned towards him, and which was turned away.

'Yes,' she said, 'I shall be glad!' And she looked beyond him into the grey-blue, shifting surface of the sea, and smiled.

Gwion had reached the guard-post, the same by which his lord had been abducted, without hindrance, and was in the very act of stepping over the threshold when the guard barred his way with a braced lance, and challenged him sharply: 'Are not you Gwion, Cadwaladr's liegeman?'

Gwion owned to it, bewildered rather than alarmed. No doubt they were keeping a closer watch on this gate, after last night's incursion, and this sentry did not know Owain's mind, and had no intention of incurring blame by allowing either entry or exit unquestioned. 'I am. The prince has given me leave to stay or go, as I choose. Ask Cuhelyn. He will tell you so.'

'I have later news for you,' said the guard, unmoving. 'For the prince has only a short while since asked that you be sought, if you were still within the pale, and sent back to him.'

'I never knew him change his mind in such a fashion,' protested Gwion distrustfully. 'He made it plain he set no store on me, and did not care a pin whether I stayed or departed. Nor whether I lived or died, for that matter.'

'Nevertheless, it seems he has a use for you yet. No harm, if he never threatened any. Go and see. He wants you. I know no more than that.'

There was no help for it. Gwion turned back towards the squat roof of the farmstead, his mind a turmoil of unprofitable speculations. Owain could not possibly have got wind of what was still at best only a vague intent, hardly a plan at all, though he had spent a long time with Ieuan ab Ifor over the detail of numbers and means, and all that Ieuan had gathered concerning the layout of the Danish camp. Too long a time, as it now appeared. He should have left at once, before there could be any question of detaining him. By this time he could have despatched his groom south to bring up the promised force, and been back within the stockade here before ever he was missed. Planning could have waited. Now it was too late, he was trapped. Yet nothing was quite lost. Owain could not know. No one knew but Gwion himself and Ieuan, and Ieuan had not yet spoken a word to any of those stalwarts he knew of who would welcome a venture. That recruitment was still to come. Then what Owain wanted of him could have nothing to do with their half-formed enterprise.

He was still feverishly recording and discarding possibilities when he entered the low-beamed hall of the farm, and made his stiff and wary reverence to the prince across the rough trestle table.

Hywel was there, close at his father's shoulder, and two more of the prince's trusted captains stood a little apart, witnesses in some business which remained inexplicable to Gwion. For the only other person in the room was the meagre little deacon from Lichfield, in his rusty black habit, his spiky ring of straw-coloured hair growing stubbornly every way, his grey eyes as always wide, direct and tranquil. They looked at Gwion, and Gwion turned his head away, as though he feared they might see too deeply into his mind if he met them fully. He found even the benevolent regard of such eyes unnerving. But what could this little cleric have to do with any matter between Owain and Cadwaladr and the Danish interlopers? Yet if the business in hand here was something entirely different, what could it have to do with him, and what need to recall him?

'It's well that you have not left us, Gwion,' said Owain, 'for after all there is a thing you can do for me, and therewith also for your lord.'

'That I would certainly do, and gladly,' said Gwion, but as yet withholding belief.

'Deacon Mark here is newly come from Otir the Dane,' said the prince, 'who holds my brother and your lord prisoner. He has brought word from Cadwaladr that he has agreed to pay the sum he promised, and buy himself out of debt and out of bondage.'

'I cannot believe it!' said Gwion, blanched to the lips with shock. 'I will not believe it, unless I hear him say so, freely and openly.'

'Then you and I are of one mind,' said Owain drily, 'for I also had hardly expected him to see sense so soon. You have good cause to know my mind in this matter. I would rather my brother should be a man of his word, and pay what he promises. But neither would I accept from another mouth the instruction that will beggar him. Otir deals fairly. From my brother's mouth you cannot hear his will made plain, he will not be free until his debt is paid. But you may hear it from Brother Mark, who received it in trust from him, and will testify that he spoke it firmly and with intent, being whole of his body and in his right mind.'

'I do so testify,' said Mark. 'He has been prisoner only this one day. He is fettered, but further than that no hand has been laid on him, and no threat made against his body or his life. He says so, and I believe it, as no violence has ever been offered to me or to those others hostage with the Danes. He told me what was to be done. And he delivered to me with his own hand his seal, as authority for the deed, and I have delivered it to the prince, according to Cadwaladr's orders.'

'And the purport of his message? Be kind enough to repeat it,' the prince requested courteously. 'I would not have Gwion fear that I have in any degree prompted you, or put twisted words into your mouth.'

'Cadwaladr entreats the lord Owain, his brother,' said Mark, fixing his dauntingly clear eyes upon Gwion's face, 'to send with all haste into Llanbadarn, to Rhodri Fychan, who was his steward, and who knows where his remaining treasury is bestowed, and to tell him that his lord requires the despatch to Abermenai of money and stock to the value of two thousand marks, to be delivered to the Danish force under Otir, as promised to them at the agreement in Dublin. And to that end he has sent his seal for guarantee.'

There was a long silence after the clear, mild voice ended this recital, while Gwion stood motionless and mute, struggling with the fury of denial and despair and anger within him. It was not possible that so proud and intolerant a soul as Cadwaladr should have submitted, and so quickly. And yet men, even the most arrogant and hot-headed of men, do value their lives and liberty high, and will buy them back even with humiliation and shame when the threat comes close, and congeals from imagination into reality. But first to dare defy and discard his Danes, and then to grovel to them and scrape together their price in undignified haste – that was unworthy. Had he but waited a few days, there should have been another ending. His own men were so near, and would not have let him lie in chains for long, even if brother and all had deserted him. God, let me have two days yet, prayed Gwion behind his dark, closed face, and I will fetch him off by force, and he shall call off his bailiffs and take back his property, and be Cadwaladr again, erect as he always was.

'This charge,' Owain was saying, somewhere at the extreme edge of Gwion's consciousness, a voice from the distance, or from deep within, 'I intend to fulfil with all haste, as he asks, the quicker to redeem his person together with his good name. My son Hywel rides south at once. But since you are here, Gwion, and all your heart's concern is his service, you shall ride with Hywel's escort, and your presence will be a further guarantee to Rhodri Fychan that this is indeed Cadwaladr's voice speaking, and those who serve him are bound to obey. Will you go?'

'I will go.'

What else could he say? It was already decreed. It was another way of discarding him, but with a sop to his implacable loyalty. In the name of that loyalty he must now assist in stripping his lord of a great part of what possessions remained to him, when only a short while ago he had been in high heart, setting out to bring an army to Cadwaladr's rescue, without this ignominy and loss. But: 'I will go,' said Gwion, swallowing necessity whole. There might still be an opportunity to make contact with his waiting muster, before ever the Danish ships loaded and raised anchor with their booty, and sailed in triumph for Dublin.

They set out within the hour, Hywel ab Owain, Gwion, and an escort of ten men-at-arms, well-mounted, and with authority to commandeer fresh remounts along the way. Whatever Owain's feelings now towards his brother, he did not intend him to remain long a prisoner – or, perhaps a defaulting debtor. There was no knowing which of the two mattered more.

The three days predicted by Cadfael passed in brisk activity elsewhere, but in the two opposed camps they dragged and were drawn out long, like a held breath. Even the watch kept upon the stockades grew a shade lax, expecting no attack now that the issue was near its resolution without the need of fighting. Only Ieuan ab Ifor still fretted at the waiting, and bore in mind always that such negotiations might collapse in failure, prisoners remain prisoners, debts unpaid, marriages delayed beyond bearing. And as the hours passed he spoke privately to this one and that one among his younger and more headstrong friends, rehearsed for them the safe passage he had made twice by night at low tide along the shingle and sand to spy out the Danish defences, and how there was a place where approach from the sea was possible in reasonable cover of scrub and trees. Cadwaladr might have submitted, but these young hot-heads of Wales had not. Bitterly they resented it that invaders from Ireland should not only sail home without losses, but even with a very substantial profit to show for their incursion. But was it not already too late, now that it was known Hywel had gone south with orders to bring back and pay over the sum Otir demanded and Cadwaladr had conceded?

By no means, said Ieuan. For Gwion was gone with them, and somewhere between here and Ceredigion Gwion had brought up a hundred men who would fight for Cadwaladr. None of these had consented to let his lord be plundered of two thousand marks, or be made to grovel before the Dane. They would not stomach it, even if Cadwaladr had been brought so low as to submit to it. Ieuan had spoken with Gwion before he left in Hywel's party. On the way south, if chance offered, he would break away from his companions and go to join his waiting warriors. On the way north again, if he was watched too suspiciously on the way south, even Hywel would be content with him for his part in dealing with Rhodri Fychan at Llanbadarn, and no one would be paying too much heed to what he did. Somewhere along the drove roads he could break away and ride ahead. One dark night was all they would need, with the tide out and their numbers thus reinforced, and Heledd and Cadwaladr would be snatched out of bondage, and Otir could take to the seas for his life, and go back empty-handed to Dublin.

There were not wanting a number of wild young men in Owain's following whose instincts leaned rather to fighting out every issue to a bloody conclusion than to manipulating a way out of impasse without loss of life. There were a few who said openly that Owain was wrong to abandon his brother to pay his dues alone. Oaths were meant to be kept, yes, but the tensions of blood and kinship could put even oaths out of mind. So they listened, and the thought of bursting in through the Danish fences, sweeping Otir and his men into their ships at the edge of the sword and driving them out to sea began to have a powerful appeal. They were weary of sitting here inactive day after day. Where was the glory in bargaining a way out of danger with money and compromise?

The image of Heledd burned in Ieuan's memory, the dark girl poised against the sky on a hillock of the dunes. Twice he had seen her there, watched the long, lissome stride and the proudly carried head. She had a fiery grace even in stillness. And he could not believe, he could not convince himself, that such a woman, one alone in a camp full of men, could continue to the end unviolated, uncoveted. It was against mortal nature. Whatever Otir's authority, someone would defy it. And now his most haunting fear was that when they had loaded their plunder, so tamely surrendered , and were raising anchor to sail for home, they would carry Heledd away with them, as they had carried many a Welsh woman in the past, to be slave to some Dublin Dane for the rest of her life.

He would not have bestirred himself as he did for Cadwaladr, to whom he owed nothing but ill. But for sheer hostility to the invaders, and for the recovery of Heledd, he would have dared the assault with only his own small band of like-minded heroes, if need arose. But better far if Gwion could return in time with his hundred. So for the first day, and the second, Ieuan waited with arduous patience, and kept watch southward for any sign.

In Otir's camp the days of waiting passed slowly but confidently, perhaps too confidently, for there was certainly some relaxation of the strict watch they had kept. The square-rigged cargo ships, with their central wells ready for loading, were brought inshore, to be easily beached when the time came, and only the small, fast dragon-boats remained within the enclosed harbourage. Otir had no reason to doubt Owain's good faith, and as an earnest of his own had removed Cadwaladr's chains, though Torsten stayed attentive at the prisoner's elbow, ready for any rash move. Cadwaladr they did not trust, they knew him now too well.

Cadfael watched the passing of the hours and kept an open mind. There was still room for things to go wrong, though there seemed no particular reason why they should do so. It was simply that when two armed bands were brought together so closely in confrontation, it needed only a spark to set light to the otherwise dormant hostility between them. Waiting could make even the stillness seem ominous, and he missed Mark's serene company. What engaged his attention most during this interlude was the behaviour of Heledd. She went about the simple routine she had devised here for her living without apparent impatience or anticipation, as if everything was predetermined, and already accepted, and there was nothing for her to do about any part of it, and nothing in it either to delight or trouble her. She was, perhaps, more silent than usual, but with no implication of tension or distress, rather as if words would be wasted on matters already assured. It might have suggested nothing better than resignation to a fate she could not influence, but there was no change in the summer gloss that had turned her comeliness into beauty, or the deep, burnished lustre of her iris eyes as they surveyed the ribbon of the shingle beach, and the swaying of the ships offshore under the urging of the changing tides. Cadfael did not follow her too assiduously, nor watch her too

closely. If she had secrets, he did not want to kn
she wanted to confide, she would. If there was any
needed from him, she would demand it. And of h
here he was assured. All these restless young men want__ __ow
was to load their ships and take their profits home to Dublin,
well out of an engagement that might have ended in disaster,
given so doubled-edged a partner.

Thus in either camp the second day drew to a close.

Faced with the authority of Hywel ab Owain, the grudging
and stiff-necked testimony of Gwion, who so clearly hated
having to admit his lord's capitulation, and holding
Cadwaladr's seal in his hand, Rhodri Fychan on his own lands
in Ceredigion found no reason to question further the
instructions he was given. He accepted with a shrug the necessity, and delivered to Hywel the greater part of the two thousand marks in coin. It made some heavy loads for a number of
sumpter horses which were likewise contributed as part of the
ransom price. And the rest, he said resignedly, could be
rounded up from grazing land close to the northern border of
Ceredigion, near the crossing into Gwynedd, in Cadwaladr's
swart, sturdy cattle, moved there when this same Hywel drove
him out of his castle and fired it after him, more than a year
ago. His own herdsmen had grazed them there on his behalf
ever since he had been driven out.

It was at Gwion's own suggestion that he was commis-
sioned to ride northward again ahead of his companions, and
get this herd of cattle, slow-moving as they would be, in
motion towards Abermenai at once. The horsemen would
easily overtake them after they had loaded the silver, and no
time would be wasted on the return journey. A groom of
Rhodri's household rode with him, glad of the outing, to bear

241

witness that they had the authority of Cadwaladr himself, through his steward, to cut out some three hundred head of cattle from his herds and drive them northward.

It was all and more than he could have hoped for. Travelling south he had had no opportunity to withdraw himself or make any preparation for his escape. Now with his face to the north again everything fell into his hand. Once he had set out across the border of Gwynedd, with herd and drovers in brisk motion behind him, nothing could have been easier than to detach himself and ride ahead, on the pretext of giving due notice to Otir to prepare his ships to receive them, and leave them to follow to Abermenai at the best speed they could make.

It was the morning of the second day, very early, when he set forth, and evening when he reached the camp where he had left his hundred like-minded companions living off the country about them, and by this little more popular with their neighbours than such roving armies usually are, and themselves glad to be on the move again.

It seemed wise to wait until morning before marching. They lay in a sheltered place in open woodland, aside from the roads. One more night spent here, and they could be on their way with the first light, for from now on they could move only at a fast foot pace, and even by forced marches foot soldiers cannot outpace the horsemen. Cadwaladr's drovers must rest their travelling herd overnight, there was no fear of being overtaken by them. Gwion slept his few hours with a mind content that he had done all a man could do.

In the night, on the highroad half a mile from their camp, Hywel and his mounted escort passed by.

Chapter Thirteen

ROTHER CADFAEL walked the crest of the dunes in the early evening of the third day, and saw the Danish cargo ships beached in the shallows below him, and the line of men, stripped half-naked to wade from shore to ships, ferrying the barrels of silver pence aboard, and stowing them under foredeck and afterdeck. Two thousand marks within those small, heavy containers. No, somewhat less, for by all accounts the sumpter horses and certain cattle were to go with them as part of Otir's fee. For Hywel was back from Llanbadarn before noon, and by all accounts the drovers would not be far behind.

Tomorrow it would all be over. The Danes would raise anchor and sail for home, Owain's force would see them off Welsh soil, and then return to Carnarvon, and from there disperse to their homes. Heledd would be restored to her bridegroom, Cadfael and Mark to their duties left behind and almost forgotten in England. And Cadwaladr? By this time Cadfael was sure that Cadwaladr would be restored to some degree of power and certain of his old lands, once this matter was put by. Owain could not for ever hold out against his blood. Moreover, after every dismay and exasperation his brother had cost him, always Owain hoped and believed that there would be a change, a lesson learned, a folly or a crime regretted. So there was, but briefly. Cadwaladr would never change.

Down on the steel-grey shingle Hywel ab Owain stood to watch the loading of the treasure he had brought from Llanbadarn. There was no haste, doubtful if they could put the beasts aboard until the morrow, even if they reached here before night. Down there on neutral ground Dane and Welshman brushed shoulders amicably, content to part with debts paid and no blood shed. The affair had almost become a matter of marketing. That would not suit the wildest of Owain's clansmen. It was to be hoped he had them all well in hand, or there might be fighting yet. They did not like to see silver being bled away from Wales into Dublin, even if it was silver pledged, a debt of honour. But steadily the small barrels passed from man to man, the sunbrowned backs bending and swaying, the muscular arms extending the chain from beach to hold. About their bared legs the shallow water plashed in palest blues and greens over the gold of sand, and the sky above them was blue almost to whiteness, with a scatter of whiter clouds diaphanous as feathers. A radiant day in a fine, settled summer.

From the stockade Cadwaladr was also watching the shipment of his ransom, with his stolid shadow Torsten at his shoulder. Cadfael had observed them, withdrawn a little to his right, Torsten placidly content, Cadwaladr stormy-browed and grim, but resigned to his loss. Turcaill was down there aboard the nearest of the ships, hoisting the barrels in under the afterdeck, and Otir stood with Hywel, surveying the scene benignly.

Heledd came over the crest, and made her way down through the scrub and the salt grasses to stand at Cadfael's side. She looked down at the activities stretching out from beach to ship, and her face was calm and almost indifferent. 'There are still the cattle to get aboard,' she said. 'A rough voyage it will be for them. They tell me that crossing can be terrible.'

'In such fine weather,' said Cadfael, matching her tone, 'they'll have an easy passage.' No need to ask from which of them she had that information.

'By tomorrow night,' she said, 'they'll be gone. A good deliverance for us all.' And her voice was serene and even fervent, and her eyes followed the movements of the last of the porters as he waded ashore, bright water flashing about his ankles. Turcaill stood on the after-deck for some moments, surveying the result of their labours, before he swung himself over the side and came surging through the shallows, driving blue of water and white of spray before him, and looking up, saw Heledd as blithely looking down from her high place, and flung back his lofty flaxen head to smile at her with a dazzle of white teeth, and wave a hand in salute.

Among the men-at-arms who stood at Hywel's back to see the money safely bestowed Cadfael had observed one, thick-set and powerful and darkly comely, who was also looking up towards the ridge. His head was and remained tilted back, and his eyes seemed to Cadfael to be fixed upon Heledd. True, one woman among a camp of Danish invaders might well draw the eye and the interest of any man, but there was something about the taut stillness and the intent and sustained pose that made him wonder. He plucked at Heledd's sleeve.

'Girl, there's one below there, among the lads who brought the silver – you see him? On Hywel's left!— who is staring upon you very particularly. Do you know him? By the cut of him he knows you.'

She turned to look where he indicated, gave a moment to considering the face so assiduously raised to her, and shook her head indifferently.

'I never saw him before. How can he know me?' And she turned back to watch Turcaill cross the beach and pause to exchange civilities with Hywel ab Owain and his escort, before marshalling his own men back up the slope of the dunes towards the stockade. He passed before Ieuan ab Ifor without a glance, and Ieuan merely shifted his stance a little to recover the sight of Heledd on the dunes above him, as Turcaill's fair head cut her off from him in passing.

During those vital night watches, Ieuan ab Ifor had taken care to be captain of the guard on the westward gate of Owain's camp, and to have a man of his own on watch through the night hours. Towards midnight of that third night Gwion had brought his muster by forced marches to within sight of Owain's stockade, and there diverted them to the narrow belt of shingle exposed by the low tide, to pass by undetected. He himself made his way silently to the guard-post, and from its shadow Ieuan slid out to meet him.

'We are come,' said Gwion in a whisper. 'They are down on the shore.'

'You come late,' hissed Ieuan. 'Hywel is here before you. The silver is already loaded aboard their ships, they are waiting only for the cattle.'

'How can that be?' demanded Gwion, dismayed. 'I rode ahead from Llanbadarn. The only halt I made was the few hours of sleep we took last night. We marched before dawn this morning.'

'And in those few hours of the night Hywel overtook and passed you by, for he was here by mid-morning. And come tomorrow morning the herd will be here and loading. Late to save anything but a beggarly life for Cadwaladr as Owain's almsman instead of Otir's prisoner.' For Cadwaladr he did not grieve overmuch, except as his plight had strengthened the case for a rescue which could at the same time deliver Heledd.

'Not too late,' said Gwion, burning up like a stirred fire. 'Bring your few, and make haste! The tide is low and still ebbing. We have time enough!'

They had been ready every night for the signal, and they came singly, silently and eagerly, evading notice and question. Glissading down the suave slopes of the dunes, and across the belt of shingle to the moist, firm sand beyond, where their feet made no sound. More than a mile to go between the camps, but an hour left before the tide would be at its lowest, and ample time to return. There was a lambent light from the water, a shifting but gentle light that was enough for their purposes, the white edges of every ripple showing the extent of the uncovered sand. Ieuan led, and they followed him in a long line, silent and furtive under the dykes of Owain's defences, and on into the no-man's-land beyond. Before them, anchored offshore after their loading, the Danish cargo ships rode darkly swaying against the faint luminosity of the waves, and the comparative pallor of the sky. Gwion checked at sight of them.

'These have the silver already stored? We could reclaim it,' he said in a whisper. 'They'll have only holding crews aboard overnight.'

'Tomorrow!' said Ieuan with brusque authority. 'A long swim, they lie in deep water. They could pick us off one by one before ever we touched. Tomorrow they'll lay them inshore again to load the beasts. There are enough among Owain's muster who grudge so much as a penny to the pirates;

247

if we start the onset they'll follow, the prince will have no choice but to fight. Tonight we take back my woman and your lord. Tomorrow the silver!'

In the small hours of the morning Cadfael awoke to a sudden clamour of voices bellowing and lurs blaring, and started up from his nest in the sand still dazed between reality and dreaming, old battles jerked back into mind with startling vividness, so that he reached blindly for a sword before ever he was steady on his feet, and aware of the starry night above and the cool rippling of the sand under his bare feet. He groped about him to pluck Mark awake before he recalled that Mark was no longer beside him, but back in Owain's retinue, out of reach of whatever this sudden threat might be. Over to his right, from the side where the open sea stretched away westward to Ireland, the acid clashing of steel added a thin, ferocious note to the baying of fighting men. Confused movements of struggle and alarm shook the still air in convulsive turmoil between sand and sky, as though a great storm-wind had risen to sweep away men without so much as stirring the grasses they trod. The earth lay still, cool and indifferent, the sky hung silent and calm, but force and violence had come up from the sea to put an end to humanity's precarious peace.

Cadfael ran in the direction from which the uproar drifted fitfully to his ears. Others, starting out of their beds on the landward side of the encampment, were running with him, drawing steel as they ran, all converging on the seaward fences, where the clamour of battle had moved inward upon them, as though the stockade had been breached. In the thick of the tangle of sounds rose Otir's thunderous voice, marshalling his men. And I am no man of his, thought Cadfael, astounded but still running headlong towards the cry, why should I go looking for trouble? He could have been holding off at a safe distance, waiting to see who had staged what was plainly a determined attack, and how it prospered for Dane or Welshman, before assessing its import for his own wellbeing, but instead he was making for the heart of the battle as fast as he could, and cursing whoever had chosen to tear apart what could have been an orderly resolution of a dangerous business.

Not Owain! Of that he was certain. Owain had brought about a just and sensible ending, he would neither have originated nor countenanced a move calculated to destroy his achievement. Some hot-blooded youngsters envenomed with hatred of the Dane, or panting for the glory of warfare! Owain might reserve his quarrel with the alien fleet that invaded his land uninvited, he might even choose to exert himself to thrust them out when all other outstanding business was settled, but he would never have thrown away his own patient work in procuring the clearing of the ground. Owain's battle, had it ever come to it, as it yet might, would have been direct, neat and workmanlike, with no needless killing.

He was near to the heave and strain of close infighting now, he could see the line of the stockade broken here and there by the heads and shoulders of struggling men, and a great gap torn in the barrier where the attackers had forced their way in unobserved, between guard-posts. They had not penetrated far, and Otir already had a formidable ring of steel drawn about them, but on the fringes, in the darkness and in such confusion, there was no knowing friend from enemy, and a few of the first through the gap might well be loose within the camp.

He was rubbing shoulders with the outer ring of Danes, who were thrusting hard to shift the whole intruding mass

back through the stockade and down to the sea, when someone came running behind him, light and fast, and a hand
clutched at his arm, and there was Heledd, her face a pale,
startled oval, starry in the dark, lit by wide, blazing eyes.

'What is it? Who are they? They are mad, mad . . . What
can have set them on?'

Cadfael halted abruptly, drawing her back out of the press
and clear of random steel. 'Fool girl, get back out of here! Are
you crazed? Get well away until this is over. Do you want to
be killed?'

She clung to him, but held her ground sturdily, more
excited than afraid. 'But why? Why should any of Owain's do
such mischief, when all was going so well?'

The struggling mass of men, too closely entangled to allow
play to steel, reeled their way, and some among them losing
balance and footing, the mass broke apart, several fell, and
one at least was trampled, and let out breath in a wheezing
groan. Heledd was torn away from Cadfael's grasp, and
uttered a brief and angry scream. It cut through the din on a
piercing, clear note, and even in the stress of battle turned
heads in abrupt astonishment to stare in her direction. She
had been flung aside so sharply that she would have fallen, if
an arm had not taken her about the waist and dragged her
clear as the shift of fighting surged towards her. Cadfael was
borne the opposite way for a moment, and then Otir's rallying
cry drew the Danish circle taut, and their driving weight bore
the attackers backwards, and compressed them into the
breach they had made in the stockade, cramming them
through it in disorder. A dozen lances were hurled after them,
and they broke and drew off down the slope of the dunes
towards the shore.

A handful of the young Danes, roused and eager, would

have pursued the retreating attackers down the dunes, but Otir called them sharply to order. There were wounded already, if none dead, why risk more? They came reluctantly, but they came. There might be a time to take revenge for an act virtually of treachery, when agreement, if not sworn and sealed, had amounted almost to truce. But this was the time rather to salvage what was damaged, and sharpen once again a watchfulness grown slack as the need seemed to diminish.

In the comparative stillness and quiet they set about picking up the fallen, salving minor wounds, repairing the breach in the stockade, all in grim silence but for the few words needed. Under the broken fence three men lay dead, the foremost of the defenders overwhelmed by numbers before help could reach them. A fourth they picked up bleeding from a lance-thrust meant for his heart, but diverted through the shoulder. He would live, but he might lack the muscular power of his left arm for the rest of his life. Of minor gashes and grazes there were many, and the man who had been trampled spat blood from injuries within. Cadfael put by all other consider-ations, and went to work with the rest in the nearest shelter by torchlight, with whatever linen and medicines they could pro-vide. They had experience of wounds, and were knowledge-able in treating them, if their treatment was rough and ready. The boy Leif fetched and carried, awed and excited by this burst of violence by night. When all was done that could be done Cadfael sat back with a sigh, and looked round at his nearest neighbour. He was looking into the ice-blue eyes and unwontedly sombre face of Turcaill. The young man had blood on his cheek from a graze, and blood on his hands from the wounds of his friends.

'Why?' said Turcaill. 'What was there to gain? It was as good as finished. Now they have their dead or wounded, too,

I saw men being carried or dragged when they broke and ran. What was it made it worth their while to break in here?'

'I think,' said Cadfael, rubbing a hand resignedly over his tired eyes, 'they came for Cadwaladr. He still has a following, as rash as the man himself. They may well have thought to pluck him out of your keeping even in Owain's despite. What else do you hold of such value to them that they should risk their lives for it?'

'Why, the silver he's already paid,' said Turcaill practically. 'Would they not have made for that?'

'So they well may,' Cadfael admitted. 'If they have made a bid for the one, they may do as much for the other.'

'When we lay the ships inshore again tomorrow,' Turcaill's brilliant eyes opened wide in thought. 'I will say so to Otir: the man they can have, and good riddance, but the ransom is fairly ours, and we'll keep it.'

'If they are in good earnest,' said Cadfael, 'they have still to do battle for both. For I take it Cadwaladr is still safely in Torsten's keeping?'

'And in chains again. And sat out this foray with a knife at his throat. Oh, they went away empty-handed,' said Turcaill with dour satisfaction. And he rose, and went to join his leader, in conference over his three dead. And Cadfael went to look for Heledd, but did not find her.

'These we take back with us for funeral,' said Otir, brooding darkly over the bodies of his men. 'You say that these who came by night were not sent by Owain. It is possible, but how can we tell? Certainly I had believed him a man of his word. But what is rightfully ours we will make shift to keep, against Owain or any other. If you are right, and they came for Cadwaladr, then they have but one chance left to win away

252

both the man and his price. And we will be before them, with the ships and the sea at our backs, with masts stepped and ready for sail. The sea is no friend to them as it is to us. We'll stand armed between them and the shore, and we shall see if they will dare in daylight what they attempted in the night.'

He gave his orders clearly and briefly. By morning the encampment would be evacuated, the Danish ranks drawn up in battle array on the beach, the ships manoeuvred close to take the cattle aboard. If they came, said Otir, then Owain was in good faith, and the raiders were not acting on his orders. If they did not come, then all compacts were broken, and he and his force would put to sea and raid ashore at some unguarded coast to take for themselves the balance of the debt, and somewhat over for three lives lost.

'They will come,' said Turcaill. 'By its folly alone, this was not Owain's work. And he delivered you the silver by his own son's hand. And so he will the cattle. And what of the monk and the girl? There was a fair price offered for them, but that deal you never accepted. Brother Cadfael has earned his freedom tonight, and it's late now to haggle over his worth.'

'We will leave supplies for him and for the girl, they may stay safe here until we are gone. Owain may have them back as whole as when they came.'

'I will tell them so,' said Turcaill, and smiled.

Brother Cadfael was making his way towards them through the disrupted camp at that moment, between the lines soon to be abandoned. He came without haste, since there was nothing to be done about the news he carried, it was a thing accomplished. He looked from the three bodies laid decently straight beneath their shrouding cloaks to Otir's dour face, and thence full at Turcaill.

'We spoke too soon. They did not go away empty-handed. They have taken Heledd.'

Turcaill, whose movements in general were constant and flowed like quicksilver, was abruptly and utterly still. His face did not change, only his startling eyes narrowed a little, as if to look far into distance, beyond this present time and place. The last trace of his very private smile lingered on his lips.

'How came it,' he said, 'that she ever drew near such a fray? No matter, she would be sure to run towards what was forbidden or perilous, not away from it. You are sure, Brother?'

'I am sure. I have been looking for her everywhere. Leif saw her plucked out of the mêlée, but cannot say by whom. But gone she is. I had her beside me until we were flung apart, shortly before you drove them back through the stockade. Whoever he was who had her by the waist, he has taken her with him.'

'It was for her they came!' said Turcaill with conviction.

'It was for her one at least came. For I think,' said Cadfael, 'this must be the man to whom Owain had promised her. There was one close to Hywel, yesterday when you were loading the silver, could not take his eyes off her. But I did not know the man, and I thought no more of it.'

'She is safe enough, then, and free already,' said Otir, and made no more of it. 'And so are you, Brother, if you so please, but I would remain apart until we are gone, if I were you. For none of us knows what more may be intended for the morning. No need for you to put yourself between Dane and Welshman in arms.'

Cadfael heard him without hearing, though the words and their import came back to him later. He was watching Turcaill so closely that he had no thought to spare for whatever his own next moves should be. The young man had stirred easily and naturally out of his momentary stillness. He drew breath smoothly as ever, and the last of the smile lingered as a spark in his light, bright eyes after it had left his lips. There was nothing to be read in that face, beyond the open, appreciative amusement which was his constant approach to Heledd, and that vanished instantly when he looked down again at the night's losses.

'It's well she should be out of today's work,' he said simply. 'There's no knowing how it will end.'

And that was all. He went about the business of striking camp and arming for action like all the rest. In the darkness they stripped such tents and shelters as they had, and moved the lighter longships from the harbour in the mouth of the bay round into the open sea to join the larger vessels and provide an alert and mobile guard for their crews and cargo. The sea was their element, and fought on their side, even to the fresh breeze that quivered through the stillness before dawn. With sails up and filled, even the slower ships could put out to sea rapidly, safe from attack. But not without the cattle! Otir would not go without the last penny of his due.

And now there was nothing for Cadfael to do, except walk the crest of the dunes among the deserted fires and discarded debris of occupation, and watch the Danish force pack, muster and move methodically down through the scrub grass towards the ships rocking at anchor.

And they will go! Heledd had said, serious but neither elated nor dismayed. They were as good as gone already, and glad to be on their way home. Now if it was indeed Ieuan ab Ifor who had inspired that nocturnal attack, perhaps after all there was no man exerting himself on behalf of Cadwaladr, neither for his person and prestige nor for his possessions, and there would be no further confrontation, on the beach or in the sea, but only an orderly departure, perhaps even with a cool exchange of civilities between Welsh and Danish by way of leave-taking. Ieuan had come for his promised wife, and had what he wanted. No need for him to stir again. But how had he persuaded so many to follow him? Men who had nothing to gain, and had gained nothing. Some, perhaps, who had lost their lives to help him to a marriage.

The lithe little dragon-ship stole round silently into the open sea, and took station, riding well inshore. Cadfael went down a little way towards the strip of shingle, and saw the beach now half dry, half glistening under the lapping of the waves, and empty until the head of the Danish line reached it, and turned southward along the strand, a darker line in a darkness now lightening slowly towards the dove-grey of pre-dawn. The withdrawing raiders had made haste away to the deserted fields and sparse woodland between the camps, into some measure of cover. There were places where the shore route would be too dangerous now, with the tide flowing, though Cadfael felt certain they had come that way. Better and faster to move inland with their wounded and their prize, to reach their own camp dryshod.

Cadfael put a ridge of salt-stunted bushes between himself and the wind, which was freshening, scooped a comfortable hole in the sand, and sat down to wait.

In the soft light of the morning, just after sun-up, Gwion arrayed his hundred men, and the few of Ieuan's raising who remained with them, in a hollow between the dunes, out of sight of the shore, with a sentry keeping watch on the crest above. There was mist rising from the sea, a diaphanous swirl of faint blue over the shore, which lay in shadow, while westward the surface of the water was already bright, flecked with the white shimmer of spray in the steady breeze. The Danes, drawn up in open ranks, lined the edge of the sea, waiting immovably and without impatience for Owain's herdsmen to bring them Cadwaladr's cattle. Behind them the cargo ships had been brought in to beach lightly in the shallows. And there, in the midst of the Danes, was Cadwaladr himself, no longer shackled but still prisoner, defenceless among his armed enemies. Gwion had gone himself to the top of the ridge to look upon him, and the very sight was like a knife in his belly.

He had failed miserably in all that he had tried to do. Nothing had been gained, there stood his lord, humbled at the hands of the Danes, exposed to the scorn of his brother, not even assured of regaining a single foot of land at that brother's hands after all this bitter undertaking. Gwion gnawed ceaselessly at his own frustration, and found it sour in his mouth. He should not have trusted Ieuan ab Ifor. The man had been concerned only with his woman, and with that prize in his arms he had not stayed, as Gwion had wanted to stay, to attempt a second achievement. No, he was away with her, stifling her cries with a hand over her mouth, until he could hiss in her ear, well away from the Danes in their broken stockade, that she should not be afraid, for he meant her only good, for he was her man, her husband, come at risk to fetch her out of danger, and with him she was safe, and would be safe for ever . . . Gwion had heard him, totally taken up with his gains, and with no care at all for other men's losses. So the girl was out of bondage, but Cadwaladr, sick with humiliation and rage, must come under guard to be handed over for a price to the brother who discarded and misprized him.

It was not to be borne. There was still time to cut him out

clean from the alien array before Owain could come to savour the sight of him a prisoner. Even without Ieuan, gone with his bruised and bewildered woman and the dozen or so of his recruits who had preferred to steal back into camp and lick their wounds, there were enough stout fighting men here to do it. Wait, though, wait until the herd and their escort came. For surely once the attack was launched, others would see the right of it, and follow. Not even Hywel, if Hywel was again the prince's envoy, would be able to call off his warriors once they had seen Danish blood flow. And after Cadwaladr, the ships. Once the gage was cast down, the Welsh would go on to the end, take back the silver, drive Otir and his pirates into the sea.

The waiting was long, and seemed longer, but Otir never moved from his station before his lines. They had lowered their guard once, they would not do so again. That was the missed opportunity, for now there could be no second surprise. Even in Hywel, even in Owain himself, they would not again feel absolute trust.

The lookout on the crest reported back regularly and monotonously, no change, no movement, no sign yet of the dust of the herd along the sandy track. It was more than an hour past sunrise when he called at last: 'They are coming!' And then they heard the lowing of the cattle, fitful and sleepy on the air. By the sound of them, fed and watered, and on the move again after at least a few hours of the night for rest.

'I see them. A good half-company, advancing aside and before the drovers, out of the dust. Hywel has come in force. They have sighted the Danes . . .' That sight might well give them pause, they would not have expected to see the full force of the invaders drawn up in battle array for the loading of a few hundred head of stock. But they came on steadily, at the pace of the beasts. And now the foremost rider could be seen clearly, very tall in the saddle, bare-headed, fair as flax. 'It is not Hywel, it is Owain Gwynedd himself!'

On his hillock above the deserted camp Cadfael had seen the sun shine on that fair head, and even at that distance knew that the prince of Gwynedd had come in person to see the Norseman leave his land. He made his way slowly closer, looking down towards the impending meeting on the shore.

In the hollow between the dunes Gwion drew up his lines, and moved them a little forward, still screened by the curving waves of sand the wind had made and the tenacious grasses and bushes had partially clothed and secured in place.

'How close now?' Even in Owain's despite he would venture. And those clansmen who were approaching at Owain's heels, who could not all be tame even to their prince's leash, must see the attack, and be close enough to take fire from it in time, and drive the onslaught home with their added numbers.

'Not yet within call, but close. A short while yet!'

Otir stood like a rock in the edge of the surf, solid legs well braced, watching the advance of the swart, stocky cattle and their escort of armed men. Light-armed, as a man would normally go about his business. No need to expect any treachery there. Nor did it seem likely that Owain had had any part in that ill-managed raid in the night, or had any knowledge of it. If he had taken action, it would have been better done.

'Now!' said the lookout sharply from above. 'Now, while they are all watching Owain. You have them on the flank.'

'Forward now!' Gwion echoed, and burst out of the sheltering slopes with a great roar of release and resolve, almost of exultation. After him the ranks of his companions surged headlong, with swords drawn and short lances raised aloft, a sudden glitter of steel as they emerged from shadow into sun.

Out into clear view, and streaming down the last slope of sand into the shingle of the beach, straight for the Danish muster. Otir swung about, bellowing an alarm that brought every head round to confront the assault. Shields went up to ward off the first flung javelins, and the hiss of swords being drawn as one was flung into the air like a great indrawn breath. Then the first wave of Gwion's force hurtled into the Danish ranks and bore them backwards into their fellows by sheer weight, so that the whole battle lurched knee-deep into the surf.

Cadfael saw it from his high place, the impact and the clashing recoil as the ranks collided in a quivering shock, and heard the sudden clamour of voices shouting, and startled cattle bellowing. The Danes had so spaced their array that every man had room to use his right arm freely, and was quick to draw steel. One or two were borne down by the first impetuous collision, and took their attackers down into the sea with them in a confusion of spray, but most braced themselves and stood firm. Gwion had flung himself straight at Otir. There was no way to Cadwaladr now but over Otir's body. But the Dane had twice Gwion's weight, and three times his experience in arms. The thrusting sword clanged harshly on a raised and twisted shield, and was almost wrenched out of the attacker's grasp. Then all Cadfael could see was one struggling, heaving mass of Welshman and Dane, wreathed in shimmering spray. He began to make his way rapidly down on to the beach, with what intent he himself could hardly have said.

Echoing shouts arose from among the clansmen who marched at Owain's back, and a few started out of their ranks and began to run towards the mêlée in the shallows, hands on hilts in an instant, their intent all too plain. Cadfael could not wonder at it. Welshmen were already battling against an alien invader, there in full view. Welsh blood could not endure to stand aside, all other rights and wrongs went for nothing. They hallooed their partisan approval, and plunged into the boiling shallows. The reeling mass of entangled bodies heaved and strained, so closely locked together that on neither side could they find free room to do one another any great hurt. Not until the ranks opened would there be deaths.

A loud, commanding voice soared above the din of snarling voices and clanging steel, as Owain Gwynedd set spurs to his horse and rode into the edge of the sea, striking at his own too impetuous men with the flat of his sheathed sword.

'Back! Stand off! Get back to your ranks, and put up your weapons!'

His voice, seldom raised, could split the quaking air like thunder hard on the heels of lightning when he was roused. It was that raging trumpet-call rather than the battering blows that caused the truants to shrink and cower before him, and lean aside out of his path, plashing ashore in reluctant haste. Even Cadwaladr's former liegemen wavered, falling back from their hand-to-hand struggles. The two sides fell apart, and thrusts and sword-strokes that might have been smothered in the encroaching weight of wrestling bodies found room to wound before they could be restrained or parried.

It was over. They fell back to the solid shingle, swords and axes and javelins lowered, in awe of the icy glare of Owain's eyes, and the angry circling of his horse's stamping hooves in the surf, trampling out a zone of stillness between the combatants. The Danes held their ranks, some of them bloodied, none of them fallen. Of the attackers, two lay groping feebly out of the waves to lie limp in the sand. Then there was a silence.

Owain sat his horse, quieted now by a calming hand but still quivering, and looked down at Otir, eye to eye, for a long moment. Otir held his ground, and gave him back penetrating stare for stare. There was no need for explanation or protestation between them. With his own eyes Owain had seen.

'This,' he said at length, 'was not by my contrivance. Now I will know, and hear from his own mouth, who has usurped my rule and cast doubt on my good faith. Come forth and show yourself.'

There was no question but he already knew, for he had seen the charge launched out of hiding. It was, in some measure, generous to let a man stand fast by what he had done, and declare himself defiantly of his own will, in the teeth of whatever might follow. Gwion let fall the arm still raised, sword in hand, and waded forward from among his fellows. Very slowly he came, but not from any reluctance, for his head was erected proudly, and his eyes fixed on Owain. He plashed waveringly out of the surf, as little wave on following wave lapped at his feet and drew back. He reached the edge of the shingle, and a sudden rivulet of blood ran from his clenched lips and spattered his breast, and a small blot of red grew out of the padded linen of his tunic, and expanded into a great sodden star. He stood a moment erect before Owain, and parted his lips to speak, and blood gushed out of his mouth in a dark crimson stream. He fell on his face at the feet of the prince's horse, and the startled beast edged back from him, and blew a great lamenting breath over his body.

Chapter Fourteen

EE TO HIM!' said Owain, looking down impass-
ively at the fallen man. Gwion's hands stirred and
groped feebly in the polished pebbles, faintly con-
scious of touch and texture. 'He is not dead, have
him away and tend him. I want no deaths, more than are
already past saving.'

They made haste to do his bidding. Three of the front
rank, and Cuhelyn the first of them, ran to turn Gwion gently
on his back, to free his mouth and nostrils from the churned-
up sand. They made a litter from lances and shields, and
muffled him in cloaks to carry him aside. And Brother Cadfael
turned from the shore unnoticed, and followed the litter into
the shelter of the dunes. What he had on him by way of linen
or salves was little enough, but better than nothing until they
could get their wounded man to a bed and less rough and
ready care.

Owain looked down at the pool of blackening blood in the
shingle at his feet, and up into Otir's intent face.

'He is Cadwaladr's man, sworn and loyal. Nevertheless,
he did wrong. If he has cost you men, you have paid him.'
There were two of those who had followed Gwion lying in
the edge of the tide, lightly rocked by the advancing waves.

A third had got to his knees, and those beside him helped him to his feet. He trailed blood from a gashed shoulder and arm, but he was in no danger of death. Nor did Otir trouble to add to the toll the three he had already put on board ship, to sail home for burial. Why waste breath in complaint to this prince who acknowledged and deserved no blame for an act of folly?

'I hold you to terms,' he said, 'such as we understood between us. No more, and no less. This is none of your doing, nor any choice of mine. They chose it, and what came of it has been between them and me.'

'So be it!' said Owain. 'And now, put up your weapons and load your cattle, and go, more freely than you came, for you came without my knowledge or leave. And to your face I tell you that if ever you touch here on my land again uninvited I will sweep you back into the sea. As for this time, take your fee and go in peace.'

'Then here I deliver your brother Cadwaladr,' said Otir as coldly. 'Into his own hands, not yours, for that was not in any bargain between you and me. He may go where he will, or stay, and make his own terms with you, my lord.' He turned about, to those of his men who still held Cadwaladr sick with gall between them. He had been made nothing, a useless stock, in a matter conducted all between other men, though he was at the heart and core of the whole conflict. He had been silent while other men disposed of his person, his means and his honour, and that with manifest distaste. He had no word to say now, but bit back the bitterness and anger that rose in his throat and seared his tongue, as his captors loosed him and stood well aside, opening the way clear for him to depart. Stiffly he walked forward on to the shore, towards where his brother waited.

264

'Load your ships!' said Owain. 'You have this one day to leave my land.'

And he wheeled his horse and turned his back, pacing at a deliberate walk back towards his own camp. The ranks of his men closed in orderly march and followed him, and the bruised and draggled survivors of Gwion's unblessed army took up their dead and straggled after, leaving the trampled and bloodied beach clear of all but the drovers and their cattle, and Cadwaladr alone, aloof from all men, stalking in a black, forbidding cloud of disgust and humiliation after his brother.

In the nest of thick grass where they had laid him, Gwion opened his eyes, and said in a fine thread of a voice, but quite clearly: 'There is something I must tell Owain Gwynedd. I must go to him.'

Cadfael was on his knees beside him, staunching with what linen he had to hand, padded beneath thick folds of brychans, the blood that flowed irresistibly from a great wound in the young man's side, under the heart. Cuhelyn, kneeling with Gwion's head in his lap, had wiped away the foam of blood from the open mouth and the sweat from the forehead already chill and livid with the unhurried approach of death. He looked up at Cadfael, and said almost silently: 'We must carry him back to the camp. He is in earnest. He must go.'

'He is going nowhere in this world,' said Cadfael as quietly. 'If we lift him, he will die between our hands.'

Something resembling the palest and briefest of smiles, yet unquestionably a smile, touched Gwion's parted lips. He said, in the muted tones they had used over him: 'Then Owain must come to me. He has more time to spare than I

265

have. He will come. It is a thing he will wish to know, and no one else can tell him.'

Cuhelyn drew back the tangle of black hair that lay damp on Gwion's brow, for fear it should discomfort him now, when all comfort was being rapt away all too quickly. His hand was steady and gentle. There was no hostility left. There was room for none. And in their opposed fashion they had been friends. The likeness was still there, each of them peered into a mirror, a darkening mirror and a marred image.

'I'll ride after him. Be patient. He will come.'

'Ride fast!' said Gwion, and shut his mouth upon the distortion of the smile.

On his feet already, and with a hand stretched to his horse's bridle, Cuhelyn hesitated. 'Not Cadwaladr? Should he come?'

'No,' said Gwion, and turned his face away in a sharp convulsion of pain. Otir's last defensive parry, never meant to kill, had struck out just as Owain thundered his displeasure and split the ranks apart, and Gwion had dropped his levelled sword and his guard, and opened his flank to the steel. No help for it now, it was done and could not be undone.

Cuhelyn was gone, in faithful haste, sending the sand spraying from his horse's hooves until he reached the upland meadow grass and left the dunes behind. There was no one more likely to make passionate haste to do Gwion's errand than Cuhelyn, who for a brief time had lost the ability to see in his opposite his own face. That also was past.

Gwion lay with closed eyes, containing whatever pain he felt. Cadfael did not think it was great, he had already almost slipped out of its reach. Together they waited. Gwion lay very still, for stillness seemed to slow the bleeding and conserve the life in him, and life he needed for a while yet. Cadfael had water beside him in Cuhelyn's helmet, and bathed away the beads of sweat that gathered on his patient's forehead and lip, cold as dew.

From the shore there was no more clamour, only the brisk exchanges of voices, and the stir of men moving about their business unhindered now and intent, and the lowing and occasional bellowing of cattle as they were urged through the shallows and up the ramps into the ships. A rough, uncomfortable voyage for them in the deep wells amidships, but a few hours and they would be on green turf again, good grazing and sweet water.

'Will he come?' wondered Gwion, suddenly anxious.

'He will come.'

He was coming already, in a moment more they heard the soft thudding of hooves, and in from the shore came Owain Gwynedd, with Cuhelyn at his back. They dismounted in silence, and Owain came to look down at the young, spoiled body, not too closely yet, for fear even dulling ears should be sharp enough to overhear what was not meant to be overheard.

'Can he live?'

Cadfael shook his head and made no other reply.

Owain dropped into the sand and leaned close. 'Gwion . . . I am here. Spare to make many words, there is no need.'

Gwion's black eyes, a little dazzled by the mounting sun, opened wide and knew him. Cadfael moistened the lips that opened wryly, and laboured to articulate. 'Yes, there is need. I have a thing I must say.'

'For peace between us two,' said Owain, 'I say again, there is no need of words. But if you must, I am listening.'

'Bledri ap Rhys . . .' began Gwion, and paused to draw

breath. 'You require to know who killed him. Do not hold it against any other. I killed him.'

He waited, with resigned patience, for disbelief rather than outcry, but neither came. Only a considering and accepting silence that seemed to last a long while, and then Owain's voice, level and composed as ever, saying: 'Why? He was of your own allegiance, my brother's man.'

'So he had been,' said Gwion, and was shaken by a laugh that contorted his mouth and sent a thin trickle of blood running down his jaw. Cadfael leaned and wiped it away. 'I was glad when he came to Aber. I knew what my lord was about. I longed to join him, and I could and would have told him all I knew of your forces and movements. It was fair. I had told you I was wholly and for ever your brother's man, you knew my mind. But I could not go, I had given my word not to leave.'

'And had kept your word,' said Owain. 'So far!'

'But Bledri had given no such word. He could go, as I could not. So I told him all that I had learned in Aber, what strength you could raise, how soon you could be in Carnarvon, everything my lord Cadwaladr had to know for his defence. And I took a horse from the stables before dark, while the gates were open, and tethered it among the trees for him. And like a fool I never doubted but Bledri would be true to his salt. And he listened to all, and never said word, letting me believe he was of my mind!'

'How did you hope to get him out of the llys, once the gates were closed?' asked Owain, as mildly as if he questioned of some ordinary daily duty.

'There are ways . . . I was in Aber a long time. Not everyone is always careful with keys. But in the waiting time he was noting all things within your court, and he could count as well as I, and weigh chances as sharply, while he so carried himself as to put all suspicion of his intent out of mind. What I thought was his intent!' Gwion said bitterly. His voice failed him for a moment, but he gathered his strength and resumed doggedly: 'When I went to tell him it was time to go, and see him safely away, he was naked in his bed. Without shame he told me he was going nowhere, he was no such fool, having seen for himself your power and your numbers. He would lie safe in Aber and watch which way the wind blew, and if it blew for Owain Gwynedd, then he was Owain's man. I called to mind his fealty, and he laughed at me. And I struck him down,' said Gwion through bared teeth. 'And then, since he would not, I knew if I was to keep faith with Cadwaladr I must break faith with you, and go in Bledri's place. And since he had so turned his coat, I knew that I must kill him, for to make his way with you he would certainly betray me. And before he had his wits again I stabbed him to the heart.'

Some quivering tension in his body relaxed, and he drew and breathed out a great sigh. He had done already almost all that truth required of him. The rest was very little burden.

'I went to find the horse, and the horse was gone. And then the messenger came, and there was no more I could do. Everything was in vain. I had done murder for nothing! What it was entrusted to me to do for Bledri ap Rhys, whom I killed, that I did, for penance. And what came of it you know already. But it is just!' he said, rather to himself than to any other, but they heard it: 'He died unshriven, and so must I.'

'That need not be,' said Owain with detached compassion.

269

'Bear with this world a little while longer, and my priest will be here, for I sent word for him to come.'

'He will come late,' said Gwion, and closed his eyes.

Nevertheless, he was still living when Owain's chaplain came in obedient haste to take a dying man's last confession and guide his failing tongue through his last act of contrition. Cadfael, in attendance to the end, doubted if the penitent heard the words of the absolution, for after it was spoken there was no response, no quiver of the drained face or the arched lids that veiled the black, intense eyes. Gwion had said his last word to the world, and of what might come to pass in the world he was entering he had no great fear. He had lived long enough to rest assured of the absolution he most needed, Owain's forbearance and forgiveness, never formally spoken, but freely given.

'Tomorrow,' said Brother Mark, 'we must be on our way home. We have outstayed our time.'

They were standing together at the edge of the fields outside Owain's camp, looking out over the open sea. Here the dunes were only a narrow fringe of gold above the descent to the shore, and in subdued afternoon sunlight the sea stretched in cloudy blues, deepening far out into a clear green, and the long, drowned peninsula of shoals shone pale through the water. In the deep channels between, the Danish cargo ships were gradually dwindling into toy boats, dark upon the brightness, bearing out on a steady breeze under sail, for their own Dublin shore. And beyond, the lighter longships, smaller still, drove eagerly for home.

The peril was past, Gwynedd delivered, debts paid, brothers brought together again, if not yet reconciled. The affair might have turned out hugely bloodier and more destructive. Nevertheless, men had died.

Tomorrow, too, the camp at their backs would be dismantled of its improvised defences, the husbandman would come back to his farmhouse, bringing his beasts with him, and return imperturbably to the care of his land and his stock, as his forebears had done time after time, giving ground pliably for a while to marauding enemies they knew they could outwait, outrun and outlast. The Welsh, who left their expendable homesteads for the hills at the approach of an enemy, left them only to return and rebuild.

The prince would take his muster back to Carnarvon, and thence dismiss those whose lands lay here in Arfon and Anglesey, before going on to Aber. Rumour said he would suffer Cadwaladr to return with him, and those who knew them best added that Cadwaladr would soon be restored to possession of some part, at least, of his lands. For in spite of all, Owain loved his younger brother, and could not shut him out of his grace much longer.

'And Otir has his fee,' said Mark, pondering gains and losses.

'It was promised.'

'I don't grudge it. It might have cost far more.'

And so it might, though two thousand marks could not buy back the lives of Otir's three young men, now being borne back to Dublin for burial, nor those few of Gwion's following picked up dead from the surf, nor Bledri ap Rhys in his chill, calculating faithlessness, nor Gwion himself in his stark, destructive loyalty, the one as fatal as the other. Nor could all these lost this year call into life again Anarawd, dead last year in the south, at Cadwaladr's instigation, if not at his hands.

271

'Owain has sent a courier to Canon Meirion in Aber,' said Mark, 'to put his mind at rest for his daughter. By this he knows she is here safe enough, with her bridegroom. The prince sent as soon as Ieuan brought her into camp last night.'

His tone, Cadfael thought, was carefully neutral, as though he stood aside and withheld judgement, viewing with equal detachment two sides of a complex problem, and one that was not his to solve.

'And how has she conducted herself here in these few hours?' asked Cadfael. Mark might study to absent himself from all participation in these events, but he could not choose but observe.

'She is altogether dutiful and quiet. She pleases Ieuan. She pleases the prince, for she is as a bride should be, submissive and obedient. She was in terror, says Ieuan, when he snatched her away out of the Danish camp. She is in no fear now.'

'I wonder,' said Cadfael, 'if submissive and obedient is as Heledd should be. Have we ever known her to be so, since she came from Saint Asaph with us?'

'Much has happened since then,' said Mark, thoughtfully smiling. 'It may be she has had enough of venturing, and is not sorry to be settling down to a sensible marriage with a decent man. You have seen her. Have you seen any cause to doubt that she is content?'

And in truth Cadfael could not say that he had observed in her bearing any trace of discontent. Indeed, she went smilingly about the work she found for herself, waited upon Ieuan serenely and deftly, and continued to distil about her a kind of lustre that could not come from an unhappy woman. Whatever was in her mind, and held in reserve there with deep and glossy satisfaction, it certainly did not disquiet or distress her. Heledd viewed the path opening before her with unmistakable pleasure.

'Have you spoken with her?' asked Mark.

'There has been no occasion yet.'

'You may essay now, if you wish. She is coming this way.'

Cadfael turned his head, and saw Heledd coming striding lightly along the crest of the ridge towards them, with purpose in her step, and her face towards the north. Even when she halted beside them, it was only for a moment, checked in flight like a bird hovering.

'Brother Cadfael, I'm glad to see you safe. The last I knew of you was when they swept us apart, by the breach in the stockade.' She looked out across the sea, where the ships had shrunk into black splinters upon scintillating water. All along the line of them her glance followed. She might have been counting them. 'They got off unhindered, then, with their silver and their cattle. Were you there to see?'

'I was,' said Cadfael.

'They never did me offence,' she said, looking after their departing fleet with a slight, remembering smile. 'I would have waved them away home, but Ieuan did not think it safe for me.'

'As well,' said Cadfael seriously, 'for it was not entirely a peaceful departure. And where are you going now?'

She turned and looked at them full, and her eyes were wide and innocent and the deep purple of irises. 'I left something of mine up there in the Danish camp,' she said. 'I am going to find it.'

'And Ieuan lets you go?'

'I have leave,' she said. 'They are all gone now.'

They were all gone, and it was safe now to let his

273

hard-won bride return to the deserted dunes where she had been a prisoner for a while, but never felt herself in bondage. They watched her resume her purposeful passage along the edge of the fields. There was barely a mile to go.

'You did not offer to go with her,' said Mark with a solemn face.

'I would not be so crass. But give her a fair start,' said Cadfael reflectively, 'and I think you and I might very well go after her.'

'You think,' said Mark, 'we might be more welcome company on the way back?'

'I doubt,' Cadfael admitted, 'whether she is coming back.'

Mark nodded his head by way of acknowledgement, unsurprised. 'I had been wondering myself,' he said.

The tide was on the ebb, but not yet so low as to expose the long, slender tongue of sand that stretched out like a reaching hand and wrist towards the coast of Anglesey. It showed pale gold beneath the shallows, here and there a tuft of tenacious grass and soil breaking the surface. At the end of it, where the knuckles of the hand jutted in an outcrop of rock, the stunted salt bushes stood up like rough, crisp hair, their roots fringed with the yellow of sand. Cadfael and Mark stood on the ridge above, and looked down as they had looked once before, and upon the same revelation. Repeated, it made clear all the times, all the evenings, when it had been repeated without witnesses. They even drew back a little, so that the shape of them might be less obtrusive on the skyline, if she should look up. But she did not look up. She looked down into the clear water, palest green in the evening light, that reached almost to her knees, as she trod the narrow golden path towards the seagirt throne of rock. She had her skirts, still frayed and soiled from travel and from living wild, gathered up in her hands, and she leaned to watch the cold, sweet water quivering about her legs, and breaking their lissome outlines into a disembodied tremor, as though she floated rather than waded. She had pulled all the pins from her hair; it hung in a black, undulating cloud about her shoulders, hiding the oval face stooped to watch her steps. She moved like a dancer, slowly, with languorous grace. For whatever tryst she had here she came early, and she knew it. But because there was no uncertainty, time was a grace, even waiting would be pleasure anticipated.

Here and there she halted, to be still, to let the water settle and be still around her feet, and then she would lean to watch the tremulous ardour of her face shimmering as each wave ebbed back into the sea. A very gentle tide, with hardly any wind now. But Otir's ships under sail were more than halfway to Dublin by this hour.

On the throne of rock she sat down, wringing the water from the hem of her gown, and looked across the sea, and waited, without impatience, without doubts. Once, in this place, she had looked immeasurably lonely and forsaken, but that had been illusion, even then. Now she looked like one in serene possession of all that lay about her, dear companion to the sea and the sky. The orb of the sun was declining before her, due west, gilding her face and body.

The little ship, lean and dark and sudden, came darting down from the north, surging out of the concealment of the rising shoreline beyond the sandy warrens across the strait. Somewhere up-coast it had lain waiting off Anglesey until the sunset hour. There had been, thought Cadfael, watching intently, no compact, no spoken tryst at all. They had had no time to exchange so much as a word when she was snatched away. There had been only the inward assurance to keep them constant, that the ship would come, and that she would be there waiting. Body and blood, they had been superbly sure, each of the other. No sooner had Heledd recovered her breath and accepted the fact of her innocent abduction than she had come to terms with events, knowing how they must and would end. Why else had she gone so serenely about passing the waiting time, disarming suspicion, even putting herself out, who knows how ruefully, to give Ieuan ab Ifor some brief pleasure before he was to pay for it with perpetual loss. In the end Canon Meirion's daughter knew what she wanted, and was ruthless in pursuing it, since no one among her menfolk and masters showed any sign of helping her to her desire.

Small, serpentine and unbelievably swift, oars driving as one, Turcaill's dragon-ship swooped inshore, but held clear of beaching. It hung for a moment still, oars trailed, like a bird hovering, and Turcaill leaped over the side and came wading waist-deep towards the tiny island of rock. His flaxen hair shone almost red in the crimson descent of the sun, a match for Owain Gwynedd's, as dominant and as fair. And Heledd, when they turned their eyes again on her, had risen and walked into the sea. The tension of the ebbing tide drew her with it, skirts floating. Turcaill came up glistening out of the deeper water. They met midway, and she walked into his arms, and was swung aloft against his heart. There was no great show, only a distant, brief peal of mingled laughter rising on the air to the two who stood watching. No need for more, there had never been any doubt in either of these sea creatures as to the inevitable ending.

Turcaill had turned his back, and was striding through the

surf back to his ship, with Heledd in his arms, and the tide, receding more rapidly as the sun declined, gave back before him in iridescent fountains of spray, minor rainbows wreathing his naked feet. Lightly he hoisted the girl over the low side of his dragon, and swung himself after. And she, as soon as she had her footing, turned to him and embraced him. They heard her laughter, high and wild and sweet, thinner than a bird's song at this distance, but piercing and clear as a carillon of bells.

All the long, sinuous bank of oars, suspended in air, dipped together. The little serpent heeled and sped, creaming spray, round into the clear passage between the sandy shoals, already showing golden levels beneath the blue, but more than deep enough yet for this speedy voyager. She sped away end-on, small and ever smaller, a leaf carried on an impetuous current, borne away to Ireland, to Dublin of the Danish kings and the restless seafarers. And a fitting mate Turcaill had carried away with him, and formidable progeny they would breed between them to master these uneasy oceans in generations to come.

Canon Meirion need not fret that his daughter would ever reappear to imperil his status with his bishop, his reputation or his advancement. Love her as he might, and wish her well as he probably did, he had desired heartily that she should enjoy her good fortune elsewhere, out of sight if not out of mind. He had his wish. Nor need he agonise, thought Cadfael, watching that resplendent departure, over her happiness. She had what she wanted, a man of her own choosing. By that she would abide, wise or unwise by her father's measure. She measured by other means, and was not likely to suffer any regrets.

The small black speck, racing home, was barely visible as

a dot of darkness upon a bright and glittering sea.

'They are gone,' said Brother Mark, and turned and smiled. 'And we may go, too.'

They had overstayed their time. Ten days at the most, Mark had said, and Brother Cadfael would be returned safe and sound to his herb garden and his proper work among the sick. But perhaps Abbot Radulfus and Bishop de Clinton would regard the truant days as well spent, considering the outcome. Even Bishop Gilbert might be highly content to keep his able and energetic canon, and have Meirion's inconvenient daughter safely oversea, and his scandalous marriage forgotten. Everyone else appeared well content to have so satisfactory a settlement of what might well have been a bloody business. What mattered now was to return to the level sanity of daily living, and allow old grudges and animosities to fade gradually into the obscurity of the past. Yes, Cadwaladr would be restored, on probation, Owain could not totally discard him. But not wholly restored, and not yet. Gwion, who by any measure had been the loser, would be decently buried, with no very great acknowledgement of his loyalty from the lord who had bitterly disappointed him. Cuhelyn would remain here in Gwynedd, and in time surely be glad that he had not had to do murder with his own hands to see Anarawd avenged, at least upon Bledri ap Rhys. Princes, who can depute other hands to do their less savoury work for them, commonly escape all temporary judgements, but not the last.

And Ieuan ab Ifor would simply have to resign himself to losing a delusory image of a submissive wife, a creature Heledd could never become. He had barely seen or spoken with her, his heart could scarcely be broken at losing her, however his dignity might be bruised. There were pleasant women in Anglesey who could console him, if he did but look about him here at home.

And she . . . she had what she wanted, and she was where she wanted to be, and not where others had found it convenient to place her. Owain had laughed when he heard of it, though considerately he had kept a grave face in Ieuan's presence. And there was one more waiting in Aber who would have the last word in the story of Heledd.

The last word, when Canon Meirion had heard and digested the tale of his daughter's choice, came after a deep-drawn breath of relief for her safety at least – or was it for his own deliverance?

'Well, well!' said Meirion, knotting and unknotting his long hands. 'There is a sea between.' True, and there was relief for both of them in that. But then he continued: 'I shall never see her again!' and there was as much of grief in it as of satisfaction. Cadfael was always to be in two minds about Canon Meirion.

They came to the border of the shire in the early evening of the second day, and on the principle that it was as well to be hanged for a sheep as a lamb, turned aside to pass the night with Hugh at Maesbury. The horses would be grateful for the rest, and Hugh would be glad to hear at first hand what had passed in Gwynedd, and how the Norman bishop was rubbing along with his Welsh flock. There was also the pleasure of spending a few placid hours with Aline and Giles, in a domesticity all the more delightful to contemplate because they had forsworn it for themselves, along with the world outside the Order.

Some such unguarded remark Cadfael made, sitting

contentedly by Hugh's hearth with Giles on his knees. And Hugh laughed at him.

'You, forswear the world? And you just back from gallivanting to the farthest western edge of Wales? If they manage to keep you within the pale for more than a month or two, even after this jaunt, it will be a marvel. I've known you restless after a week of strict observance. Now and again I've wondered if some day you wouldn't set out for Saint Giles, and end up in Jerusalem.'

'Oh, no, not that!' said Cadfael, with serene certainty. 'It's true, now and again my feet itch for the road.' He was looking deep into himself, where old memories survived, and remained, after their fashion, warming and satisfying, but of the past, never to be repeated, no longer desirable. 'But when it comes down to it,' said Cadfael, with profound content, 'as roads go, the road home is as good as any.'

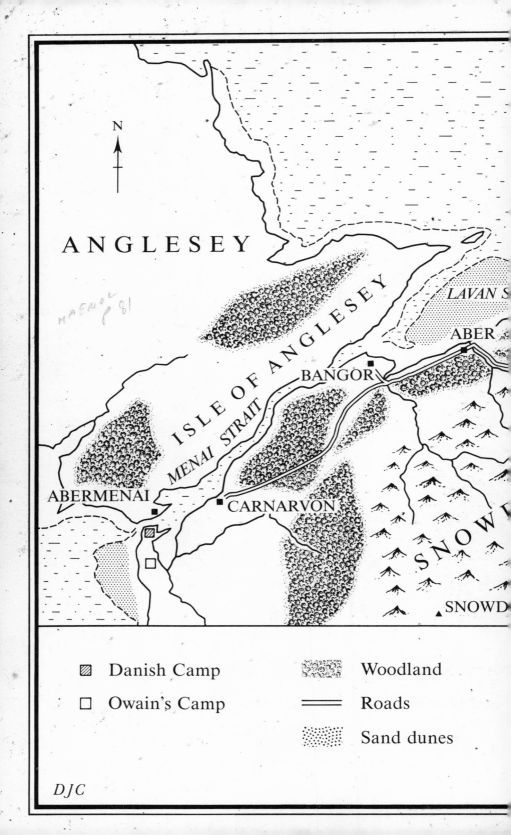

N

ANGLESEY

MAENOL p.81

ISLE OF ANGLESEY

LAVAN S

ABER

BANGOR

MENAI STRAIT

ABERMENAI

CARNARVON

SNOWD

SNOWD

	Danish Camp		Woodland
	Owain's Camp	===	Roads
			Sand dunes

DJC